KARA McDOWELL

SCHOLASTIC PRESS
NEW YORK

ISBN 978-1-338-65454-7

1 2020

Printed in the U.S.A.   23

First edition, October 2020

Book design by Yaffa Jaskoll

For my mom,
who took me to see *You've Got Mail* when I was nine,
who raised me on romantic comedies,
and who has always supported my dream

Fitz Wilding is an idiot and a love addict, and I enable both.

Get out of the car? Or stay in the car?

The familiar uptick in my heart rate is the first sign that something is wrong.

No, that's not true. The letter in my back pocket, and the fact that I felt compelled to write it, is the *first* sign. The racing heart is an inevitable side effect of seeing Fitz. And of making a hard decision.

The driving rain has slowed to a misting, and I flip off the windshield wipers. Twinkle lights from the neighboring restaurants cast a hazy yellow glow across the slick pavement. My headlights have been off since I pulled into the parking lot three and a half songs ago, because I didn't want him to see me. I *don't* want him to see me. Not until I've decided what I'm going to do with the letter.

Get out of the car?

Stay in the car?

My palms break out in a cold sweat as my phone buzzes with a text from Fitz. **Quit stalling, Collins. It's not that cold.**

Followed quickly with: **I'm dying.**

I've been caught. A smile tugs at my lips as I tap out a quick response. **You're not.**

Poor Fitz. Always so dramatic.

I take the keys from the ignition and open the door to the chilly December air. It's tempting to be disappointed in myself, especially when I spent the evening sitting in my room penning the world's most unnecessary breakup letter, but the reality is this: It wasn't ever a choice. He asked me to come, so of course I was going to come. That's what best friends do.

I pull the sleeves of my sweater over my palms and walk slowly through the festive stretch of downtown Gilbert. Christmas lights are strung in shop windows and the old-fashioned streetlamps proudly display a dozen matching wreaths. Joy and cheer ooze from every brick and windowpane, a stark contrast to the sludgy sick feeling pooling in my stomach.

Despite my slow tread, I reach the water tower in no time at all. Certainly not enough time for me to have made a decision. I stop short in front of the ladder that ascends five stories into the air.

Climb or don't climb?

Another decision to make. I run an inventory of my physical symptoms. Increased heart rate? Check. Sweaty hands? Check. Numb lips? Not yet.

I might avoid a panic attack, after all.

"Paige!" I hear the smile in Fitz's voice. In the dark, I can just make out the brim of his baseball hat sticking over the platform as he looks down at me. "Be careful. The ladder is slick."

"If I die because of you—" I mutter as I put my foot on the bottom rung and begin to climb.

"I'll serve gummy worms at your funeral." He flashes a dazzling smile, and my annoyance begins to slip. At the top, he holds an umbrella over my head with one hand, using the other to help me step from the wet ladder to the platform.

"Hang on," he says before I sit. He shrugs out of his jacket and dries a place for me on the narrow aluminum ledge. When that's done, we sit side by side, our legs dangling in the night, our backs leaning against the cold silo.

"Based on the fact that I'm here right now, I'm assuming tonight didn't go well," I say.

"It did not," he agrees, grim faced and sullen again.

"And what was the plan?" A gust of wind blows, whistling through nearby trees. Without his sodden jacket, goose bumps erupt over his forearms. I pretend not to notice.

"It was supposed to be romantic," he moans, rubbing his hands over his face.

"Rain is a romance staple," I say indulgently. "What happened?"

"I blindfolded her, told her I had a surprise. I set up this whole picnic." He motions to the damp basket next to him, filled with soggy sandwiches and limp chips. "As it turns out, she's deathly afraid of heights."

I can't help but laugh. Fitz is always creating elaborate romantic scenarios, but they go up in flames at least as often as they're successful; .500 is a great batting average but less impressive in the grand gesture department.

"You didn't know that?" I ask. A touch of pink blooms on his cheeks. "No wonder she dumped you." He and Molly have been dating for seven months and ten days, and that's plenty of time to discover his girlfriend's deepest fears. I don't say that part out loud, though. Don't want him to know I'm counting.

"Is there something wrong with me? Why does this keep happening?" His tone is self-deprecating, but the current of truth running under his words makes my chest swell.

My instinct is to take him by the shoulders and say: *No. You're perfect. It's the girls who are wrong.* Instead, I keep my hands to myself and say: "Maybe you're trying too hard."

He scoffs. "What does that even mean? Trying too hard? How can you try too hard for something or someone you really want?"

"Don't ask me. I don't try for anything I want." It's meant to be a joke, but it's too true to be funny.

Maybe coming here tonight was a bad decision, after all.

The average person makes thirty-five thousand decisions every single day. I read that somewhere and it stuck in my brain, because that number? It's big. Overwhelming. Paralyzing. Enough to make me stay in bed all day and pull the covers over my head. I also read that super successful people like Barack Obama and Mark Zuckerberg wear the same clothes every day to avoid decision fatigue.

Decision fatigue is something I understand. I feel it in my soul. Take school, for example. I couldn't decide which elective to take this year. Drama? Clay? American Sign Language? What if I'm destined to be a famous sculptor, but I waste my talent reciting poorly memorized Shakespeare instead? Or what if taking clay, which is only available fourth hour, means that I get put in the opposite lunch period as all my friends, and I spend the entire year eating alone in the bathroom? Or what if there's a carbon monoxide leak in the languages corridor and all the ASL kids drop over dead in first period? Grim. But possible.

"I thought she was the one," Fitz says quietly as he lets his head fall to my shoulder.

My heart collapses. Not because he's talking about another girl. I'm used to that by now. But because he can *lean his head against my shoulder* without combusting. Being this close to him makes my hands shaky and my heart wild. In contrast, his touch is casual and thoughtless; when he observes the metadata on his activity tracker tonight, skimming it for peaks in his heart rate, this physical contact won't even register.

"The one who what?" I snap. The amount of energy I expend to not look jealous or insecure when he talks about other girls could power an entire city, but tonight, with the letter in my pocket, my mask is slipping. "Did you think you were going to get married and have tiny, gorgeous babies?"

Fitz's role models are two disgustingly in love parents and three sisters in their twenties and thirties, all of whom raised him on a steady diet of nineties rom-coms. No wonder he's constantly stumbling into love, trying to one-up himself with the grandest of all the grand gestures. For any guy not blessed with Fitz's effortless good looks and impressive batting average, his romance obsession could be fodder for locker room teasing. As it is, almost everyone I know (guys included) has been in love with Fitz at some point.

Molly is not the first girl who he's called "the one," and she won't be the last either. I'm horribly jealous. Practically dripping with poison-green envy. Not only because of those other girls (although that's part of it) but also because he has a fearless heart. It's the thing I love most about him.

It's the thing I hate in equal measure.

"She is gorgeous, isn't she?" Fitz says longingly.

Not actually my point. I allow myself an eye roll, thankful to the dark sky for hiding it. "What was the final straw? The height, the rain, or the unfortunate combination of both?"

"I don't want to talk about it." He lifts his head and fiddles with the band on his activity tracker. The school baseball coach makes all the players wear them, even in the off-season.

"Since when?" I ask, thrown by his departure from our usual script. This is the part where he relays every last word and brutal text, describing in heart-wrenching detail how her tears rolled down her cheeks while she yelled at him or kissed him or whatever it is that happens during a breakup.

Fitz looks up at me from under his lashes and my breath catches in my throat. Why does my breath *still* catch? Like one of those girls in one of his movies. When will my brain accept the fact that I'm not the heroine in Fitz's love story? His expression shifts from mopey to serious, his blue eyes trained on mine. Even after all this time, one look from him can make my stomach falter and my mouth dry. And suddenly I want to burn the letter in my pocket, the one that highlights all the reasons why we can't be friends anymore. It's messy and vulnerable and written in excruciating detail, and it boils down to this: I hate how much I love him. For the first time all evening, I'm certain I won't give him the letter, because I don't want to live in a world where he doesn't look at me like this.

"Wanna see something cool?" he asks, turning his attention to his phone. His bad mood vanishes and the weird tension between us breaks. He opens his weather app and pulls up the forecast for Williams, Arizona, a tiny mountain town near

Arizona's northern border where Fitz's family owns a cabin. Snowflake icons begin the day after Christmas and continue for the rest of the week.

"Are you trying to kill me?" I moan enviously. As a born-and-raised Gilbert kid, snow is nothing more than a fairy tale. Only as real as the stories Fitz tells me.

"I know it's a few days early, but merry Christmas."

"Excuse me?"

"This is your present." He gestures to the screen.

"What do you mean?"

"It's about time I made good on my promise." His eyes search mine, looking for the answer to a question he hasn't asked. I'm transported back to a night two years ago. My face flushes hot, despite the chill nipping at my cheeks. I wonder if he's thinking about it too.

"Are you serious?"

"It's not Venice, but—"

"Who needs Venice?" I grip the railing in front of us with both hands to stop myself from throwing my arms around him. Hugging Fitz is a clear violation of my rules.

My rules for touching are as follows. It is only acceptable when it is:

- accidental (bumping my knee against his when we're watching a movie)
- helpful (brushing a bug from his hair)
- or necessary (swatting his shoulder when he's being annoying).

Maybe I should add another category for spontaneous, cannot-be-helped touching. How many categories is too many?

"You do," Fitz says, bringing my attention back to our conversation. "You need Venice and Florence and Milan and Rome. And that's just one country."

"Okay, okay, I get it." I laugh, giddy at the thought of spending winter break with him and his family.

"I can't give you those places, but I can show you a snow-covered town at the mouth of the Grand Canyon. You in?" He rubs his hand on the back of his neck, a dead giveaway that he's nervous. As if I'd say no.

"Of course! I don't expect you to give me all of Europe." I laugh again, because how ridiculous would I have to be to turn my nose up at his cabin because it's not nestled in the Swiss Alps?

Fitz knows as well as anyone how deep my wanderlust runs. When I lie in bed at night, surrounded by pictures ripped out of travel magazines, I imagine future lives as a ranch hand in Montana and a sheepherder in Ireland and a churro maker in Spain. I don't know if I love sheep or even churros, but nothing summons a panic attack faster than the realization that if I'm extremely lucky, I'll get one of those imagined futures.

One.

I'm paralyzed by the fact that walking through one door essentially means slamming shut fifty or a hundred or a million other ones.

"When do you leave?" I ask.

"Tonight. The truck's packed and ready. I'll pick you up early the day after Christmas; we'll turn around and be back before the snow hits."

"*Snow!*" I shake my head, still in disbelief. "Do I need special clothes so I don't freeze to death?"

"My sisters have plenty that you can borrow."

"As long as my mom says yes, which you know she will, I guess I'll see you in a few days." I get to my feet, unable to suppress my grin. I've been dying to go to Fitz's cabin for ages, and he's invited me up a few times during the summer, but the timing never worked out. Until now.

"What's that?" Fitz plucks the letter out of my back pocket, raising an eyebrow at his name scrawled across the envelope.

"Hey!" I lunge for it, my feet slipping on the damp aluminum. My arms scramble through the air, my fingers slipping off the metal railing.

"Whoa!" He grabs me by the waist, steadying me. "Are you okay?"

I nod, too shaky and breathless to say anything.

"Holy shit. I thought you were gonna fall." He tilts his wrist so we can both see how high his heart rate has spiked.

"So did I."

He slowly removes a hand from my waist and gently presses two fingers to my neck, tracking my pulse. I nearly stop breathing. A lazy smile spreads across his face. "Damn. You *were* scared."

"Mm-hmm," I agree, secretly thinking that the feel of his warm fingers on my cold skin is having more of an impact than the near fall. His hand drops, and he releases my waist.

We both look over the edge, taking in the fifty-foot drop.

Get out of the car or stay in the car?

Climb or don't climb?

Tell him or don't tell him?

This is what I mean about decisions. I could be smashed against wet cement at this exact second, and it's impossible to untangle the reason why. Is it because Molly dumped Fitz? Because I drove out here to either break off our friendship or cheer him up? Because I climbed this tower?

When bad things happen, I want to know where to put the blame. I hate the swampy maze of endless regret that comes with wondering.

"So." I take a shaky breath, steeling myself for the trek down the ladder. "I'll see you after Christmas?"

"Unless you bail on me again," he says softly. Surprised, I meet his eyes. We don't ever talk about *that* night, and I'm not sure what to say. "Never mind." He shakes his head. "See you after Christmas."

I'm sorry. I messed up. I regret it.

I could say any of those things, and mean it. But I'm dealing with a racing heart, shaky hands, and only a fraction of the bravery I'd need to say the words out loud.

My mind spins as I retrace my steps backward: down the ladder, past the warmly glowing twinkle lights, and into my car. I think about decisions and paralysis and regret the whole way home, and it's not until I pull into my driveway that I realize tonight's tragedy will not be almost falling off the water tower.

It'll be the fact that I left the letter with Fitz.

I mark my life by the moments that ruined it.

The panic attack in front of my classmates when I was fourteen.

The "snowstorm" when I was fifteen.

That night I bailed on Fitz, ruining any chance we might have had.

And today. The day I wrecked the best relationship of my life with a piece of notebook paper and a hasty decision that I can't take back.

I have these moments cataloged for easy recall thanks to SIM—shorthand for "secretary in my mind." He's nerdy-buff, wears tragically uncool round glasses, and makes my life a living nightmare, what with his never-ending lists of all the ways my life could implode in a giant trash fire of suck.

This doesn't make me weird. (I'm pretty sure.) I figure we all have voices in our heads that whisper or shout certain things, telling us what to do and why. It just so happens that the loudest voice in my head never stops yakking about all the ways my life is poised to go wrong. I know SIM is really *me*, but I hate that it's me, so I gave that part of myself a different name.

Sweat prickles the back of my neck as I tear through the car. I check under the seats and rummage through old gas receipts and bobby pins in the center console. I search my pockets half a dozen times, open the glove compartment twice, and even lift up all the floor mats. But it's useless, and I knew it would be. I left the letter on the water tower with Fitz.

I can still see it lying on the wet platform, his name scrawled across the front as if it was an afterthought, as if the contents of the letter don't include words that will change everything. Words like *I* and *love* and *you*. And I was too distracted by his hand on my waist to pick it up.

I turn the key in the ignition, ready to drive to the water tower or to Fitz's house or to the cabin or to the ends of the earth to get it back. My hands are sweaty and slick on the steering wheel as my heart thumps painfully in my chest. The rising tide of panic is quick, and if I don't fix this immediately, it'll overwhelm me.

I send Fitz a text. **Did you find the envelope I left on the water tower?**

I wait one minute, and I'm okay. I wait two minutes, and I'm holding it together. I wait three minutes, and I'm falling apart.

He opened the letter and he's never going to talk to me again.

The raw ache in my chest is worse than panic, deeper than regret. It's so bad I don't even have a word for it.

He's probably driving to Williams right now, thinking about how— Oh. He's driving to Williams. Right now. Fitz never texts and drives, and that's why he's not answering. I'm shaky with relief as I pull up his number and press call. He doesn't text and drive, but he's not against answering a call.

"Hey! Did you get the okay to come to the cabin?" His voice is friendly, and warm relief spreads through me like honey.

"Not yet. But listen. Did you find the letter I left on the water tower?"

"Yeah. I've got it."

"Don't open it, okay?"

"I didn't. But why not?"

"It's part of your Christmas present." *The part where I tell you why I love you and why I hate you and ask you to leave me alone for the rest of my life.*

If he reads it . . . I shudder at the implications as SIM sharpens his pencil and starts a new list.

All the ways my life will fall apart if Fitz reads that letter:

- My invitation to the cabin will be rescinded.
- I'll lose my best friend.
- Life as I know it will end.

Fitz clears his throat. "I willed a blizzard into existence for you, and you got me . . . an envelope?"

"I know! That's why I didn't give it to you before. It's not . . . ready. I need more time."

"Can I open it on Christmas?"

"No. Wait until I get there. Please?"

He pauses for longer than I'm comfortable with. "Is everything okay?"

"Yeah! Why wouldn't it be?" My voice goes all high and screechy. A dead giveaway. "Promise you'll wait."

"Fine, Collins. See you in a few days."

We hang up, and I sag with relief. Crisis averted. For now. I'm going to have a permanent stomachache until that letter is back in my hands. Not even Christmas will be able to take my mind off this disaster. That's the thing about my brain. It latches onto the bad, digs its fingernails in, and refuses to let up even for a second.

I'm still shaky with nerves and regret as I walk in the front door. Mom is sitting on the couch in the small family room, her legs tucked under her and her ear pressed to the phone. She waves and then holds a finger to her lips, her eyes bright with excitement. She's in her navy scrubs from her shift at the hospital, her hair piled on her head in a messy bun.

I give an obligatory nod hello and retreat to my room, flopping onto my bed and pulling a pillow over my face. Once I'm sure I'm not going to explode from embarrassment and shame, I slide the pillow off and look around.

My bedroom is a tribute to the places I've never been and the things I've never done. It's a shrine to the lives I'm scared I'll never have.

The western wall is covered in photos of Seattle and Chicago and New York and Boston and Atlanta. Maybe it's a cliché, but I romanticize tall buildings and bright lights the way Fitz romanticizes, well . . . romance. But I also dream of ranches in Wyoming and farms in Nebraska and mountains in Colorado. And that's just the United States. Moving along the wall, you'll run into a collage of Western Europe. Picture after picture of castles and cobblestone roads. Gondolas on the canals of Venice, crumbling colosseums in Rome, waterfalls in Iceland. Each wall is a portion of the world. Japan and Thailand and the Philippines.

Argentina and Brazil and Peru. My bedroom is *my* world, but it's also *the* world.

Above my bed is a picture of Aomori, Japan, that I printed from a HuffPost article about the snowiest places on Earth. The photo is a winding mountain road surrounded by walls of blinding white snow. It looms over a group of travelers, easily three times their height. The snow won't be like that in Williams, obviously, but it'll be new to me. An adventure in an otherwise tame life. Maybe I'll even write about it. Figure out a way to turn it into the start of my imagined travel-writing career. The way I see it, travel writing is the one way I can be paid to live all the lives I've imagined.

Later, I'm almost finished packing when Mom knocks lightly on my door and leans her head in. "Can I come in?" In addition to working as a CNA, she's also a full-time student in nursing school, a ridiculous schedule that has given her permanent shadows under her eyes and a weariness to her posture that I worry nothing can fix. Today, though, she looks happy. Finishing school for the semester has that effect.

I nod. "How was work?"

"Busy. You know how people get around the holidays." She moves into the room and leans against the wall.

"Drunk and sad and stupid?"

"Exactly. A recipe for injuries and accidents. Plus, the flu virus is nasty this year, so the ER was extra packed. But tomorrow's my last shift for more than a week and I'm in the mood to celebrate. So—" She pauses dramatically, her whole face lit up. "Do you want to see your present?"

"What's with people today? Isn't it a little early for that?"

"This gift is time sensitive." Her eyes flick to the open duffel bag on my bed and the mound of discarded clothes next to it. "What are you doing?"

"Oh." I pause, suddenly unsure how to approach this. I assumed she was working all week and wouldn't care if I left after Christmas. Other than our annual Christmas Eve trip to ZooLights, we don't have elaborate traditions. But now that she has the week off, I'm less confident that she'll let me go. New Year's Eve is already the most depressing day on the calendar—even worse than Valentine's Day, which allows for the moral high ground of spouting phrases like "manufactured" and "Hallmark holiday." If I'm gone, what will she do?

"Where's my present?" I ask. She takes the bait and pulls an envelope out of her pocket, waving it back and forth with a grin. I tear the envelope open, expecting to see a couple of twenty-dollar bills, and am stunned to see a plane ticket to New York City.

My heart sputters. "What? How? When? *How?*" We don't ever have extra money, especially at Christmas. Every year Mom buys a real tree because I love the smell, and there are always a few presents underneath, but this is beyond anything I've ever received. Better than the year she found an almost-new stand mixer at a garage sale.

"I won a contest at work. One week off and two tickets to New York City for Christmas. No one will admit it, but I think the odds may have been tipped in my favor. The nurses know how badly I wanted to win for you." She clasps her hands together in front of her mouth, anticipating my reaction.

"When do we leave?"

"Day after tomorrow."

New York. My eyes stray to the brightest glittery city on my wall. "Where are we staying?"

Mom smiles again, but I sense a shadow of hesitation in it. *Of course.* Here comes the part where she breaks the news that the only place we can afford to stay is a rented cell on Rikers Island. "Do you remember my old friend Tyson?"

"No?"

"Sure you do." She clears a spot on the edge of my bed to sit. "His family visited for spring break that one time. We went to a Diamondbacks game, remember?"

"Kind of. His wife spent the whole time complaining about the sun? And the kid, like, inhaled that popcorn we were supposed to share."

She nods. "Tyson and Jenna divorced last year; she moved out of the city, but Tyson and the 'kid'—now a Columbia student— have an apartment in Manhattan. We'll be staying with them!"

"Won't that be awkward?" Sleeping on a random couch is a long way from my fantasy New York trip. I don't need five-star hotels. Far from it. But I also don't want to get stuck playing Secret Santa with strangers. *Here's a candle from the airport gift shop. Hope you like it!*

"No! I promise it won't be. Tyson's excited. To be honest, I've been wanting to visit him. He was recently diagnosed with multiple sclerosis, and this will be a good distraction for Harrison and him."

"Harrison?"

"The popcorn thief."

"I don't know—" I hesitate, my eyes scanning my walls. This trip has potential disaster written all over it. I don't care what Mom says, spending Christmas with strangers will never not be awkward. On the other hand, I might never have enough money to travel to *any* of the cities on my wall, New York included.

"Don't change your mind now! You're mostly packed already. What ruined the surprise?"

"Wait. What?" I snap out of my daydreams of snowy carriage rides in Central Park. Mom gestures to the mound of clothes next to us.

Fitz.

Fitz and the cabin.

Fitz and the cabin and the letter.

Oh no. "Fitz invited me to his cabin for the break."

Mom's face softens and a look of understanding dawns on her features. "You want to go."

"No! I mean, I did, but this is New York." I wave the ticket in front of my face. "I can't—I mean, are the tickets transferable?"

She shakes her head. Because of course. Because I can't ever have anything good without it also being terrible.

"I don't talk much about you and Fitz," she says, choosing her words carefully.

My face flames.

Please don't say it.

"But it's clear as day that you're in love with him."

"I'm not!"

She raises her eyebrows, and I don't have it in me to argue.

"He's important to you, and I can see why. He's charming and handsome and thoughtful—"

"*Mom.*"

"He's also showy and dramatic, but you love who you love. If you want to spend Christmas with him, I won't stop you from going. I'll miss you, but at least I'll have New York to distract me."

"It's not Christmas. They invited me up the day after."

She purses her lips, considering this development. "I'm sure your dad would be happy to have you until then."

I hate to say it, but Christmas with my dad is another plus to the New York column. I know he loves me, but he's a bit highstrung, and being around him winds me tighter than I already am. Mom's personality is much more chill. When it comes to keeping SIM under control, that balance is important.

The first few years after the divorce, I was shuffled back and forth for holidays. But when Dad got remarried, he either stopped asking me to come for Christmas, or Mom stopped offering to send me. It's undetermined. All I know is that the thought of Mom alone on Christmas is too sad for words.

"I don't know." I pick at a hole forming in the knee of my jeans. "Going to New York has always been my dream. One of them, anyway." Even if this is the dream-lite version.

What about the letter? SIM demands. Stupid SIM.

Williams with *Fitz.*

Or *New York* for Christmas.

"Tell me what to do."

"Not this time, Sweets. You're smart and beautiful and sensitive and—"

"Mom!" I sag under the weight of her compliment avalanche.

"You'll figure it out." She kisses the top of my head and stands to leave.

"What if I don't?"

She gazes at me thoughtfully. "I know making decisions is hard for you, but I still have the number for that therapist—"

"Never mind. I'll figure it out on my own."

She frowns as she squeezes my hand in her own. "Let me know if you change your mind."

I won't, but I nod anyway. *Seeing a therapist? For this?* It'd be a waste of everyone's time, and especially Mom's money.

Despair creeps into my chest, filling my lungs. It's too much. I can't choose. If I go with my mom, I get to travel, but I leave the letter with Fitz. And honestly? I'm not sure if I'll even enjoy New York, knowing that Fitz is in possession of the letter that could blow up our relationship.

If Fitz were here, he'd walk me through one of his games, the ones he uses when I'm spiraling out of control. But he's not here, and I have a decision to make. I set my alarm for an early wake-up and text Clover to pick me up in the morning. I need to clear my head, which means I need yeast. And since I won't have the car, it looks like I'll be joining Clover at goat yoga.

Making a hard decision feels like this:

- a racing heart
- cold sweat
- numb lips
- tingly fingers
- queasy stomach
- weak limbs
- dizziness

Panic, in other words. Making a decision feels like panic.

(I once asked Fitz if this visceral response was normal. He didn't respond, which makes me think the answer is no.)

I've been sweaty and crampy and sick since last night, and that's why I'm on a yeast-finding expedition. Because I need help, and baking always helps.

"Are the goats going to be okay in this weather?" I wrap my hands around my hot chocolate and take a sip, fiddling again with the broken heater in Clover's old Prius, on the off chance that today is the day my poking and prodding become effective. (Spoiler alert: It's not.)

"It's only fifty-five degrees," Clover says.

"*Only?* Fifty-five degrees is practically subarctic."

"It's going to be much colder than this wherever you end up for Christmas."

I groan. "What would you do, if you were me?"

Clover turns off the car and pulls a pink beanie with a fuzzy pom-pom over her long ice-blonde waves. We're both in yoga clothes because, like I predicted, her condition for driving me to the store is that I attend goat yoga with her. The class is put on by her youth group and run by her boyfriend, Jay. I rarely join Clover at her youth group activities, but when she first mentioned goat yoga, it was too weird and too hilarious to pass up. She was also nervous, she confessed before our first class, that she didn't have the "right" body type for yoga. Naturally, she smashed that fear in about point two seconds, proving that curvy girls can do whatever they want.

"You know what I would do."

"You would choose the boy."

She grins. "I always choose the boy."

"What would your mother say if she could hear you?"

Clover rolls her eyes. "My mother chose the boy too, once upon a time. And she still chooses him, 'every single day,' as she likes to remind me."

"Did you tell them about your Christmas Eve plans?" I ask her.

"Blah. No. I'm putting it off as long as I can. Better to ask forgiveness than permission, right?"

"Is that what they teach at that church of yours?" I tease while we exit the car and cross the cold, crowded parking lot. Three days before Christmas and everyone has last-minute errands to run. "Only in your house would you have to lie about serving Christmas Eve lunch at the women's shelter."

"It's not about the service or the shelter. My mom served there herself half a dozen times when she was campaigning, and half a dozen more since she was elected to the state house."

Clover's mom is the junior representative of Arizona's Twelfth District, and I vividly remember the campaign pictures of her "happily unmarried" parents and her brother, Heath, in aprons and hairnets serving soup to the women and children in the shelter who were fleeing domestic abuse. Bethany James is a total bleeding heart, but she also disapproves of much of Clover's new lifestyle.

"If Jay wasn't there—"

"If Jay wasn't there, she'd still be weird about it. Church gives her hives. But it's the serious boyfriend thing that really freaks her out," she says.

"Sorry, Clove. She'll come around," I say, even as I remember her grimacing the whole way through her daughter's baptism this summer.

"That's what I've been telling Jay, and myself, for the last nine months. But I swear it's gotten worse. If she's not careful, she's going to push us both away for good." Glass doors slide open and we step into a rush of warm air. A stack of cinnamon-scented pine cones sits near the door, giving the air a warm, spicy aroma.

I frown as I grab a grocery basket, unsure of what to say. Sure, it was a little weird *for me* the first time I saw Clover passing out flyers for the Christian Youth Group, but her life is not about me.

Going to church makes her happy. Dating Jay makes her happy. But sometimes she hints about a distant future with Jay, and my skin itches at the prospect of making that commitment at such a young age.

"Enough distracting yourself with my problems. Did you make a pro-con list?"

"You have to ask?" Pro-con lists are a sham. The pro of one thing is inevitably the con of another thing, making it all a wash.

"Spell it out for me anyway."

We bypass rows of candy canes and wrapping paper, sidestepping a disgruntled employee with a mop and a bucket on our way to the baking aisle. "If I go to the cabin with Fitz, I can destroy that horrible letter before he has the chance to read it. If I go to New York, well, that's self-explanatory. I'd be in *New York*. But how can I enjoy New York if I'm worried about the letter?"

"Huh." She picks up a jar of yeast and tosses it into my basket.

"What?"

"If you don't want Fitz to read the letter, why'd you write it?"

"Because!" I huff. She folds her arms and waits. "Because I knew he was planning some romantic thing with Molly and I was sad and jealous and felt like I would explode if our relationship continued as-is for another day. I was tired of being his consolation prize, the girl he calls when his relationship goes up in flames."

"What changed?"

"I saw him." I flash back to his damp hair in the rain, the way he carefully held the umbrella over my head, his strong hands as he kept me from falling.

"That's all it took to break down your resolve? *Looking* at him?"

I shrug. "That's all it ever takes."

I put the last few supplies in my basket and we exit the aisle.

"Mom asked me to grab wrapping paper and Scotch tape, then we can go," Clover says. We weave our way through a trail of wet-floor signs and follow the explosion of red and green to the Christmas aisle, where I yelp at the familiar sight of glasses and shiny black hair. I grab Clover's arm and pull her into the greeting card aisle.

"What are you doing?"

"Molly!" I whisper.

"What?"

"Molly's in the Christmas aisle."

"No way." Clover pokes her head around the endcap and gasps.

"What's she doing?" I ask.

"Holding a stuffed teddy bear. Do you think it's for Fitz?"

"She forfeited the right to buy Fitz a present when she dumped him." I edge near her and peek around an endcap displaying last-minute stocking stuffers. Molly Nguyen is standing forlornly in front of a shelf of cheesy teddy bears in Santa hats. Clover moves to walk into the aisle but I pull her back. "Wait for her to leave!"

"We're gonna be late for yoga," Clover says too loudly. Molly looks up and catches us staring at her.

"Oh! I didn't think I'd see anyone I knew." Molly gestures to her sloppy ponytail and baggy Minnie Mouse sweatshirt as we move awkwardly into the aisle.

"You look fine," Clover says. And she does. It's true that Molly's usually more put together than this, but she still has an effortlessly cute vibe. If I were a more evolved human or a better feminist, I wouldn't be jealous of her flawless beauty or the way her face was made for those chic black frames, but I'm not better, and I am jealous.

"Christmas shopping?" I gesture to the bear in her hand.

Her cheeks redden. We're friendly, but not friends. Before she started dating Fitz, she hung out with the band and orchestra kids. She plays the viola and has always been shy around me. "It's silly, but I was thinking, for Fitz . . ."

"He said you broke up with him."

She bites her lip and shrugs. "It's not a big deal."

I grind my teeth to keep from snapping at her. "Maybe not to you, but it is to him."

She hugs the bear to her chest. "I guess I didn't think he'd care all that much. You know how he is."

"He's the best guy I know."

"He's dated a lot of people," she says, not unkindly.

And okay, it's not like I haven't thought something very similar once or twice or a hundred times, when I'm feeling jealous or insecure. But as his best friend who's also in love with him, I'm allowed to think that. As the girl who broke his heart, she's not.

"Only a few of them were serious. And anyway, who cares? At least he tries."

Molly's face falls. "Do you think I screwed up?"

"Honestly, yeah. Fitz is one of the good ones." I grab tape from the shelf and turn to leave while Clover picks out rolls of shiny gold wrapping paper.

"Wait!" Molly calls. I halt in my tracks.

"I'll meet you up front," Clover says as she takes our purchases and leaves.

I turn to see Molly dabbing at tears with the sleeve of her sweatshirt. "I did screw up with Fitz."

I groan inwardly, feeling guilty. Molly's never been anything but nice to me, and I could have been more understanding. "I'm sorry. It's none of my business what happened between you two."

"He didn't tell you?" She sets the bear on the shelf.

"Well—" I hesitate. *Is her fear of heights a secret?* Maybe she doesn't want people to know. "Not much," I say truthfully. He usually divulges way more info after a breakup. Jealousy and disappointment rush through me, eroding some of the goodwill I was feeling toward her. *Why didn't he say anything else?*

She sniffles, somehow reminding me of Ivy and Ruby and all the other girls Fitz's dated or flirted with or written love notes to over the years. Like Priya, the five-foot-eleven tennis prodigy who was his date for junior homecoming, or Dani, the short and snarky pitcher who ate lunch with us before she moved to Indiana. She and Fitz never *dated*, but I had to watch him make moon eyes over her for a month during sophomore year. By the time she crossed the state line, his gaze had already landed on Luna, the frizzy-haired little thing who sat next to him in Spanish class.

The thing about Fitz is that he doesn't have a type. On my worst days, it bothered me because I had no idea who to be jealous of. Blondes? Yes. Brunettes? Them too. He's had crushes on girls taller than me and shorter than me and skinnier than me and curvier than me and it soon became painfully clear that Fitz would work his way through every girl in the school before he'd consider dating me.

Molly wrings her hands. "Are you doing okay?"

Me? "I'm fine."

"Are you sure?" Her eyes are full of meaning as they search mine, but I have no idea what that meaning is.

"Yep." I lie. I mean, I'm obviously not fine, what with the Fitz vs. New York decision looming and the stomachache I've had since last night, but she doesn't need to know that.

Molly sighs, clearly frustrated with my response.

"How are *you?*" I'm not sure what else to say.

"I'm good. Other than the Fitz thing, obviously," she says dully.

I have to laugh at her disclaimer. *Good, other than the Fitz thing* is my homeostasis. I should put it in my Insta bio.

"Yeah. Well, I should find Clover. We have to meet some goats; it's a whole thing." I move to leave, but she stops me with her hand.

"Fitz said . . ." Her eyes shift nervously.

"What'd he say?"

"Ready to go?" Clover appears, grocery bag in hand.

"What did Fitz say?" I ask Molly again.

She hesitates. "Never mind. I'll see you around." She rushes out of the aisle, leaving the teddy bear on the shelf.

"Ugh. She was about to tell me something important."

"Sorry, but we've got yoga to do, and then you have bread to bake and a decision to make." Clover smiles at her rhyme, but my pulse spikes at the mention of my impending decision. My traitorous heart pumps poison through my body, infecting every cell with stone-cold dread. Zero to catastrophe. It's a thing that happens sometimes.

I bend over with my hands on my knees and take several deep breaths. The tips of my fingers go numb. "Please tell me what to do."

"Why do you really want to go to the cabin?"

"To get the letter."

"Yeah, but why else?"

"To see the snow."

Clover exhales loudly. "Lord help me, we're gonna be here all day," she mumbles. And then louder, she says, "Those reasons aren't good enough. If that's all you've got, go to New York."

"What else would there be?"

She gapes at me like I'm an idiot.

(I'm not sure she's wrong.)

"A week alone with Fitz? A romantic, snowy cabin? Mistletoe? Crackling fires? Don't pretend like you haven't thought about it."

Something comes to life in my chest. It feels stupidly like hope. "Do you think there's a chance he has feelings for me?"

She smiles sadly. "I don't know if he does *now*. But he definitely did once."

I push away the memory of *that* night, the one from sophomore year, because it always sends me into a spiral of deep regret. "*If* he ever did, I ruined it for good."

Her eyes are full of sympathy as she says, "You won't know for sure unless you let him read that letter."

My cheeks flush. "But what if—"

"What if you go to the cabin and accidentally burn it down while trying to start a cozy fire? What if you go to New York and fall in love with a Brooklynite hipster and never come home? This game goes in circles. It never ends, and you make yourself miserable in the process. The thing you have to ask yourself is, what do you want?"

"I don't want to end up like Molly, another ex-girlfriend to add to his list."

"You're thinking like a person who's scared. Block out the fear and tell me what you want more than anything else."

I imagine I'm the type of person who doesn't make Lists of Doom, who *can* make a decision without the use of the words *what if* and *missed chances* and *ruined life*, and I ask myself the following:

What do I want?

Well. As terrifying as it is to admit to myself, Clover is right. I want snuggly fireside chats and Christmas cookies with Fitz. I want to see snowflakes land on the ends of his thick, dark lashes. I want him under the mistletoe, today and tomorrow and every day for the foreseeable future. But I also want travel and adventure and a life bigger than this town.

Sometimes I cannot breathe for how much I want, and for how scared I am. And that's the point. How am I supposed to choose between the two best things? How can I be sure neither one will ruin my life?

"I wish it were possible to have them both," I say.

Clover furrows her brow. "Do you want to go to the cabin, get the letter, then fly to New York?"

"No. I want to be in two places at once."

"Like in the multiverse?"

"The what?"

"It's the idea that there are different versions of ourselves in different universes— " She sees my bewildered expression and cuts herself off. "Never mind. Listen. If you spend your life paralyzed by fear, you'll miss out on everything. Not only Fitz and New York, but all the other good things too. Jay and I are together because I had the courage to say hi to him that first night at Youth Group. And now we're in love, and I spend every Saturday morning with goats climbing on top of me. Because I made a choice. You're not making any choices, and as your best friend, I refuse to watch you throw away opportunities like this."

"Maybe I should ask Fitz."

"No one wants to feel like an opportunity cost. Trust me." Clover grabs my phone and taps on the screen. When she hands it back, an app called Magic 8 is open. "Whatever it says, that's what you do. Deal?"

"But what if— "

"Paige, listen to me. This takes all decisions out of your hands, but it forces you to act. It's perfect."

But what if it sends me down the wrong path, flinging my life so far out of its natural orbit that it ruins my future forever and ever amen? is what I want to say. But Clover is looking at me with a mixture of hopeless frustration and don't-mess-with-me-or-I'm-gonna-feed-you-to-the-goats.

Well. If my life is going to collapse like a loaf of underbaked bread, it'd be nice to know where to put the blame.

"Deal." I type my question before SIM can change my mind.

Should I go to New York?

I shake my phone and it vibrates between my fingers. The animated ball spins faster and faster, matching the beat of my heart.

I hold my breath and wait. The ball slows to a heartrending stop, but Clover covers it with her hands before I get a view. "No matter what the app says, you should keep using it."

"Permanently?"

"Yes."

It's completely ridiculous, but I don't hate the idea. Without the weight of a hundred possible life-altering decisions dragging me down, I could enjoy Christmas vacation more than I've enjoyed anything in a long time.

"I'll do it," I say, before I can second-guess myself.

Clover removes her hands from the screen, revealing my fate.

Grinning, I speed across the slick grocery store floor, eager to get to yoga, and after that—

"Wait for me!" Clover calls at the same time the employee with the mop yells, "Be careful!" My foot slips out from under me and I crash into a wet-floor sign, falling forward onto the floor. My head bangs hard against the ground and dueling images of Fitz and New York flash before my eyes, just before my vision goes black.

FATE ONE

December 23 | 5:52 a.m. | Sky Harbor Airport

The thing about passport photos is this: They're terrible.

Tragic.

Universally unflattering.

I could fix this problem. Let the people show their teeth! Let them be happy! Let them be excited for their global adventure! The disastrous nature of passport photos is not a mystery is what I'm saying. A forced neutral expression is never going to be a good look.

"Take your shoes off, put them in a bucket, and step through the metal detector," the TSA agent says. She looks stern but bored, impatient and indifferent. Doesn't she understand that everyone around her is embarking on a trip that could alter the entire trajectory of their lives?

"Do you want to see my passport?" I ask.

"You're on a domestic flight, miss."

"It's my ID."

"We don't require minors to show identification."

"Oh. Well, I have it. In case you want to see it."

She narrows her eyes. "Is there some reason you're trying to get me to look at your passport?"

"This is her first flight. She's excited." Mom takes me gently by the shoulders and steers me to the security line. "The first rule of air travel is to not upset the TSA agents."

"Roger that." We dump our loose belongings in a bucket, take off our shoes, shuffle through the line, endure a pat-down. I love it all.

"Aren't you glad I had the foresight to ask for a passport for my tenth birthday?" I ask as we settle into chairs outside our gate.

"Mm-hmm."

"Because if I recall, you didn't appreciate it at the time."

"I did not." Her eyelids droop. I'm not deterred.

"I'm pretty sure that's the year you sat me down and told me we couldn't afford to purchase a passport for, quote, 'no reason.' Which was pretty harsh, by the way."

It's six a.m., but I've never felt so awake in my life. My heart is pumping in my chest, my blood thrumming through my veins. It's all happening. I'm spending Christmas in New York with a family I haven't seen in more than a decade. I'm preparing for a career as a travel writer. I'm going to be a braver, more adventurous version of myself. All because some app said yes when it could have said no.

Of course, SIM can't leave it at that. He rudely reminds me that Fitz might open the letter and find out that our friendship is built on a delicate lie, where one of us cares too much and the other cares too little.

I pull up yesterday's texts with Fitz and scroll through the conversation. After Magic 8 decided I'd be coming to New York, I

explained that it was an opportunity I couldn't pass up, and Fitz
was cool about it. But then this happened.

**11:30 a.m. FITZ: Does this mean I can open your letter
without you?**

11:30 a.m. ME: What?! No!

11:40 a.m. ME: Promise me you're not going to open it!

11:45 a.m. ME: I'm serious.

11:47 a.m. ME: Fitz?

**11:48 a.m. FITZ: I won't. No promises about Gray, though.
That kid is sneaky.**

Yesterday, it read like an offhand comment. A joke about his
three-year-old nephew. Today, I'm not so sure. My stomach churns
at the thought. I need a distraction, ASAP. I turn to Mom.
"You're lucky to have me for a daughter, is what I'm saying."

She gives me a Very Serious Look. "Paige. Do you know that
New York is in the United States?"

"It's close to Canada. You never know what could happen."

You never know what could happen? I mean, obviously. That's
my whole thing. But that's never felt like a good statement
before.

"And you're lucky to have a mom who shelled out $115 for a
dream I wasn't sure I'd ever be able to give you." She smiles wistfully, eyes still closed, and I'm struck all over again by the

unlikelihood of us being here. This time two days ago, I was destined to spend another winter break in Arizona, waiting for Fitz to come back to town and for Clover to schedule hangouts with me around her boyfriend's schedule.

"Thanks, Mom." I flip back to the front of the passport and study my photo. The photographer was impatient with me and my forbidden grin. I tried to smother it, I swear. But it became one of those things where the harder you try not to smile, the more impossible it becomes. I finally managed to clamp my lips around my teeth, but the smile in my eyes is obvious. Ten-year-old me was bursting with the possibility of adventure.

Even back then, I knew I wanted a life outside Gilbert, Arizona, because I hadn't met the one boy who might make me want to stay.

Mom and I are at the end of the last boarding group and the seats aren't assigned, so we have to split up. The flight attendant directs us to an empty middle seat near the center of the plane and tells us there's still an aisle seat in the last row. "Which one do you want?" Mom asks as she searches for room in an overhead bin to store our luggage.

"Hang on." I pull up Magic 8 and type. **Should I sit in the middle seat?** I shake my phone and wait.

Doubtful.

"Aisle, please." Done. Easy. No stress or angst about my potential seatmates or armrests or leg room or even the view. I think I'm going to like this new system. I settle into the last aisle, next to the bathroom. Which, okay. Maybe not the best seat in the house.

But I'm on my first flight ever, and not even the thin wall between the toilet and me is going to dampen my mood.

My stomach clenches in excitement as the plane rumbles down the runway. I crane my neck to look out the window, but after a few seconds the woman in the window seat pulls the shade closed and slips a sleep mask over her eyes. All around me, people look tired and annoyed and bored, like they don't realize or care that in less than eight hours we'll land at LaGuardia Airport in New York. Well, New York by way of Atlanta, but still! Don't these people realize how lucky they are?

I pull a small notebook from my backpack and examine the New York City at Christmas bucket list I made for myself.

Ice-skating in Central Park
Rockefeller Christmas tree
Holiday window displays
Holiday markets
Santaland at Macy's

I cobbled it together from half a dozen online articles sometime between the hazy hours of late last night and early this morning. Like Clover said, I'm taking charge of my life, and I'm not at all thinking about the week I'm missing with Fitz or which girl he'll be in love with by the time I get home. Not much, anyway.

An hour into the flight, one of the attendants makes an announcement. "Good afternoon, passengers! Please direct your attention to row twenty-four for a special surprise." I crane my neck around the bathrooms, where the flight attendants are smiling conspiratorially at each other.

"What's going on?" I ask them.

"Watch." An attendant with a name tag that says JULIE points to the middle of the plane.

A sweaty-looking guy with floppy hair is standing in the aisle. He wipes his forehead with the back of his hand and clears his throat. "Four years ago, I was on a flight from Phoenix to Atlanta for a work trip."

"I can't hear you!" A shout comes from up front.

Sweaty guy clears his throat and starts again. "Four years ago, I was on a flight from Phoenix to Atlanta!" He's practically shouting. "It was almost Christmas, and I was pissed off that my boss was making me travel, and I resolved to make everyone in my vicinity as miserable as I was. Until I sat in my seat, and laid eyes on the most beautiful girl in the world." He bends and I think he dropped something, but then he's on one knee. There's a collective gasp. I lean forward, desperate to get a glimpse at the woman's face. But all I can see is the man beaming at her as if she were every good thing on the planet Earth. My poor, lovesick heart squeezes, and I wish that Fitz were here to witness this. This is exactly the type of emotional candy he lives for.

"Makayla Rios, I love you, and I want to spend the rest of my life with you. Will you marry me?" He fumbles with the box, dropping it on the ground. It slides under a seat. Friendly laughter ripples through the plane, because no one has realized that she hasn't said yes. And she's not going to.

I know this because I know Fitz, and Fitz knows rom-coms.

When a man proposes, there are only two reasons a woman does not immediately accept. The first reason is that she's too busy crying or gasping to coherently form words. The second is that she's not going to.

Makayla Rios leans into the aisle, her black hair falling forward to obscure her face. She whispers something into sweaty guy's ear.

Let's talk about this. I'm sorry. I can't. I care about you. I wonder which of the thousand equally terrible ways she's breaking his heart.

He's frozen, unable to get up from his knee or close the ring box or wipe the gutted look from his face. Whispers spread like a naked selfie in a locker room.

"What did she say?"

"She said no!"

"Poor guy."

"So awkward!"

I turn to the flight attendants. Julie is holding a bottle of champagne, watching this whole nightmare unfold with a horrified expression. "What do I do?" She turns to the other attendant, a bald guy with CrossFit muscles and a name tag that reads ADAM.

"Nothing! Put it away. I'll distract them," he whispers, and grabs the speaker.

"It is currently eight forty-five a.m. That would be, uh, Phoenix time. We're flying at, um—thirty-six thousand feet and are on pace to land in Atlanta at twelve fifteen local time. If you're continuing on to LaGuardia, please stay on board so we can count you as a through passenger. Thank you."

The announcement gives proposal guy time to close the ring box and return to his seat. I squirm uneasily, overwhelmed with vicarious embarrassment. If it's this bad for me, he must be dying.

"What do you think is happening?" I ask Julie as she readies the drink cart.

"I'll find out and report back." It takes approximately twelve hundred years for her to push the drinks all the way to the other end of the plane, but eventually she comes back, handing me a second hot chocolate when she sees I've finished my first. "They're fighting. He's crying," she whispers as she crouches next to me under the guise of organizing the drink cart.

My heart shatters for him. I'm trying to think of some way to help when Makayla stands. "She's coming back here! What do we do?" I whisper.

"Stop talking about her!" Julie whispers back as she clears the aisle.

I'm flustered as Makayla stops outside the bathrooms, which are both flipped red to OCCUPIED. She sighs heavily and leans against the wall. I sneak glances at her: early to midtwenties, thick black eyeliner, butterfly tattoo below her ear, blunt bangs across her forehead. Check, check, check. I make mental notes about all her characteristics, as if they'll add up to something meaningful. Or maybe I'm looking for a warning sign. Something that says: *This is what a person looks like right before they stomp on your heart.*

She catches me staring. "Do you have something to say?"

Surprised, I turn around, half expecting her to be talking to someone else. But the woman beside me is still asleep.

"Are you talking to me?"

Her gaze lingers on the bruise on my forehead, still fresh after yesterday's embarrassing fall. "You were gawking, like everyone else on the plane."

I wince. "Sorry."

She shrugs. "I get it. It was completely awful, like a car wreck you can't look away from."

"Oh, yeah, I guess, I mean— Did you break up?"

She nods.

"So you *really* don't want to marry him." *Wow. Brilliant observation, Paige.*

She blows her bangs out of her eyes with a sigh. "I've been meaning to break up with him for ages, but it never seemed like the right time."

"Is it ever?"

"No, but it's *especially* a bad time right before Christmas. And when his dog just died."

Fair enough. I pull a bag of sour gummy worms out of my backpack and offer it to her. She takes a few with a small smile. "Can I ask you a question?" I ask.

She shrugs again. An invitation to be nosy.

"How is it possible that you two were in such different places?" Something shifts uneasily in my stomach. I'm asking about them, but maybe some part of me wants to know about Fitz and me too. How is it possible that two people who call themselves best friends can view their relationship so differently?

"We've been together a long time. Things have always been so comfortable and easy between us, you know?"

I nod.

"How old are you?" she asks.

"Seventeen."

She purses her lips. "Don't fall in love for, like, ten years, okay?" I laugh uneasily and she continues. "I was only nineteen when Ben and I met. We were too young then and we're too young now. It's too soon to decide our future." She says this last part quickly, tossing it in the air without any conviction, testing the words out loud. When she tells this story to her friends and family, that's the line she'll choose. Too young. Too soon.

The bathroom door opens and Makayla disappears behind it. When she returns, her eyes and nose are red, her eyeliner smudged on the wrong side of smoky. "Can I hang out back here?" she whispers to Julie.

"I'm sorry, you need to take your seat."

Makayla groans and runs her hands through her hair. She glances warily at her ex. He's hunched over, head in his hands like an Eeyore impersonator. She looks like she'd rather jump out the window than spend the next few hours sitting next to him, and I'm hit with another wave of sympathy. He shouldn't have to suffer through the rest of the flight sitting next to the girl who publicly ripped his heart to shreds.

"Switch seats with me?" I offer.

She hesitates. "Are you sure?"

"Yes." I toss my hot chocolate cup in the garbage behind me, grab the bag of gummy worms, and move up the aisle. Ben lifts his head at the sound of my footsteps.

"Who are you? Where's Kay?" He's deflated. Even his

knees look saggy. He moves to the side to allow me to pass.

"I'm Paige. Makayla is at the back of the plane."

"Did she say—?"

"I didn't want you to have to sit next to her for the rest of the flight, so we switched seats."

"Well, that's embarrassing." His face droops lower. He's entering basset hound territory.

For the next hour, Ben plays a game on his phone while I live through a time loop of Fitz opening the letter. I imagine it all: Surprise at learning I love him. Anger at learning I hate him. Hurt at the fact that I told him to stop talking to me. Each daydream adds another knot to my already twisty stomach. He agreed to wait, but now that plans have changed and I'm en route to New York, it's not a stretch to imagine he'd give in to curiosity and see what all the fuss was about.

Ben sets his phone down with a heavy sigh and scrubs his hands over his face. I don't want to get called out for staring again, but . . .

"Are you okay?" I blurt.

He gives me that look adults sometimes get around kids. The one that says: *You have no idea what you're talking about.* "Just wait, kid."

"What's it feel like?"

"Rejection?"

"Heartbreak." The word is shaky on my lips. It matches my hands and the tremble in my stomach.

He spins his phone between his fingers. His eyes are haunted, and he's silent for so long I give up hope of an answer. I'm suddenly aware of the sweat dripping down my back, and the freezing air blowing in my face from the vents. I try to swallow back my panic, but it's no use. I can feel it building, escalating, demanding attention.

I made a huge mistake.

No. Scratch that. I've made a hundred mistakes. Writing the letter. Leaving it with Fitz. Going to New York. Take your pick. My life is the Russian roulette of bad decisions, except in this game, every chamber is loaded.

"It's every bad thought you've ever had about yourself." The quiet pain laced through his words shoots me straight through the heart. "It's a boulder sitting on your chest, squeezing the air from your lungs. It's the feeling of losing something. It's tearing your house apart brick by brick to find it, even though you know it's not there."

Whoa.

"I have to make a call. It's an emergency." My heart slams against my ribs, desperate to break free and escape the inevitable pain.

He checks the time on his phone. "Hope it can wait an hour."

"Not really."

"Relax, kid. You want to hear a story?"

"Sure. Yes. Please distract me. Anything."

He settles in his seat. "I met Makayla on my twenty-second birthday . . ."

I groan silently and clutch my phone in my hands.

This trip was a mistake that's going to tear Fitz and me apart. I can feel it. There's no coming back from this.

FATE TWO

Fitz Wilding wears confidence like a crown. He's quick with a lazy grin, comfortable in every situation, and so adaptable it makes my head spin. He's everything I'm not, and I hate him for it. Of course, I don't hate him enough. Not nearly. If my hate were born of actual resentment and not of heartbreak, I'd be immune to the fact that he looks so heart-stoppingly good all the time. Take baseball, for example. Fitz looks *real* good at third: knees bent in a crouch, blue eyes serious, glove ready, brown hair curling under the edge of his hat.

Fitz watching a movie is equally phenomenal, because every emotion plays out on his face. I've probably spent entire days of my life watching Fitz watch movies. The proximity of his body to mine is always more interesting than the actors on the screen.

My favorite Fitz, however, is him behind the wheel of his pickup truck. All our best conversations have taken place in the cab of that truck. It's where he confessed that he wants to play professional ball and where I confessed that I want to travel the world, and we bonded over the tragedy of having impossible dreams.

We're admittedly an odd pair: the jock with a team full of baseball friends and a new girl in his DMs every week, and me. The girl with one other friend and no inclination to play sports. Fitz and I met in seventh-grade English class, and likely would have stayed classroom-only friends if his sister wasn't always late picking him up from practice and my mom's shifts didn't end until thirty minutes after whatever after-school activity I joined to avoid being home alone. Those hot afternoons sitting with him on the curb outside school quickly became the best part of my day. And when I saw him turn down a ride from another parent to wait with me, I realized he was enjoying them too.

My breath catches at the sight of him now: hat on, windows down, left arm bent at the elbow, fingers lightly tapping the top of the frame. No matter how many girls he dates, I'm convinced that vulnerable, thoughtful, silly Fitz-behind-the-wheel is someone very few people know. I'm sick at the thought that I'm one letter away from losing access to my favorite version of him.

Give it some time, I remind myself as I cross my front lawn on shaky legs. *Be patient.* If I make a big deal about getting the letter back, he's going to realize that the letter is a Big Deal.

"I could have driven," I say as I open the door and hoist myself up into the passenger's seat. His truck is one of those giant monstrosities with enormous tires that's killing the planet. It belongs to his father's landscaping company, but it's basically Fitz's to use as he pleases. The only vehicle access I have is Mom's old sedan, but because she's on a plane to New York, she agreed to let me drive to the cabin.

"No way." He checks his mirrors and pulls away from the curb. "On the off chance the storm hits early, I want you safe in a four-wheel drive with snow tires." He glances at me and frowns. "What happened to your head?"

I rub at the small lump on my forehead. "Slipped and fell. I'm fine. And thanks again for letting me come up a few days early and crash your family's Christmas. Are you sure your parents don't mind?"

"Mom's hyped. She lives for hosting big holiday celebrations. But I feel bad that *your* mom had to leave last minute like that."

So the thing is—I lied. Fitz knows how badly I want to travel, and he wouldn't understand why I chose not to go to New York. I told him an abbreviated version of the truth—that Mom won a ticket at work (not a lie!) and was using it to visit her sick friend (also not a lie!).

"What about your dad?"

"He's . . ." I hesitate, wondering if I can get away with another evasion. The fact is, my dad's uninformed about this last-minute turn of events. "He's busy," I say, feeling decent about the probable truth of my response. Most adults I know love to talk about how busy they are.

Fitz frowns in sympathy and my stomach squirms. I hate pseudo-lying to him, despite the fact that I lie by omission every day of my life.

"So, did you bring that letter I wrote?" I aim for casual and fall spectacularly short, just on this side of eager.

"No. Was I supposed to?"

"No. But I need it back. Where is it?"

Fitz looks at me sideways, his face hesitant. "On the counter? Maybe?"

"You lost it?"

"No! It's definitely *in* the cabin. I'm just not sure where." He shrugs, the corners of his mouth turning up in a sheepish smile.

I take a deep breath as liquid dread oozes through my belly.

Don't panic.

Easier said than done.

Because what if the letter is sitting on the counter, and a glass of water spills, soaking the envelope, and Mrs. Wilding tears it open to allow the letter to air dry, but as she sees the ink slowly spreading she takes a picture of it to preserve it forever, and while snapping the picture sees an incriminating word or sentence or paragraph and reads it, then tells the whole family, and by the time I get there, everyone will know my secret.

What. If.

This is my worst nightmare, and I felt it coming in my bones. I opened my eyes this morning with a feeling of unease looming at the edge of my mind, whispering that I've done something wrong, or am about to do something wrong, or have done everything wrong my entire life. It happens more often than I'd like to admit, and the worst part is the unpredictability. I'll go to sleep feeling perfectly fine, only to wake up feeling like I've been sucker-punched in the stomach.

"What's wrong?"

"Nothing," I say, because how can I explain it to him when I don't have the words to understand it myself?

His hand twitches, his face uncharacteristically serious. "It's been a while, but do you wanna do the thing?"

I grimace at the window in lieu of responding. My reflection is terrible.

"Describe five things you can see right now."

Eyes still trained on the passing highway, I answer in a dull voice. "Cars, road, sky, overpass, cactus."

"Four things you can touch."

My gaze flicks to him. I press my hands against my thighs, focusing my concentration on the feel of my soft leggings. "Cotton-Lycra." I place my hand on the cool window. "Glass." I hold it in front of the vent. "Heat." My eyes flick to Fitz again. He lifts his right hand from the steering wheel and holds it palm up over the center console. He used to hold my hands during this part, giving me something solid and warm to focus on while everything in my brain feels chaotic and out of control.

I pretend not to notice his gesture and I run my fingers through my straight brown hair, naming it as my fourth thing.

"Three things you can hear." He doesn't skip a beat, just casually returns his hand to the steering wheel.

"Your voice." I cringe before I can stop myself. "Tires on the road." I strain to hear the radio, which is turned down low. "'Baby, It's Cold Outside.'"

"This song is atrocious. He basically drugs this girl," he says as he reaches to turn up the volume.

"Say, what's in this drink?" the woman croons.

"Get out! Get out now!" we both shout at the radio. I lean back in my seat, grinning.

"Do you want to keep going?" Fitz asks.

"I'm okay." The looming dread has loosened its grip on my chest, and anyway, he's about to ask me to name two things I can smell, and I'll be forced to admit that I'm slowly inhaling his smoky-sweet scent.

The desert landscape gives way to mountain terrain as we drive, cacti dropping from view only to be replaced by tall pine trees. I lean my head against the window as Fitz and I talk about Christmas music and baseball season and his family and mine. Uncharacteristically, Molly's name isn't mentioned even once. If I were a better person, I'd tell him her teary-eyed confession, the one hinting that she regrets dumping him.

But I'm not. So I don't.

I close my eyes outside Flagstaff, trying to picture the landscape blanketed in a thick layer of snow. Instead, sheer force of habit pulls me into a two-year-old memory. I had spent all Christmas break lying sick in bed with strep throat. Due to a combination of strong bacteria and weak antibiotics, my strep morphed into scarlet fever.

"Knock, knock." Fitz rapped his knuckles on my door frame. "I hear you've gone and gotten yourself some dramatic illness."

Fitz! My heart sighed in relief. "Just call me Beth March," I said, not caring that the words tore at my throat. For the first time in days, I was unbothered by the fire in my throat or my throbbing headache or the fact that I couldn't seem to get warm. Fitz had always had that effect on me. He could turn my bad mood into a good one simply by allowing me to exist in his orbit.

He flopped himself across the foot of my bed. "I'm sorry, I will not stand by and let you convince yourself that you're a tragic literary heroine."

"Beth wasn't the heroine. She was the sister."

"You're not dying."

"I never said I was."

"But you thought it." His eyes glinted with mischief, and I couldn't deny it.

"Did it snow?" I asked, impatient to hear about his week at the cabin.

"Tons."

I whimpered pathetically.

"They had to close the roads," he said.

"Stop."

"The power went out."

"No!" I groaned, covering my face with a pillow. He pulled it away and smiled at me, eyes sparkling like he knew a secret. He leaned toward me conspiratorially.

"I'm horribly contagious," I said. *Come closer*, I thought.

"I'll risk it."

My heart throbbed in my chest as an as-yet-unnamed emotion swelled inside me. *It's the fever*, I reasoned. What else could it be?

"Am I hot?"

Fitz's eyes widened in surprise. "What?"

"I think I still have a fever. I'm feeling feverish. I'm feeling—" His palm touched my forehead, the contact rendering me speechless.

"You're burning up."

"I told you I'm *very* hot."

He rolled his eyes while I giggled deliriously. "This sucks," he said.

"Are you worried about me? I should be better soon." I smoothed the wrinkle between his eyes with my finger.

"It's not that. I know you're not dying. But I have this surprise set up, and I was excited to show you—"

"A surprise?" I sat up and my head protested. "For me? I'm in."

"No, you're too sick."

"Nonsense." I threw the mound of blankets off and stood up, stumbling as the room spun. Fitz grabbed my hand until my head felt less loopy. In that moment, I knew I didn't care what the surprise was, because the important thing was this: Fitz had a surprise. For me. The thought made me dizzier, somehow. Fitz wasn't the type to plan surprises for me, not like when Tommy Weisman sent me a Valentine's Day candygram in seventh grade and then cried when I promptly ate it.

I sat on the handlebars of Fitz's bike while he steered. At his house, he ducked into the garage and retrieved a bulky garbage bag. "Quick wardrobe adjustment before we go in," he explained as he opened the bag. He slid a beanie over my hair, brushing a stray tangle out of my face with his fingers. My skin blazed under his touch. He wrapped a scarf around my neck while my heart hammered in my chest. He slipped gloves over my fingers, and I nearly passed out.

"What are you doing?" I whispered through searing pain.

"You'll see. Now close your eyes."

"Why?"

"I imagined it with your eyes closed. Please?"

"You imagined it?"

Fitz sighed and placed his hands gently over my eyes before leading me from the freezing porch into the still-freezing house.

"Why's it so cold?"

"Because you're delirious with fever."

"I'm not."

"You are. But it's okay. I think it's going to work in my favor. Open your eyes."

He moved his hands and I opened my eyes to snow.

In the house.

I tried to blink away the blinding white, but it didn't go anywhere. Fitz's living room was transformed. Piles of white, fluffy "snow" covered the coffee table, end tables, and tile floor. I bent to run my fingers through it.

Snow.

It wasn't, of course, but in all the ways that matter, it was.

"How'd you do it?"

"Aw, don't ask me that. It's better if you don't know." He rubbed the back of his neck. "Sorry it's not cold," he added sheepishly.

"It's perfect," I breathed.

He smiled extravagantly, his cheeks pink with embarrassment or cold underneath his ball cap.

He was the most beautiful thing I'd ever seen, and I was in love with him.

The force of the revelation buried me like an avalanche. I dropped to my knees, sending tiny white flecks of fake snow fluttering in all directions.

I loved him. Of course I loved him. How had that never occurred to me before? He made me a snowstorm. How could I do anything other than love this boy?

"I'll show you the real thing someday," he said as he crouched next to me.

"Promise?" The room was spinning again. I needed to lie down.

"Pinkie swear." He winked.

I lay down and made a snow angel, breathing in the scent of baking soda. He leaned back on his arms, watching me with an amused smile. My eyes found his and we stayed like that for several breaths, my heart pumping hope and fear through my body like a drug. My fever was 103 and I hadn't eaten in five days, but I felt happier than I ever had in my life. "I could stay here forever."

"I should get you home."

"Already?" My voice was thick with wounded disappointment.

"You should be in bed, and Ivy's on her way over."

Ivy? Ivy McGuire? Ivy McGuire from third-period world history? "Why?"

His grin turned wolfish. "I'm going to woo her." He spread his arms wide.

"I don't get it. Is she obsessed with snow or something?"

"I don't think so."

"Isn't she from Chicago?"

"Um, I don't . . . yeah, that sounds right."

"So she's seen plenty of snow."

"Probably."

"Then why did you make this for her?"

"I made it for you."

"Then why show it to her?" I snapped. If I focused on my anger instead of my crushing disappointment and jealousy, maybe I wouldn't cry.

"This is my grand gesture!"

I rolled my eyes. "Why can't you do something else? Why can't it be enough to show the snow to me?"

"Because I'm not trying to make out with you."

Clearly. I blinked away the white-hot tears. "I don't feel good."

"I kept you too long. But hey, I'm glad you loved it."

"Hopefully Ivy will too."

"That's the plan." He winked again, creating an ache in my heart that would set up permanent residence for the next two years.

Fitz shakes me out of my half slumber and painful memories as he turns off the main road and pulls down a long dirt driveway that winds deeply into a grove of pine trees. At the end of the driveway is a large multistory wooden cabin.

"We're not exactly roughing it," I say, taking in the high, peaked roof and the wraparound porch. It resembles a ski lodge more than a rustic cabin. "So, what do I need to know?" I ask Fitz.

"What do you mean?"

"About your sisters. What do I talk about? What don't I talk about? I want them to like me."

"Everyone already knows and loves you."

"Not Darcy." Fitz's eldest sister is the only one in his family I haven't met. She lives in Boston with her new wife and, from what I can tell, only visits at Christmas.

"Don't worry about it. You'll be fine." His eyes meet mine across the warm car, and I swear there's something different in the way he's looking at me. Maybe it's the heat blasting at my cheeks or the gingerbread cabin in front of me or the Christmas music on the radio, but suddenly the warm air feels charged. "Are you ready?" His eyes spark as he looks at mine.

No, I'm not at all sure I'm ready for this. But I don't exactly have a choice in the matter, so I open the door. A blast of arctic air fills my lungs as we step outside, pushing out any notions of electricity or sparkling eyes and grounding me in reality.

Reality. The universe in which Fitz was just dumped by the girl he called "the one."

We crunch across fallen pine needles and up the porch steps. He turns to me. "I lied. You do need to prepare yourself."

Anxious nerves hit me straight in the gut. "You're scaring me."

"You should know that what's behind this door is overwhelming," he says with a stone-faced expression.

"Oh no. Which sister? It's Darcy, isn't it?" I frown at the remembered image of his oldest sister's profile picture. She's all razor-sharp angles and dark, piercing eyes.

"It's not that." He takes a steadying breath. "It's the décor. It's very . . . cozy."

"Mm-hmm."

"And Christmassy. It's like the North Pole on steroids."

"And you thought this would scare me?"

He huffs out a laugh and it transforms into white puffs of air between us. I roll my eyes, shoving him hard in the shoulder, and open the door myself.

Fitz wasn't wrong. My eyes are drawn to a towering behemoth of a Christmas tree, strung with lights and ribbons and mismatched ornaments. Garlands drape from every wooden banister and stockings are hung from the large stone fireplace. Crackling flames lick the logs inside, and squashy leather sofas strewn with fuzzy blankets beg me to collapse into them. Christmas cheer touches every inch of the cabin, and I've never loved a place more.

"I told you." Fitz's whispered words tickle my neck, sending electric shocks down my spine. "Stay here where it's warm. I'll grab your bags." He doubles back out the door, and I tentatively move into the room.

A man I recognize as Fitz's brother-in-law is the first to see me. He feeds a spoon of orange mush to a baby in a high chair and tosses a friendly smile in my direction.

"Molly! You made it!"

FATE ONE

December 23 | 12:27 p.m. | Hartsfield-Jackson
Atlanta International Airport

The jury is still out on airplanes.

On the one hand, this giant steel contraption is making one of my oldest dreams come true. On the other hand, Ben talks a lot. Too much. He drones on for so long that *I* want to break up with him. But the thing about airplanes is that you're stuck. And I hate feeling stuck.

"Well, I guess I can't stall any longer." He claps his hands on his thighs before standing up. "Time to face the music." He nods to me before ambling slowly down the aisle. The plane is about half-empty now. Insert Fitz joke about how he'd consider it half-full.

Gosh. I miss him.

I wanted to bolt from the plane as soon as it touched down on the runway, but it seemed rude to push my way through the aisle when other passengers had connections to make. Plus, my phone is already dead and my charger is in my carry-on bag, which is at the back of the plane. So, I had to wait.

But now Ben is gone and I retrieve my bag from the overhead

bin near the bathrooms and then find Mom. "Hey. I'm gonna get off the plane real quick."

"No, Sweets. There's not time."

"I have to make a phone call."

"They're boarding soon. They just announced it."

"I heard the announcement, but I have to charge my phone. It's important."

Mom sighs. "Clover will be fine without you for a few hours."

"I'll be fast." I take off, not waiting for an answer. I race down the long tunnel, brushing past boarding passengers, and am stopped at the gate by a frowny employee.

"No running."

"Seriously?" That *cannot* be an airport rule. Watch the last ten minutes of any rom-com for proof. But then I remember Mom's advice not to anger airport employees. "Sorry, it's just that I need to charge my phone before the plane takes off."

"You're going to New York?"

"Yeah."

"Get back on the plane. It's leaving soon."

"I know, but—"

"We're not holding the plane for you. I'll lock this door whether you're here or not."

"But—"

"Which side do you want to be on?"

I turn with a grumble and trudge down the tunnel, taking my place in line behind the boarding passengers. And lucky me, I once again get the seat by the bathrooms.

* * *

The flight from Atlanta to New York is torture. Why didn't anyone tell me that airplanes are kind of boring? That they're small and there's nothing to eat and the temperature always feels wrong, and you'll have nothing but time to think about the one thing you don't want to think about? When we finally touch down in LaGuardia, I'm a sweaty (but also somehow freezing?) anxious mess.

And since I'm at the very last row and everyone is impatient and no one has any sympathy for the complete and total destruction of my life, I'm once again the last person off the plane. And my phone is still dead, and my charger is smashed somewhere in the depths of my carry-on, and Mom is ushering me toward baggage claim, and *my phone is dead*, and I need to call Fitz and tell him to stay away from that letter but I can't because MY PHONE IS DEAD.

I sputter out a bunch of protests while Mom retrieves our luggage, but she's too busy reading subway maps and flagging down taxis and Google Mapping to pay attention. Before I know what's happening, I'm in the back of a cab.

I rummage through my bag and find my charger, spinning it between my fingers while Mom chatters to the driver about our flight and our first time in New York. The big gray city whizzes by my window. I look up at the buildings, marveling at their size, but I can't enjoy it, not really, because what if Fitz (or his nephew) is opening my letter *right now*?

By the time we pull up in front of a redbrick apartment building, I'm a twisted ball of knots, practically turned inside out from stress. "What apartment are they in?" I ask.

"5B."

"Can I meet you up there?" I want to run ahead and charge my phone ASAP in Tyson's apartment.

"No. You can stay right here and help me with the bags."

I growl a frustrated sigh and step out of the cab. My foot lands in a taffy-thick pile of dirty sludge, and I'm soaked up to my ankle. "Gross! What is this?"

Mom steps gently over the muddy brown sludge. "Leftover snow."

"This is snow?" I shake my foot, wishing I had a bucket of sanitizer to dunk it in. Snow is decidedly less magical than I expected.

"It was snow. Now it's snirt. Snow plus dirt." The trunk pops open and I help Mom pull out our luggage, careful to avoid stepping in the mounds of "snirt" piled next to the curb.

We lug our bags up five flights of stairs and stop in front of door 5B. Mom knocks, and a guy answers the door. He has messy brown hair pulled into a low ponytail and a bored expression.

"Harrison! You're so big now! This is Paige. Do you remember her?"

Harrison sort of grunts in response as Mom and I drag our bags inside. "My dad's in the other room." He jerks his thumb down the skinny hallway toward a small living room. Mom heads toward it, but I follow Harrison into the clean but shabby kitchen at the back of the apartment.

"Is there an outlet I can borrow?" I hold up my charger and phone. By this point I'm practically leaping out of my own skin, and it's a huge effort to keep my voice in a normal register.

"You can unplug the toaster," he says flatly.

I do, and then I plug in my charger and attach it to my phone. "Thanks. I have to make a phone call. It'll be quick."

"Okay." He sits at a small table in the breakfast nook, props his feet on the chair next to him, and pulls a clunky textbook onto his lap. The chapter heading reads "Introduction to Philosophy." An open bag of Flamin' Hot Cheetos sits next to him. He grabs a handful and tosses them in his mouth, crunching loudly.

"Um . . . it's kind of private?" I hate the way my voice goes up at the end.

"That's what texts are for."

"This is too delicate to deal with over text."

"Okay." He doesn't move. Doesn't even think about it. He resolutely *does not budge*. I could try to find another room, but it seems weirder for me to barge into one of the bedrooms than to stay here.

"I hate to ask, but can you leave?"

He cocks his head for a moment, considering this. Or at least, pretending to consider it. "Nah."

I sigh and pull up Fitz's number. Fine. Whatever. I don't have time to debate with him, and I don't have time to rummage through the apartment looking for another outlet. I dial.

Fitz picks up after the first ring. "Hey, Collins!"

My face breaks into a smile and all my senses heighten. Fitz may as well be in the same room with me, for how happy I am to hear his voice. "Hi," I practically sigh, the word breathy with relief. Harrison looks from his book; I angle my body away from him. "I need to ask you for a favor. And I can't explain why I need it, but it's important."

I swear I can hear Fitz sit up on the other end of the phone. "What's wrong? Are you okay?"

"I'm in New York and I'm fine." I glance at Harrison, who's listening with open curiosity.

"What's going on?"

"Don't open the letter."

He pauses for too long. "I already said I wouldn't."

"But you said Gray might—"

"It was a joke."

"Please get rid of it. It's embarrassing." My cheeks flame. This is awful. He's going to figure it out.

"Paige—"

"I wrote you a letter that said something it shouldn't have. I did something without thinking—"

"Is this a murder confession?" he asks playfully.

"I'm serious. I can't explain it right now. But please, as your friend, I'm asking you to do this for me."

Another pause, and then he says, "If that's what you want." My muscles unwind for the first time since I witnessed the failed proposal on the plane. "How's New York?"

We chat for a few minutes about his sisters and my flight, until his nephew pulls him away from the phone for an epic superhero battle. I turn, expecting to find Harrison still watching me, but his gaze is back on his book.

"Thanks again."

"I'll forward you the next electric bill," he deadpans.

"I'm Paige, by the way."

"I know." His gaze flits up to me. "We've met."

"Right. It was, what, like ten years ago?"

"Eleven."

"I didn't think you'd remember!"

"What can I say? The popcorn made quite an impression on me." He smirks as my cheeks redden. "That and the heat. It was brutal for March."

"I don't think heat will be a problem here," I joke. He doesn't comment, so I keep talking. "This is my first time in New York." Again, nothing. Not so much as an eyebrow raise. I barrel on. "I'm really excited to be here. I made a list; I want to do everything. My mom is thrilled to be here too, obviously, but she told me they wouldn't get out much."

He sighs and finally looks at me, but I wish he wouldn't. It's more of a withering stare than an actual look. "Yeah, I reckon my dad's degenerative disease is going to keep him from traipsing all over the city." His voice is icier than the biting wind outside. My insides shrivel in embarrassment.

"Yeah. Sorry. I didn't mean . . . it's just that . . ." I trail off, hoping he'll save me from this excruciating moment with a "don't worry about it" or "it's cool."

He doesn't.

I recognize a loss when I see one. It's time to take my mumbled apologies and hide out until Harrison is in a better mood. My fingers close around my phone, and I'm hit by a thought.

No. I didn't come here to hide inside with a dirty, wet foot and nothing to do. I'm here to make myself into a different kind of person with a different kind of life.

"No."

"No, what?"

"No, I didn't abandon the snowy, romantic Christmas of my dreams to sit in an apartment. I have a New York bucket list. It's filled with all the things I want to do while I'm here. I was hoping you'd help me out, maybe show me around a bit."

He blinks slowly. My pulse kicks up a notch as my skin flushes. "Not that you have to —like, spend your whole break chauffeuring me around the city."

"Oh?"

"Yeah. Um. Obviously I don't expect that. Wouldn't ask for that. But your dad told my mom you'd be willing to show me Christmas in New York." I hold my breath, waiting. "I've never been anywhere," I add as an afterthought. An appeal to his sense of humanity.

He studies me for an uncomfortable length of time before he says, "Nah." He flips his book closed and stands.

"Nah? That's it?"

"It's a complete sentence." He shrugs and moves to leave the kitchen. I step in front of him, blocking his path.

"*No* is a complete sentence. *Nah* isn't anything."

"Fine," he sighs indulgently. "Ask me again."

"Will you go with me to the Central Park ice-skating rink?" I ask. He takes a deep, slow breath, and my hope soars ridiculously high. He's going to say yes, because how could he not?

"No." The corner of his mouth twitches. An almost smile? He

dodges me and leaves the kitchen. "Oh, and Paige—" he says, turning suddenly.

"Yeah?"

"That guy you were talking to? He knows you're in love with him." He disappears down the hall as my embarrassment licks my insides like a wildfire.

For a full second that feels like twenty, I cannot breathe. And then common sense kicks in. What does Harrison know about me anyway? Nothing. He knows nothing about me or about Fitz, and also, he sucks. He sucks and I cannot believe I gave up my chance at spending Christmas with Fitz, in an actual winter wonderland, to be stuck here in a cheerless apartment with him. I pick up my wounded pride and head to the room where my mom and Harrison's dad are laughing loudly.

They're sitting on opposites ends of an old, worn couch. On the end table is a small, fake, scraggly Charlie Brown Christmas tree with no ornaments. It's the only sign of Christmas in the house. There's no delicious pine scent or stockings hanging on the wall or spicy gingerbread in the oven. Tyson is wearing worn jeans and an old Oasis T-shirt. He has shaggy brown hair that looks unintentional.

If I didn't know he was sick, I wouldn't be able to tell. I did the basic Google thing when Mom first told me about his diagnosis. He's in the early stages of multiple sclerosis, so he might be experiencing vision loss, numbness and tingling, or fatigue. Or maybe not. His legs are propped up on the coffee table and he relaxes fully into the sofa in a way that I can imagine him doing every day for the last ten years. And now he's still doing it, only everything is different. My heart pangs for him, and maybe even a little for Harrison too.

"Hey, Sweets! Come meet my friend Tyson. Tyson, this is my talented and beautif—"

"Mom!" I roll my eyes, desperately thankful that Harrison is not here for this. I know him approximately 0 percent, but I'm willing to bet he'd scoff at my mother's deluge of compliments. I assume it's an only-child thing. If I had siblings, Mom would *have* to spread some of her lavish praise and compliments among the group. Unfortunately, all she's got is me and I have to fill the role of talented and beautiful and whatever half-truths she's prepared to sprinkle all over the floor like glitter. Obnoxious, hard-to-get-rid-of glitter.

"This is Paige." She smiles indulgently. But not for me. She's smiling for Tyson, I realize with a start.

"Hey, so I think I'm gonna go out for a bit. Check out the city," I say.

"Paige, I don't know. It's freezing out there, and you don't know your way around."

"Mom." I plead with my eyes. This is what I make them say:

This is my first day in New York.

This is my chance to finally do something interesting with my life.

The boy I'm in love with might know that I'm in love with him, and he doesn't love me back, and our entire friendship might be falling apart right this very second.

"Take Harrison with you," Tyson says before taking a sip from his mug. Steam rises from the top, and he closes his eyes, savoring the hot liquid.

"Yeah—about that . . ."

"Did he say no?"

I shrug in response as Tyson groans. "I'm sorry, Paige. Between us, his girlfriend dumped him last week, and he's been having a rough time."

"Oh." Is there no escaping sad boys with wounded hearts? I glance to Mom for help.

"Maybe we could . . ." She glances at Tyson, who winces and shakes his head. She turns to me. "I'll come with you," she says with a forced smile, and it's obvious she'd rather spend her evening on the couch with her old friend.

"No, it's fine. I'll go unpack. It'll be fine. I mean fun. Where are we staying?"

"You'll be in Harrison's room," Tyson says.

I blink. "Where's he sleeping?"

"In my room, across the hall. His is the last door on the right, next to the bathroom. If every surface is covered in books, you're in the right place. I tried to make as much space for you as possible, but—" He laughs. "The kid has a thing for books. Who knows where he gets it from. I tried to pass on my record collection but he wasn't all that interested."

"So, I'm, uh—sleeping in his bed?"

"Sorry it's not a bigger place," Tyson says. "Your mom has the guest room, but I thought you would want your own space. The sheets are new, at least."

"Don't apologize. We're so happy you invited us here for Christmas," Mom says.

As I walk down the drab hall, I can't help but wish for the

garland and the twinkle lights and the stockings inevitably hanging in the Wildings' cabin. I also sort of hate myself for listening to Magic 8. Which defeats the whole purpose of the app. It's supposed to free me from paralyzing doubt, and yet. I found my way here anyway.

Turns out I can't outrun my problems, not even in the greatest city in the world. I nudge open the door at the end of the hall and prepare myself for an avalanche of books. Instead, I find Harrison lounging on the bed.

FATE TWO

December 23 | 1:45 p.m. | Williams, Arizona

Molly! You made it!

My body has an immediate, visceral reaction to Whit's words. Warm anticipation is replaced with icy disappointment.

"I'm not Molly."

"Huh?" Whitney Farnsworth struggles to keep the spoon of baby food away from the squishy girl in the high chair in front of him. She giggles and screeches as she tries to snatch it from his hand. Orange mush is splattered across everything in an eighteen-inch radius.

"I'm not Molly," I repeat, louder this time.

Whit looks baffled. He has indistinct, brownish-blond hair, a slight receding hairline, and a unironic ugly Christmas sweater. "I could have sworn Fitz said he was bringing his girlfriend."

I shrug, like, *no big deal.* My heart plummets out of my body, like, *really big freaking deal.*

I told you this would end badly, SIM whispers in my ear as he scrawls a list of everything wrong and bad and scary about this situation.

Before I can make sense of anything, Fitz's middle sister

bounds down the stairs. Her beachy blonde waves bounce and her diamond nose stud glints in the light. "Hi, Paige!" She reaches the bottom step and squeezes me in a quick, friendly hug. She's ten years older than Fitz and was already out of the house by the time Fitz and I became friends. She lives in Colorado with Whit and their kids, but I've met her a few times.

"Wait. You knew this wasn't Molly?" Whit addresses Meg as he points to me.

"We've both met Paige," she tells him. "At his baseball game a couple of years ago? And last year on the Fourth of July?"

"My memory sucks," he says to me.

"Ignore my husband. Please. How was the drive? Where's Fitz?"

"Getting my stuff."

"But you *are* the girlfriend, right?" Whit asks, struggling to keep up.

"Nope. Just a girl. And a friend." My face heats in eternal embarrassment from which I'll never recover.

"We don't have to worry about scaring you off, then. Fitz gave us this whole lecture about being on our best behavior because his girlfriend was coming, but I guess that doesn't apply now." Whit plucks the baby out of her seat and takes her to the sink to wash her off. She splashes happily in the water.

"Whit. Seriously, stop talking," Meg orders.

"No one tells me anything!"

"I tell you; you don't listen!"

Fitz appears at the door, my bag in his hands. He takes one look at my face and groans. "What'd they say?"

"What happened to Molly?" Whit interjects. Meg looks like she wants to murder him.

"Whit. Back off," Fitz growls. He turns to me. "Ignore him. Everyone does. Come on, we're staying downstairs." He nods toward the stairwell leading to the basement. "The light switch has been broken forever, so watch your step." I follow him down the first step and then hang back, eavesdropping on Whit and Meg.

"Correct me if I'm wrong, but his text said he was bringing his *girlfriend*, Molly—"

"I know," Meg interjects.

"And now he shows up with a completely different girl, no warning? Is this the one who was all over his Instagram last Halloween?"

"No."

"That's right. She was gone before the candy ran out."

"Leave him alone. You know how he is. Besides, he's only eighteen. He can date around if he wants."

"I never understood the impulse."

"Not everyone meets their soul mate at seventeen. In fact, most people don't," Meg says.

"I feel bad for most people," Whit teases. I peek around the corner and see Whit plant a big kiss on Meg's lips.

My heart sinks as I follow Fitz into the dark, thoughts of Fiona Rowe crowding my brain. To Whit's credit, Fiona *was* all over Fitz's Instagram a year ago on Halloween. They wore a couple's costume to some jock party, and three days later he told her they were better off as friends. He then picked me up and we drove around town with the windows down, eating sour gummy worms until we were sick.

The basement is colder than the main floor, and I shiver involuntarily as Fitz fumbles along the wall to find the light switch. He flips it on, revealing two threadbare couches, an empty fireplace, a mini fridge, and a pool table in the corner. He drops my duffel by the couch. "It's pretty drafty down here, but it'll warm up once the fire's started. You're welcome to anything in the fridge, obviously. You're staying down the hall, across from Jane." He stacks wood in the fireplace as he talks. When I don't respond, he glances over his shoulder expectantly. "What's wrong?"

"That was awkward."

"What was?" He frowns.

"That conversation with your brother-in-law. Everyone here is expecting Molly."

"No, they're not. I told everyone that you were coming. Whit doesn't pay attention." He laughs, like the thought of me as his girlfriend is the biggest joke in the world.

I clear my throat, forcing my voice into a totally calm, not-at-all-jealous register. "You didn't tell me that you invited Molly to the cabin."

"Oh." His eyes flick to mine. "Is that important?"

"Depends."

"On?"

"When you did it."

Fitz watches me steadily, weighing his response. "That night on the water tower."

Of course. He wanted her to come, and she said no, which

makes me nothing more than a consolation. Second choice, forever and always. I knew this trip was too good to be true. I'm not the girl who gets a romantic mountain getaway with the boy of her dreams. I'm the girl building her life on an endless parade of wrong choices. It's all I can do to blink back my tears, too mortified to say anything at all.

"Hey. No. *No.* Whatever you're thinking is wrong," Fitz says. The tenderness in his voice makes my bones ache. He stands, grabbing a fuzzy blanket from the couch, and tosses it to me. I wrap it tightly around my shoulders, wishing I could believe him.

My phone buzzes with a text from Mom. **Landed safely in New York! Are you at the cabin yet?**

My heart sinks.

Why am I here when I could be there?

My throat burns with the Herculean effort of holding back tears as I tap out a quick reply to Mom.

"Are we okay?" Fitz asks.

No. "Yep." I keep my eyes glued to my screen so he won't see the building tears.

Footsteps sound on the stairs and Mrs. Wilding appears. She's in her late fifties, with elegant gray streaks in her brown hair. "You made it! I was thinking—" She cuts herself off, hesitating as she takes in my teary expression. "Should I come back?"

"No! It's fine. I'm fine!" I swipe a hand across my nose and force a smile.

"Did you get all your stuff in okay? Fitz showed you your bedroom?"

"He was just about to. Thanks, Mrs. Wilding."

"Call me Noelle, please," she reminds me for the hundredth time. "And if you need anything, let me know."

"Actually, if I want to get back to the valley this week, is there a bus or something?"

"Hold up. You're leaving?" Fitz asks.

"Oh no! We're so excited to have you here, and I promised your mom we'd take care of you."

"She's not leaving," Fitz says.

"I just remembered . . . I have to feed the neighbor's dog."

"Really? That's the excuse you're going with?" he asks dryly.

Mrs. Wilding's eyes dart from her son to me. "I'll leave you two to talk." She retreats back to the main floor.

"What was that?"

"I should probably visit my dad," I say weakly.

He narrows his eyes. "I know when you're lying."

I sigh, exhaling all the built-up tension from my body in a single breath. *I can do this. I can be normal and fine and not completely devastated to be the replacement girl. It's fine. I'm fine.*

"You're right. I'm here, and I'm staying."

Relief shines big and bright in his eyes. "Let's go upstairs. Gray is so much bigger than last time you saw him, and Meg is excited to hang with us."

Meg's words ring in my head: *You know how he is.*

What she meant, of course, is that Fitz dates too much and brings home too many girls. And now they think I'm one of them. Their expectation alone might kill me. I picture Fitz's sisters sitting around the fire, gossiping about me, making bets about how long before I become Fitz's next project.

"I can't go up there. Your family has the wrong idea about this trip. They think I'm here as one of your girls—"

"What does that mean?"

"Don't play innocent. I want them to know I'm not your next heartbreak."

Hurt flashes across his features. "Fine. What exactly would you like me to tell them?"

"Tell them we're just friends, and nothing is ever going to happen between us." I train my gaze on my shoes so he won't see what the words cost me.

"Is that all?" His voice is flat.

I nod, pulling the blanket tighter around my shoulders.

"Done. Follow me. Your room's this way."

The small room is at the end of a short hall, next to the bathroom. It has a queen-sized bed with a patchwork quilt, a narrow strip of window that looks out on the forest floor, and a bedside table with a baseball glove that Fitz probably hasn't worn in years. I run my fingers over the soft quilt, trying to imagine a younger Fitz sleeping here, spending his summers playing catch and running through the surrounding pine trees.

"I don't want to take your room. I can sleep on the couch, or—"

He waves away my comment. "I wasn't planning on sleeping here anyway."

Right. *Molly.* He wanted her in this room, sleeping in his sheets. Fresh tears build behind my eyes, only this time there's no anger. Only hurt. Will I ever stop allowing myself to be disappointed by this boy?

I sink down onto the bed and wrap my arms around my

stomach in a desperate attempt to keep myself from crumbling. This is too much. I can't do this. I underestimated how it would feel to spend Christmas with Fitz's family. To have them mistake me for his girlfriend, to sleep in his bed, to know that lost somewhere in this cabin is a letter highlighting every embarrassing thought and feeling I've had over the last two years.

"Paige," Fitz breathes. In one long stride he's next to me on the bed, holding my gaze. I tear my eyes from his, afraid that if he looks too closely, he'll see my secret.

"Cities you want to visit," he says.

"Fitz—"

"In alphabetical order. Go." He picks up my hand and squeezes gently, breaking down the last of my defenses.

"Amsterdam. Bangkok. Copenhagen. Dublin . . . El Paso?" He scoffs.

"It's harder than it looks! Especially when I'm—you know." I gesture to the disaster that is me.

He drops one hand to swipe a single tear from my cheek, but he keeps his fingers threaded through my other hand.

"You're touching me," I say, my eyes focused on his calloused palms.

"Sorry." He drops my fingers and steps away.

"No, it's okay. It's just . . . you didn't really do that when you were with Molly. Or Ruby. Or Ivy." There were others too, but those three stuck around the longest.

He winces. "Keeping that separation felt like the right thing to do."

"Yeah. Obviously." I clear my throat and shove him in the

shoulder. He watches me warily, probably scared that I'm not going to be able to function like a normal human.

Maybe he has a point.

"Do you want to unpack while I start the fire?" he asks.

I nod, and he leaves, closing the door behind him. The room feels colder without him in it. I add a thick sweatshirt over my cardigan and place the rest of my belongings in the cedar dresser. It doesn't take long, and a few minutes later I wander into the room with the couches.

Fitz is crouched over the fire, coaxing a bright spark to life. He leans forward and tenderly blows on the small flicker, and something about the gentleness of his movements brings a lump to my throat. I return his blanket to the couch and watch, transfixed, as the small flames quickly ignite. Soon, they're blazing, warming the air around me.

He turns, unsurprised to see me watching. "What do you want to do now?"

It's a small question, but I already feel raw and tender and vulnerable. Magic 8 didn't come with rules, per se, but Clover encouraged me to use it whenever I'm feeling stuck or unsure. I type my question. **Am I ready to face the firing squad?**

The ball spins.

"What's that?" Fitz reaches for my phone, craning his neck to see the screen.

I tuck it against my chest and shake my head.

He sighs but doesn't push it.

Answer: *Not likely.*

My stomach flips. How foreboding. I try again.

Should I go upstairs?

The ball spins again, and this time I'm rewarded with a simple *Yes*. I like that. I can follow directions.

"Let's go." I pocket my phone.

Fitz flips off the light, illuminating us both in the soft glow of the fire.

"You go first," he says.

"No, it's okay." I wait for him to lead the way, to act as my shield against Whit. We both hesitate, waiting for the other. It starts to get ridiculous, and I step forward at the same time he does. The dark staircase is narrow, and as we walk, I'm all arms and elbows and hips, gently bumping into Fitz and then quickly springing in the other direction. Our feet land on the top step at the same time.

Fitz looks up, his eyes wide. I follow his line of sight, and nearly trip over my own feet at the fresh sprig of mistletoe hanging directly above our heads.

FATE ONE

December 23 | 5:38 p.m. | Upper West Side, Manhattan, New York

"What are you doing in here?"

"Relax. I had to grab something I forgot." Harrison closes the paperback in his hand, his index finger acting as a bookmark.

My skin bristles. I hate being told to relax or to calm down. It always has the opposite effect. "You're on the bed. The bed with new sheets." *And this is a room. A room in an apartment.* I sound like a lunatic. "Why are you on the bed with new sheets if you were just 'grabbing something you forgot'?"

"I got distracted." He shrugs and pushes himself to a standing position. "My bad. I didn't mean to make you uncomfortable in *my* room."

Tears prick the corners of my eyes as all my emotions from the past forty-eight hours come crashing down on me.

How did I end up here? In this strange room with a strange boy in a strange city?

My stomach pangs, a new ache blossoming inside me. Half my life has been spent claustrophobic in my own town, the desire for something new so stifling and so strong that I want to claw out of my own skin and wake up in another life. And now? The hollow gulf opening in my chest longs for something familiar. Maybe I'm not cut out to be a travel writer, after all. One hour in NYC and I'm already homesick for warm gingerbread and glowing twinkle lights and Fitz.

Especially Fitz.

Always Fitz.

"Do you think he'll read it?" Harrison asks, bringing my attention back to him. I properly assess his appearance for the first time. Like I do with everyone, I find myself defining him in relation to Fitz. The differences between the two are stark. Fitz is all golden-boy charm: an easy smile, wavy hair, and piercing blue eyes. Fitz has lean baseball-boy muscles and an effervescent energy that demands attention.

Harrison is—not that. Then again, is anyone, really? While Fitz is an obvious homecoming king, Harrison strikes me as too cool for basic popularity, in a judgy, annoying sort of way. He's way taller than I am, and probably has a couple of inches on Fitz too. He has dark brown eyes and a long face with lots of angles, giving him a dark, broody look that is not unattractive, if I'm being honest with myself.

"What?" I ask, having completely lost the thread of this conversation.

"The guy on the phone. Do you think he'll read the letter?"

I hate that he overheard our private conversation. That he thinks he knows something about me. It gives him the upper hand and makes me feel unbearably young. "No."

"Maybe you're right. But I meant what I said before. He doesn't need to read it to know that you've got it bad."

"Why would you—what are you—I'm not—"

"You are." He picks up three more books off his nightstand—which is piled with several precarious stacks. "You wrote him a letter confessing your feelings, then thought better of the whole thing. If he didn't know before, he does now."

"He doesn't. I would've heard it in his voice."

"Then he's lying to himself."

"You don't even know me. Or him."

"You guys spend a lot of time together? Do you consider him your *best friend*?" His voice is dripping with sarcasm.

"One of," I say begrudgingly.

Harrison's answering smile is wry, mocking. I feel about two inches tall. "Then he knows. He doesn't need to read your bullshit Hallmark movie letter." He pauses for a moment before asking, "Am I wrong?" He smirks at my nonresponse.

A thousand insults come rushing to my mind. I choke them down. "Is this a joke?" I look up at the ceiling of the dark apartment. "Seriously. Is this a freaking joke?"

"Freaking. How cute."

"Get out."

"Of my own room?"

"Please." My voice cracks embarrassingly and my eyes swim with tears. "Please, leave me alone."

"Okay. Yeah." He walks to the door. "Sorry, I—"

"Just go."

As soon as he's gone, I peel off my shoes and socks so my wet foot can warm up. Then I sink into the bed and bury my face in the pillow, feeling bereft. This isn't how this trip was supposed to go. I had plans and a list and a lifetime of expectation and buildup, and so far, the most exciting thing to happen to me was the *snirt*. I inhale deeply and catch a whiff of something spicy. Harrison's shampoo, probably. I bolt upright and look around.

His room is small, and his dad may have undersold the books; they're everywhere. On shelves, stacked in towers on the floor, piled high on his desk. Hardcover novels and textbooks and cheap paperbacks all mixed together. I crouch down to inspect the stack next to his bed. Classics like Joyce and Bukowski and Kerouac and McCarthy: the kind of books that people talk about when they want to sound smart. Maybe the books themselves aren't pretentious, but the boys who worship them are.

Of course.

I wrap my hands around my stomach, desperate for a distraction, for something to get rid of the clawing, gnawing, awful anxiety pooling in the pit of my stomach. I press my hands to my chest, trying to slow my thundering heart. It doesn't work. Obviously. If I could wish away my own neuroses, I wouldn't be such a basket case.

Only a few things calm me when I'm starting to unravel. The first . . . well, the first is on the other side of the country, maybe reading my letter or maybe falling in love with someone new.

The second method for Calming Paige's Brain is baking. Right now, homemade gingerbread sounds especially lovely. I drop my bag and look online for the nearest market. Mom said that the Blairs live in the Upper West Side, but that means nothing to me now as I stare at the crisscrossing grid of lines on the digital map. I'm hopeless with directions. Can't even tell north from south in my own town, let alone somewhere as big and chaotic as New York. Luckily, I don't have to. My phone uses my GPS location and highlights a small grocery store down the street. I make a list of the ingredients I need for gingerbread, plus a few other recipes in case this week is as bad as I'm fearing it will be.

All I have to do now is convince Mom to let me leave. SIM writes a very detailed script in my head.

I need to make homemade gingerbread. I need it because the process calms my brain and my heart and my hands, and it makes everything a little easier. I need it because the recipe is a specific set of instructions and if I follow them exactly, I'll have a perfect loaf at the end. I need it because nothing is ever as easy and straightforward as it should be, except for baking. There's a little store a few blocks from here, on this same street. Can I dart down there, pick up the ingredients, and come right back? I promise not to talk to strangers or take my shirt off for money.

Obviously, I don't say any of that. I tell her that I want to bake gingerbread as a thank-you gift for the Blairs. I do add the part about not taking my shirt off, though, and Mom and Tyson laugh as they shoo me out the door.

I escape the apartment, and my eyes are immediately drawn up to the tall buildings looming on all sides, and beyond that, to the dark, starless sky. A gust of cold wind whistles through the narrow corridor between Harrison's building and its neighbor, slicing clean through my flimsy Arizona sweatshirt. I have a distinct feeling that this city could chew me up and spit me out if I let it. I stick my hands into my pockets and pull my hood over my head, determined to make it to the store and back without incident.

The street is busier than expected, even with the weather. I check my phone: forty degrees. Temperatures like this in Gilbert would send everyone flocking to their phones and computers to repost memes about Arizona winters: *We salt margaritas, not sidewalks!* and *Time to break out the winter clothes!* superimposed over a picture of a dude in socks and sandals. They're as silly as they are true. We get it. Arizona is hot. Move on, already.

Despite the bone-chilling forty degrees, the streets are busy and everyone rushes by without seeming to notice me. But not in a hostile way. Just like everyone is busy doing their own thing, arms full with shopping bags or leashes or small children, sometimes all three. Over and over again, my gaze wanders up without my permission, my neck craned to take in the unfamiliar sights, and I have to force my eyes down to avoid bumping into people. But once I do, I realize there are signs of Christmas everywhere. Live trees being sold on the corner. Wreaths hanging from doors and streetlights, twinkle lights in shop windows. My mood lifts considerably.

The grocery store isn't a long walk, and I'm careful to avoid more than a few piles of dirty snirt pushed into gutters or up against buildings. I duck inside the warm store and wander around until I find the spices. I drop cinnamon and ground ginger into my basket, followed by yeast. I can't find golden syrup, so I settle for honey as a substitute. It's all more expensive than it is back home, but Mom gave me her credit card, and if I'm stuck inside all week, at least I'll have a warm oven for company.

At the checkout line, I wait behind two men with ice skates slung over their shoulders. My pulse spikes.

Ice-skating in Central Park.

The first item on my New York bucket list. I lean forward to catch snatches of their conversation. I definitely hear the word *park*. Or maybe it was *bark*. But what else would they be doing with ice skates, two days before Christmas?

They leave, turning right outside the shop, and I step forward. The older man ringing me up grunts hello but otherwise doesn't make small talk. Good. I keep my eyes on the door, the ghost of a plan forming in my mind.

I should go.

Now.

My heart starts beating quickly again, but this time in antici-pation. I pay for the food with Mom's borrowed credit card and leave the store while my heart pounds *go go go.*

But.

She told me not to. And what if—

No.

I halt that train of thought in its stupid, unproductive tracks and pull out my phone.

Should I go to Central Park?

Signs point to yes.

I grab the reusable bag that I had to pay extra for and run out the door. The Blairs' apartment is to the left, but the skaters turned right, and I want to follow them. I came to

New York to change my life, to make myself different. *Braver.* I desperately *want* to be the kind of person who can be impulsive and daring in the middle of New York City.

I call Clover on the phone and she answers quickly. "Hey, City Girl! What's up?"

"I want to do something kind of reckless, but I'm scared."

"How reckless are we talking?"

"Visiting Central Park."

"That's not reckless, that's why you're in New York. Did you ask the app?"

"Yeah. It told me to do it."

"Then do it."

"But what if—"

"Stop! Carpe diem. Seize the day. You don't know when you'll be in New York again."

"I want to do it, but I don't think I'm strong enough."

"No decisions, no thinking. Just follow the app."

No decisions. No thinking. We both hang up, and my feet turn right.

I race down the street, dodging shoppers and families and dogs, and am blessed with the glimpse of the ice-skating couple, holding hands as they descend the steps into a subway station. I follow them without thinking, pleasantly surprised by the rise in temperature but less pleased by the aroma of metal and urine.

The men I was following step onto a train, vanishing from sight. "Excuse me!" I stop the next person I see, a girl with her nose stuck in her phone. "How do I buy tickets?"

"MetroCard." She nods to a kiosk in the corner without lifting her eyes.

I stand in line at the kiosk, antsy with anticipation, grocery bag hanging on my wrist. It takes a minute, but it's not difficult to follow the prompts and push the right buttons, once again using Mom's credit card to fund my purchase. When my yellow-and-blue card is dispensed, I can't smother my broad grin. I turn just in time to see doors slide closed and the ice-skating train pull away.

What do I do now?

And that's the magic question, isn't it? Use the app. Clover's rules.

Should I go back to Harrison's apartment?

Something low in my gut protests angrily as I type. I didn't come all this way and purchase my first MetroCard just to turn around and go home. So, I'm incredibly relieved when the Magic 8 app says *No*. With that option off the table, I have no choice but to get on the next train. It's almost empty, but I stand and hold on to the pole, like they do in movies.

I'm awash in the fantasy of my new metropolitan lifestyle as the train rumbles along the track; it's never been easier to slip myself into the role of rom-com heroine, the one coming home from a long day at the office when she spies a cute boy reading pensively on the other end of an empty train car. No. Scratch that! The train car is crowded, and we're holding on to the same pole, and at an abrupt stop I stumble into him, the contents of my purse spilling everywhere (rom-com heroines are terribly clumsy, didn't you know?) and our eyes meet . . . and it's Fitz.

Every daydream, every scenario. It's always Fitz.

I listen for the words *Central Park* over the speaker, except I don't hear them. It's only after my fourth elaborate daydream (Fitz and me stumbling into each other ten years in the future, me with a bad engagement ring on my left hand, him with his dream career in the major leagues and no one to come home to at night) that I begin to worry I've gotten on the wrong train. I glance at the map on the wall of the subway, but as I have no idea where I am or where I'm going or where I've been, it means less than nothing. Seeing all those lines crisscrossing across the busiest city in the world makes me feel worse than if there were no map.

I turn back to the app. It instructs me to get off on the next stop, so I do. And then I exit the subway and turn right at the app's discretion, breezing past a liquor shop covered in graffiti and stepping over a large pile of dog poop. I don't stop, I don't question it. I keep my feet moving, my fingers flying, typing faster than I can process what's happening. I know myself well enough to know that the second I stop and pay any sort of attention to what's happening, I'll have a panic attack, alone on a dirty street filled with grumpy faces.

Doubt crawls up my spine. *What if I was wrong about New York?*

I walk for a long time. Too long. Past not one but two pizza places. My grocery bag digs into my wrist and I consider abandoning it on the sidewalk, but I keep it, cringing with every bump and bang into my thigh. If things were different, I'd stop to admire every brick and building of whatever neighborhood I've landed in. As it is, all my energy is spent trying to smother the

89

rising tide of fear. But on the corner of two dark streets in a place I've never been, it reaches me. One second, I'm breathing. The next, I'm drowning.

I've been very, very stupid.

The sun must be low on an invisible horizon, the temperature is steadily dropping, and my phone battery is at 9 percent.

My shaky hands fumble over my phone as I call Mom.

"Hello?" A male voice answers the phone, sending another hot thread of panic clean through me.

"Where's my mom?"

"I'm sorry, who's calling?" Harrison asks primly.

"Give the phone to my mom now. It's important."

"She's not here. Our parents went for a walk, and it looks like she accidentally left her phone in the apartment."

"Did she say when she'd be back?" I hate how high-pitched and screechy I sound. A large man bumps into me, sending me stumbling back into a wet, sticky pile of snirt. I'm soaking from the shins down, and I want to cry.

"Nah."

If I wasn't so busy panicking, I'd be annoyed by his nonanswer answer. "Will you give her a message for me?"

"Sure."

"Tell her that I tried to get to Central Park but I got lost and my phone is at, uh"—I check the battery—"three percent and it's cold and I don't know where I am and I don't remember where you live." I jam the palm of my hand into my eyes to wipe away the tears as my heart throbs painfully in my chest.

"Walk to the nearest corner and look up at the street signs."

"Okay, I, um, I'm at Franklin and Lincoln."

"That's way down by Julian's place. How'd you get to Brooklyn?"

"I was on the train for a long time."

He curses under his breath. "I think there's a Starbucks nearby. Do you see it?"

I scan the block, and I do see it. I breathe a small sigh of relief. "Yeah." I check the battery again. Two percent.

"Go inside. Do you have money?"

"A little."

"Order something cheap, find a seat, and *stay there*. Do not move. You got that?"

"Yeah, but what about—"

"I'll be there are soon as I can. Whatever you do, don't—"

My phone dies. I grip it with frigid fingers and do my very best not to freak out.

As if that's ever been an option.

FATE TWO

December 23 | 3:00 p.m. | Williams, Arizona

The thing about Magic 8 is this: I'm pretty sure it's trying to destroy my life. Thanks to my question and its regrettable response, Fitz and I are wedged in a dark stairwell beneath a sprig of mistletoe.

Because of course we are.

Because obviously this day hasn't been stressful enough.

Because I'm *completely* in the right mind-set to handle the fact that his chest is brushing up against mine every time he breathes and that his knee is resting against my thigh—said no girl ever. Not in respect to Fitz Wilding.

"Did you know that mistletoe is poisonous?" I say desperately.

An amused glint sparks in Fitz's eyes, smoldering right through me. He crooks his mouth to the side, lazy grin growing. I sense the joke coming. It's the eyes that give him away; they're shining in anticipation of a punch line.

I get there first.

"Name five things you see right now."

His lips part. I watch, mesmerized.

"Other than the mistletoe," I add.

His mouth snaps shut, and he grins. "I can't. It's the only thing I see. I'm pretty sure it's the only thing in the whole damn room."

I roll my eyes. What a typical Flirty Fitz thing to say.

I lean back against the wall, creating an illusion of space between our bodies. But that's all it is: an illusion. Because the fact is this: Awkward or not, being close to Fitz lights my senses on fire, and I never want it to end. "On a scale of one to *The Notebook*, how romantic is this place?" I ask. Fitz cocks an eyebrow. "I don't want to be falling into any more of these dopey rom-com traps," I amend, slanting my eyes to the mistletoe.

Fitz's cocky, lazy grin wilts, only to be replaced with an eye roll. "Very romantic. Why do you think I invited Molly?" I have no idea what to make of the challenge in his voice. He leans toward me, his lips a breath from my ear.

My heart stops in my throat.

"We have an audience," he whispers, sending electric shivers across my skin.

My eyes dart to the main room and heat floods my cheeks. Whit and the baby are lying on their stomachs on the plush white rug near the Christmas tree, openly staring at us while Gray drives toy trucks up and down Mr. Wilding's leg. "Maybe wait until the kids are asleep before getting cozy under the mistletoe," Whit jokes as he suggestively wiggles his eyebrows. The baby girl next to him whines and shoves all her fingers in her mouth. "No crying at Christmas, Sienna!" Whit says as he picks her up and bounces her in his arms.

"There will be no 'under the mistletoe' for Paige and me," Fitz says.

I told him to say it, but it hurts as if I didn't.

"Don't underestimate the power of 'Santa Baby.' That one always puts me in the mood. Right, honey?" Whit calls to Meg, who's preparing dinner in the kitchen with her mom. She smiles and slowly shakes her head, but doesn't deny it.

I stifle a laugh while Fitz clutches his stomach and pretends to gag. Then he holds my gaze but projects his voice out to Whit. "Don't worry about us. Paige has absolutely no romantic interest in me. Isn't that right, Paige?" My face gets so hot, it feels like I stuck my head in the fire. "And anyway, in five months she's leaving Gilbert and is going to conquer the world as a travel writer, so it's a moot point." Fitz finally breaks eye contact. I hold on to the stair rail, feeling dizzy.

"Since when have any of your relationships lasted five months?" Whit asks.

"Molly was seven months," Fitz fires back.

"Be nice!" Meg throws a dinner roll at Whit's head from the kitchen.

He catches it and tears off a bite with his teeth. "Thanks, love!"

Fitz looks at me. "Was that everything?"

"You didn't have to make it so awkward," I whisper as his family grows bored with our strange tension and returns to their respective activities.

"I'm sorry, but explaining to my family that you'll never be interested in me is inherently awkward."

"No, it's not!"

"Sure it is. It's like explaining that you don't like ice cream. But I did it. For you. You're welcome." He smirks.

"Wow," I say slowly, drawing out the word. "The ego on you is astounding." I shove him in the shoulder and move from the stairwell to one of the leather couches. "And what does my travel writing have to do with anything? It's embarrassing to talk about." I fiddle with the frayed edges of a large plaid blanket.

"No, it's not. You're gonna be amazing out there in the real world. And anyway, I was warning my family not to get too attached to you," he says quietly. Between his nephew playing loudly on the floor and the commotion in the kitchen, no one can hear us now.

"Right." I roll my eyes. Fitz's speech left me feeling flustered, confused, and annoyed. I grasp on to annoyance, sinking my heels into the feeling. If I can convince myself I'm annoyed at Fitz, maybe I can forget everything else that's happened since I got here.

I mean, it's not likely. Especially not with SIM and his near-constant stream of intrusive, terrible thoughts, most of which focus on that stupid missing letter. But a girl's got to try.

"Uncle Fitz!" Gray jumps onto Fitz's back, wrapping his little arms around Fitz's neck and nearly strangling him. Fitz laughs and swings Gray around while he tickles his stomach. They stop wrestling and settle into a game of driving cars up and down Mr. Wilding's leg. He startles awake, sees the boys playing, and sinks back into sleep.

When Fitz and I first became friends, waiting to be picked up on that school curb, I was fascinated by the curly-haired sister who rolled up late every day with fuzzy dice hanging from the rearview and empty Polar Pop cups littering the back seat.

Sometimes in my head I'd pretend she was mine, that I had someone other than my parents who was responsible for me. One day Jane took pity on me and brought me home to eat dinner with their family. I kept my eye on their digital picture frame during the meal, transfixed by Fitz's gorgeous, grown-up sisters and his parents, who were way older than mine. According to Fitz, his parents were told they'd never have biological children, and so they happily adopted three girls over the space of several years. When his mom did get pregnant with him much later, it was a total shock to everyone.

"Where are your other sisters?" I ask.

"Jane's at work. She goes to school in Flagstaff and works here at the train depot during the holidays. We'll see her later tonight. And Darcy—"

"Hope you don't mind an early dinner," Mrs. Wilding calls from the kitchen. "We want to finish in time for the kids to catch the train."

"What train?"

"The Polar Express train. You'll see." Fitz smiles at me as he stages an elaborate car crash for Gray. I wander into the kitchen and offer to help. Meg hands me a stack of dishes and silverware and directs me to the large farmhouse table with bench seats.

"Have either of you seen a letter with Fitz's name on it?" I ask, and this time, I manage to sound casual.

"Where was it?" Mrs. Wilding asks as she chops tomatoes for the salad.

"I'm not sure. He thinks he left it on the counter. It's part of my Christmas present to him." *Is that even a little bit believable?*

I've repeated that excuse so many times that it's lost all meaning.

"I bet it was tucked away with the rest of the presents," Meg says.

"Where are the presents?"

"At the North Pole," she says seriously.

"Um—"

She points to Gray and then covers her mouth with a finger.

"Right. Of course." I move closer and lower my voice to a whisper. "But seriously, where are they?

"In Mom and Dad's closet, safe from Gray's cute but destructive little hands."

I turn to Fitz's mom. "Can I look in the closet?"

"We'll bring the presents out on Christmas Eve, after all you kids are in bed." Her words are a decree, an explanation of The Way Things Are Done. It doesn't feel like my place to argue with her.

I try a different tactic. "Great! I'd love to help play Santa."

Meg laughs. "Good luck with that. Mom won't even let *me* see the presents early."

"But, um—" My mind blanks. *What's a valid excuse for needing that letter back, like right this second?* I glance at Fitz, wondering if I could convince him to sneak into the closet and find it.

"Don't even think about it," Meg says, guessing my plan. "That place is more secure than Fort Knox."

Well then. "I guess I'll wait until Christmas."

Mrs. Wilding smiles as she tosses the salad, but my stomach squirms in desperation. It's only two more days . . . but how am I going to survive two more days of this torture?

And look. I know Clover urged me to let Fitz read the letter. And I did consider it, honestly. For a good, solid ten minutes this morning I allowed my mind to wander down that path—the one where he reads the letter, ignores the part about how I hate him, realizes he loves me, and kisses me under a thousand gently falling snowflakes.

Almost every single day of this last year, I was convinced I needed to tell Fitz the truth. When I'm not with him, I can't imagine anything worse than continuing to live this carefully constructed lie, pretending that I don't love him half as much as I do.

And then I see him. I'll spot a glimpse of him through the crowd at school, or he'll catch my eye when our econ teacher says something painfully embarrassing, and the force of his attention on me is like a drug. I can't imagine any better feeling in the world.

My phone buzzes in my pocket with a text from Clover.

How's Magic 8 working out?

Right. *That.* The reason I'm here and not in New York.

The question of the letter is exactly the type of thing Clover would want me to ask, but I'm 100 percent certain I'm not prepared for the potential response.

TBD, I reply.

Do I need to come up there and smack some sense into you?

"You ready for dinner with the fam?" Fitz appears at my elbow, his eyes on my screen.

I stash my phone in my pocket and glance at Whit. "Hardly."

"You don't have to try to impress them," he says.

Another casual reply, a second unintentional bruise. Of course, I don't need to impress them. *How silly of me.* That's something only girlfriends or potential girlfriends need to worry about. No one cares about the best friend, especially not the best friend who is *definitely* not romantically interested.

Right?

I sit between Fitz and Gray at dinner. Gray wiggles next to me on the bench, swinging his legs and bumping his feet against me under the table. I'm a bit terrified of him and his little-kid strangeness, but also, he's cute. I cross my eyes and stick my tongue out, which he seems to like. I try it on Sienna next, but she squawks unhappily in response.

"It's not your fault," Meg says to me. "She's been fussy all day." Whit hands the baby a sippy cup, which she promptly swats away. "I don't know if we should take her on the Polar Express tonight."

Whit places his hand on Sienna's forehead. "She feels okay to me. What do you think?"

Meg touches the baby's neck with the back of her hand. "She doesn't feel warm, but I'm not sure she'll make it through the ride without throwing a fit. Do you two want our tickets?" She looks from Fitz to me.

"Tickets to what?" I ask.

"I'll stay home and watch her," Mrs. Wilding says. "Gray's so excited to meet Santa. Aren't you, Gray?"

"Santa!" Gray cheers, both fists in the air.

"But Paige has never been, and the tickets have been sold out for months." Meg frowns.

"Don't worry about us," Fitz tells his sister. "I have something else planned."

"You do?" I ask.

He winks, sending happy bursts of electricity straight through my veins. Then he wolfs down a dinner roll in two bites. "Not bad, but yours are better."

"You bake?" Meg asks me.

"Yeah! I really love it."

"Have you seen *The Great British Baking Show*?"

"That's actually how I started." On my worst days, I'd binge-watch entire seasons of the show on Netflix. Everything about it soothed my chaotic brain. Once I'd been through the entire series three times, I decided to give actual baking a try. Turns out, it's even more relaxing than the show.

"We love that show! You'll have to show us what you can do, Molly," Whit says.

"Whit!" A chorus of groans erupts.

"I'm sorry! I suck at remembering names, and I drilled *Molly* into my head. Sorry, Paige." He shrugs, not looking particularly sorry. I suspect he's doing it to mess with Fitz.

"Don't worry about it, Whitney," I say.

He blinks, and I swear the room stops breathing.

Maybe I didn't think this through. Fitz told me how much Whit hates his full name. I'm opening my mouth to grovel when Meg howls with laughter, followed quickly by the rest of the family. "You so deserved that," Meg says to Whit as she wipes tears from her cheeks.

"I like anyone who has the guts to take on this guy,"

Mr. Wilding says as he claps his son-in-law on the shoulder. Heads around the table nod in agreement. Fitz squeezes my knee under the table, nearly giving me heart palpitations.

The front door opens and Darcy glides in, looking as beautiful and chic as she does in photos. Her shiny black hair is cut in a long, A-line bob, the ends grazing her collarbone. Her pointy, upturned nose and sharp cheeks are both red from the cold. She looks like a dainty, elegant Christmas mouse.

"Darcy darling! You made it!" Mr. Wilding springs from his seat to help his eldest child with her luggage.

"It smells delicious, Mom," Darcy says as she sheds layers of winter clothing.

"I'm glad you made it!" Mrs. Wilding smiles, but there's an unnatural tightness to it. Looking around, her expression is mirrored on Meg's and Whit's faces. Only Mr. Wilding and Fitz look truly happy to see her.

"Paige! I'm so happy you're here!" Darcy smiles warmly as she takes the seat across the table. "Fitz's told me a lot about you."

I raise an eyebrow at Fitz but he ducks his head, avoiding my gaze. "It's nice to meet you too." I pass her the salad, and as she accepts it, the diamond ring on her left finger catches the firelight, sparkling brightly. "Oh! Congratulations on your wedding. Fitz showed me a picture. You and April both looked gorgeous."

"Thank you," Darcy says as her eyes dart to her sister.

Meg stands, blinking away tears. "Excuse me. I'll be right back." She darts into the bathroom off the hall. Everyone around the table frowns sympathetically.

"Did I say something wrong?"

"It's not you. This is the first time Darcy's been home since the wedding," Fitz explains.

"But it was over Thanksgiving, right? It hasn't been that long . . ."

Mrs. Wilding dabs her eyes with a napkin as Whit becomes invested in cutting the lasagna into tiny bites for Sienna.

"Ignore your sister. She loves you, but she's being selfish," Mr. Wilding says to Darcy.

"That's not fair—" Whit begins. Mr. and Mrs. Wilding cut him off at the same time, arguing amongst themselves.

Darcy leans toward me over her plate. "April and I eloped, so we didn't invite our families. Meg hasn't forgiven me for that, and I don't really blame her."

"Oh, wow. I'm sorry I brought it up. Fitz didn't tell me—"

"I didn't realize how upset she was." Fitz frowns in the direction of the bathroom door. It opens and Meg walks out, her neck and chest blotchy red. The room falls silent as she joins us back at the table, and I feel a weight of responsibility for ruining dinner. I take a cue from the others and pick silently at my food.

To my left, Gray takes a huge bite of lasagna and groans in happiness. "Mmmm. MMMMM. MMMMMMMMMMM!" He closes his eyes and leans back in his chair happily.

"I'll have what he's having," I deadpan.

Darcy laughs and slaps her hands on the table. "*When Harry Met Sally . . . ?*"

I nod. Out of the corner of my eye, Fitz shakes his head with a smile, and the conversation turns into a passionate debate about rom-coms: the good, the bad, and the so bad they're good.

After a long diatribe about *Overboard*, an old movie that Darcy calls a "problematic fave," Meg notices the time and claps her hands together. "We should head over to the train station. You ready, Gray?"

"Santa!" Gray cheers again, and there's a small flurry as people clear plates and leave the table.

I glance at Fitz, who's watching me thoughtfully. "What's the plan for us?"

He surveys me, taking in my leggings, sweatshirt, and black boots. "You'll need warmer clothes. Scarf, gloves, and a hat. Your boots are good. Meet me out back in fifteen." He throws me a scheming, dimpled smile. It's the same grin he had before he showed me the indoor snowstorm he made for Ivy, the elaborate homecoming proposal he set up for Priya, and the rowboat he rented for Ruby.

It's a smile that means he's planning something, and for the first time ever, the plan is for me. I grip the bench on either side of me, suddenly unsure how I'm going to get through this evening. Fitz clears our plates from the table and disappears out the back door, leaving Darcy and me alone.

"How worried should I be?" I ask Darcy.

She raises one perfectly sculpted eyebrow. "With Fitz in charge? Very."

A kaleidoscope of butterflies dances in my stomach. *It's fine*, I tell myself as I head into the basement to raid the stash of winter clothes that Mrs. Wilding left in my room.

It's fine. Nothing is different. Everything is exactly the same as it's always been.

I turn those words into my mantra, repeating them again and again.

It's fine. Nothing is different. Everything is exactly the same as it's always been.

As if summoned, SIM appears with his clipboard and his pencil and his annoyingly perfect necktie. *Liar,* he whispers. When it comes to making me feel terrible, no one does it better than my own stupid brain.

The rumble of an engine roars above me. I stand on the bedside table and peek out the small curtained window. Four massive tires pull into view. Fitz is sitting on an ATV, flexing his hands as he revs the engine. My throat dries.

It's fine. Nothing is different. Everything is exactly the same as it's always been.

I add another sentence to my mantra.

What could go wrong?

SIM clears his throat and starts a list.

FATE ONE

December 23 | 7:45 p.m. | Brooklyn (apparently),
New York

Whatever you do, don't —

Don't what, Harrison? DON'T WHAT?

Possibilities:

"Don't order the hot chocolate, because it'll give you food poisoning."

"Don't forget to look both ways before you cross the street, or you'll get hit by a car."

"Don't expect me to show up, because I'm too busy reading Chaucer to remember you."

Since my phone is dead and I can't ask its opinion, I wait for traffic to stop and cross the street to the brightly lit Starbucks. A blast of warm, coffee-scented air hits me and a jingle bell tinkles as I walk through the door. After ordering the smallest hot chocolate on the menu, I sit by the window and watch the street. My mind wanders to Fitz, as it usually does when I'm in situations that are scary or new or boring or exciting or . . . anything, really. There's no situation that couldn't be improved by a smile or a joke from Fitz Wilding, and I wish I could text him and ask if there's snow at the cabin. Or how many rom-coms he's watched with his sisters. Whether he misses me. Whether he misses Molly. Tell him about how hard I'm failing. My first day in New York, with nothing to show for it except a freak-out on the airplane, a second one in the apartment, and a failed attempt to see Central Park. The travel blog practically writes itself.

A sharp knock on the store window draws my attention. Harrison stands outside with his hands shoved in the pockets of his long coat, scarf wound loosely around his neck, dark hair falling over his eyes. He fits in with the surrounding crowd, looking like he's on his way to poetry night at the coffee shop. I'm so happy to see him that my bones go slightly rubbery and I grin through the window. Instead of returning my smile, he nods for me to meet him outside. I hold up a finger, asking him to wait, purchase another drink, and join him in the dark.

"Thanks for coming." I give him the drink, swinging my bag of groceries in my free hand. Now that I know I'm not doomed to spend the night wandering the city streets with wet socks, I feel instantly better.

He takes a sip and wrinkles his nose. "Is this hot chocolate?"

"Is that bad?"

"No, but I was expecting coffee. Hot chocolate is . . . quaint."

Quaint. Like I'm some farm girl from a one-stoplight town. How embarrassing.

"How'd you end up way out here, anyway?" he asks after a long silence.

"Oh, you know . . ."

"Dad said you went to the bodega."

"I did. And then I tried to find my way to Central Park. Got on the wrong train, I think."

"So, this is my fault then? Because I wouldn't take you ice-skating?" He glances at me, half-amused, half-annoyed.

"The truth hurts." I shrug.

Harrison effortlessly locates the train that'll take us back to Manhattan, and we board. We don't talk much as we stand side by side on the subway, each holding a different pole. My gaze wanders to an advertisement for a new Hallmark movie, a holiday rom-com that I have no doubt Fitz and his sisters will watch soon, if they haven't already. For once in my life, I tried to be like the girls in those movies: alone in New York, searching for adventure. I pretended I could be a different person with a different life, but the fact is, I'm a sheltered, small-town, anxious mess of a girl who crashed and burned her first day in the city. I'm exactly as *quaint* as Harrison thinks I am.

He sees me gazing wistfully at the movie poster and raises an eyebrow.

"What do you have against Hallmark movies anyway?" I ask.

"That's a joke, right?"

"Humor me."

"The diversity sucks, for one."

"Fair point."

"Other than that?" He scratches his chin. "The plots are all the same."

My skin bristles automatically. I feel the need to defend Fitz, despite the fact that he's not here and this conversation isn't actually about him. "If you've seen enough of these romantic movies to make sweeping generalizations about them, tell me about this recycled plot."

"It's, you know, nice boy meets girl, nice boy falls in love with girl, minor obstacles get in the way, nice boy wins girl. Excuse me if I expect more out of my art."

I flash back to the stack of classics on his nightstand and peg him as the kind of guy who only likes things that make him seem cool or smart or sophisticated. "I bet your cinematic choices lean toward overly long Oscar bait. The kind of movies filled with drab colors and depression," I tease. He rolls his eyes, but not before I catch the lift in the corner of his mouth. "What's wrong with happy endings, anyway?" My stomach squirms in a not unpleasant way, and I can't help but marvel at the fact that I'm in New York, bantering about romance movies with a boy who isn't *my* boy.

"It never happens that way in real life. Take my parents, for example. They get married, my mom cheats on my dad with her boss, then he gets diagnosed with a central nervous system disease six weeks before Christmas. Show me *that* Hallmark movie."

"I'm sorry—" I reach, placing my hand on his arm.

"Don't," he says sharply.

I withdraw my hand, and with it, my instinct to play nice. "That movie you described? It exists, just in a different genre. Don't fault romance movies for not telling the story of your life. That's not what they're for, that's not why they're made, and that's not what romance fans want. That's not a problem with the movie. It's a problem with your expectations."

He gives me a sidelong glance as we exit the train. "Call them what they are—fantasy."

"Not always." Fitz is living proof that nice guys exist. He's the guy in the movie, even if I'm not the girl.

"Yes. Always. And I think you agree with me."

"Why?" I walk faster to keep up with him, stuffing my cold hands into my pockets.

"If you believed in true love and happily-ever-afters, you wouldn't be so scared to let the guy read your embarrassing declaration of love. As it is, you're walking down a dirty, frozen street with a near stranger. And you want to tell me I'm the cynic?"

"That's a lot of assumptions considering you don't know me. Not to mention big talk for someone moping over his ex."

"Are you always this bad with directions, or only in New York?" He evades my accusation as we turn the corner and pass the market where I bought bread ingredients all those hours ago. I let it slide.

"There's not much in the way of public transportation where I'm from," I say. And then, because I have no sense of self-preservation, I add, "Plus, there's this app."

"What app?"

"I didn't know where to go, so I asked it for directions?" I cringe at the way my voice goes up at the end. I cringe at the fact that I'm telling him this at all.

"Google Maps? I've heard of it," he says dryly.

"Not a directions app." I roll my eyes. "It's a—" I press my lips together, regretting this entirely.

He stops in his tracks and turns to me. "A what?"

"A decision-making app." I speak slowly, choosing my words carefully.

"What the hell is that?"

"Never mind. I'm cold. Let's go." We walk in silence the rest of the way home, although he practically has to drag me away from the man selling Christmas trees on the corner.

When we get back to the apartment, his dad and my mom are rinsing takeout Chinese food from their dinner plates. The heavy scent of kung pao makes my mouth water.

"Paige! What happened? Are you okay?" Mom slips her plate into the dishwasher and then crosses the kitchen and pulls me into a tight hug. "Harrison sent Tyson a text, something about you ending up in Brooklyn. I called a dozen times but your phone went straight to voicemail." She pulls back and holds me at arm's length.

"I got a little lost, but I'm okay."

"Are you?" She furrows her brow and inspects my face, probably for mascara tracks or some other sign that I'm in distress.

"I'm fine. Thanks to Harrison," I say begrudgingly.

"Good." She hugs me again. "Thank you, Harrison. And you, Paige, are not going out alone again. Understand?" I nod.

When she finally releases me, Tyson instructs Harrison and me to help ourselves to dinner, and he and my mom clear out of the room, leaving me once again with the uncanny impression that I'm going to be spending a lot of time alone this vacation.

We pile our plates high with sticky rice and beef and broccoli.

I sit and take a huge bite, relishing the warmth. "I meant what I said to my mom," I say quietly. "Tonight could have been a total disaster, if it wasn't for you." I glance up from my plate to see Harrison shrug off the comment. "Seriously. Thank you."

He finally meets my gaze, holding eye contact for a beat. I clench my fork tightly, waiting. Anticipating. Finally, he lets out a breath, gives me a quick nod, and stuffs a handful of fortune cookies into his pocket. "See ya later."

I'm too surprised to respond. It's not that I think we're suddenly best friends or anything, but it felt like we'd come to some kind of truce out there. Guess I was wrong. He retreats down the hall, leaving me alone in a sad, dark kitchen with a giant plate of Chinese food.

At least it tastes good.

After I've devoured dinner, I rinse my plate, scroll through the pictures Fitz sent while I was out, text him and Clover a quick update, and set out the ingredients for gingerbread. I find a stand mixer in the back of a cupboard and cream together the butter and sugar. The soothing whir of the machine works its way into my brain. My hands fall into the familiar rhythm of measuring, pouring, and mixing, and by the time the bread is sliding into the oven, I've almost convinced myself that this trip isn't the worst decision I've ever made.

"Merry Christmas Eve," Mom shouts as she cracks the door to Harrison's room. "Get up! Get showered! Get ready to go!"

"I thought you'd want to stay in?" I sit up, squinting through the muted morning light that slants through the shutters.

"Not today! You're sweet to be understanding of Tyson, but you and I are spending the day together. Bring your list to breakfast and we'll map out a plan."

I stumble into the hall, still jet-lagged and half-asleep, and push open the bathroom door to find Harrison brushing his teeth. He's shirtless, with skinny joggers slung low on his hips. "Oh! I, uh, didn't realize—"

He tucks his damp hair behind his ear and spits, then moves over to make space for me in front of the sink. "No worries. You need to brush?"

I nod, because I *do* need to brush my teeth, but also because I'm not about to say out loud that I also need to pee and shower and put on deodorant and brush my hair and generally become less like a zombie and more like a human.

The bathroom is not big, and as we crowd the sink, I try my very best not to look at Harrison at all, but the only other place to look is in the steamy mirror, and my eyes keep straying from my own reflection to his surprising abs. I wouldn't have suspected a tall, thin bookworm would have defined ab muscles.

The revelation does unsettling things to my stomach.

"Whatcha looking at?" Harrison smirks.

I tear my gaze from his chest as my cheeks heat. "What's the tattoo?" I gesture to the black ink over his heart. It's an intricate, swirly design, but I don't let myself stare long enough to decipher any of the shapes or symbols.

"Just a thing," Harrison says maddeningly. He rinses his mouth a final time and brushes behind me to leave.

"What is the point in getting a tattoo if you don't want to talk about it?" I slam my toothbrush on the counter with more force than I intended.

"It reminds me who I am," he says. It's as cryptic and frustrating as ever, but I can't shake the feeling it might also be the most revealing thing he's ever said to me.

When I emerge from the bathroom, showered and dressed, Harrison is nowhere to be seen, which is fine by me. The last thing I need is to be caught gawking at his chest again. Mom and Tyson are eating breakfast at the table, and I help myself to a plate of pancakes and scrambled eggs.

"Did you bring the list?" Mom asks as she slides a bottle of maple syrup toward me.

I nod and smooth out my list next to my plate. "How many of these do you think we could get done in a day?"

"I'm not sure. Tyson, how long does it take to get from Central Park to Rockefeller Center?"

"Don't tell me you're visiting the two most generic, overpopulated, touristy attractions on Christmas Eve," Harrison says as he steps into the kitchen. I cover the paper with my hands, but he lasers in on it immediately.

"Bad idea?" Mom asks.

"It'll be crowded," Tyson says as he adds another pancake to his plate.

"We don't mind crowds," Mom says, throwing a smile my way. "We're here for the whole New York Christmas experience."

"Great! We'll all go together," Tyson says while Harrison rolls his eyes.

"Are you sure you're feeling up for it?" Mom asks.

"Positive. Harrison, grab some food and lace up your skates. We're taking these girls to Central Park."

As luck would have it, Central Park is embarrassingly close to Harrison's apartment. As in, no subway needed. As in, if I had turned ninety degrees and walked straight, I would have run smack bang into the park.

I try not to dwell on it.

"Is it everything you thought it'd be?" Harrison deadpans as we stand in front of the enormous, sparkling white rink. Lush pine trees and bare branches dot the land around us, and above the tree line, hulking buildings tower over the park. I love it instantly. The air smells like pine and nutmeg and cloves, like the best loaf of bread I've ever baked.

"It's better," I breathe reverently, my breath fogging in icy puffs.

The danger of wanting something as much as I want to travel is the possibility of unmet expectations. Ever since the plane touched down yesterday, a growing, shifting, creeping doubt took hold of me, whispering that New York isn't the magical city I've fantasized about for years. Yesterday, it felt dirty and frozen and foreign, leaving me full of regret. Regret for coming here, yes. But also regret for pinning all my hopes and dreams on the *idea* of something I've never experienced.

Yesterday, I was wrong, which means every day before that, I was right. This frozen skating pond in the middle of a bustling metropolis, like a scene lifted directly from one of those Christmas movies Harrison hates, feels like something special. From another world entirely. In this world, I'm different, not doomed to live my entire life in the same city where I was born, watching my best friend fall in and out of love with every girl but me.

"Are you coming?" I ask Harrison. He has skates slung over his shoulders, but he sits on a bench with his back to the pond and pulls out a book. "Of course not," I answer for him. "Why experience Christmas cheer when you could be reading something stuffy and dull."

He lifts his book from his lap to reveal the cover of a thick novel with a dragon on the cover. His lip twitches, but he doesn't say a word. I lean closer, and see two characters riding on the beast's back. The boy's up front, in what I assumed is the dragon-steering position, and the girl is behind him, holding an awesomely scary sword.

"Oh." So maybe it's not as boring as I assumed. "Well, have fun with your book."

"Have fun with your skates."

I wobble onto the ice, smiling at the memory of the year Clover and I became deeply invested in the Winter Olympics. We took turns making Fitz lift us in the air and pretend to be our skating partner. He dropped me, and when my head banged into his mouth, his tooth cut my forehead and left a small scar above my right eyebrow. Closest his mouth is ever gonna get to my face, and it was the exact opposite of romantic.

Mom and I hobble along together while Tyson skates circles around us. "How are you so good at this?" Mom moans as she grabs my hands and we almost topple over each other. I glance at Harrison to see if he's watching, but he's focused on a large yellow

Labrador that has its head in his lap. He scratches behind the dog's ear, laughing as the creature licks his face.

"Are you forgetting the years I played ice hockey?" Tyson asks.

"Yes, I am forgetting that," Mom confirms as we right ourselves.

"Come on, I'll help you out." He takes Mom's hand and gently leads her around the rink.

I circle the rink two more times on my own, soaking in the jingly Christmas tunes and the couples holding hands. It's tempting to throw myself a solo pity party, but the truth is that everything is festive and lovely, and the cold, fresh air feels like sharp magic in my lungs. Tyson drops Mom off at the side of the rink and goes out on his own, skating quickly past me. I'm about to cheer when he wipes out, clutching his knee as he goes down. Mom and I skate to his side as Harrison races across the rink, beating us there. Tyson groans a bit in pain, but it doesn't seem serious.

"Dad! Are you hurt?"

"Just my pride." Tyson smiles. It doesn't reach his eyes.

"*Dad.*"

"I'm fine. I had a spasm in my leg, don't worry about me." Tyson waves off his son's concern.

Harrison's face falls. "I knew this was a stupid idea. Let's go home." He reaches out a hand to help his dad up, but Tyson brushes him off and stands on his own.

"I told you, I'm fine. I—" He steps forward and stumbles again, this time grasping Mom's hand for support. "I'll go home and rest."

"I'm coming with you," Harrison insists.

"No," his dad says flatly as he exits the rink. He sits carefully on a bench and unties his skates.

"I'm not letting you walk home alone. You're—"

"I'm fine, Harry. You've been moping around the house for two weeks, but you're finally outside, breathing fresh air. You'll stay here and enjoy the day with Paige and Tilly."

Tilly? Matilda Collins hasn't gone by Tilly since . . . ever, as far as I know.

"Don't be silly. I'm coming with you; the kids can stay and have fun," Mom says. "Is that all right, Paige?"

"Yeah, of course."

She pulls out her wallet and hands me two twenty-dollar bills and her credit card. "Do not come home until you've seen everything on that list. And stay with Harrison so you don't get lost again."

"Same goes for you, Harry," Tyson says.

I mutter an agreement while Harrison mumbles his protests, and two minutes later we're standing alone but together in the middle of Central Park.

"Give me your list," he sighs.

"Nah." I shrug.

"I'm worried about my dad, because he likes to pretend that he's tough and fine but I know he's not. Give me the list so we can get this over with." His eyebrows are pinched together, stress etched in every feature. My heart softens toward him ever so slightly and I hand over the list.

He scans it quickly, his frown deepening. "Okay. We'll start with the tree. Ready to go?"

My stomach clenches. *Be braver. Be different.* But yesterday went so badly, and I still don't trust myself at all.

I angle my body away from him and ask the phone. My heart scatters as the ball spins, and I'm not entirely sure what I want the answer to be.

Yes.

Yes, go with this boy I haven't seen in eleven years. Yes, go see New York. Yes, I failed once, but this is my chance to try again.

"Sure." I match his indifference with a shrug of my own, despite the foreboding tightening in my stomach.

FATE TWO

December 23 | 5:30 p.m. | Williams, Arizona

All the things that could go wrong if I get on the back of Fitz's ATV:

- He crashes into a pine tree and we die.
- He crashes into the train and we die.
- I put my arms around him while we drive, and the contact sends me into early-onset cardiac arrest.
- Somehow, some way, Fitz realizes that I've been desperately in love with him every day for the last two years and life as I know it is over.

These thoughts and a dozen others race through my brain as I climb the basement steps and open the back door. Icy air assaults me, and my heart freezes.

But not because of the cold.

My heart freezes because Fitz was built to sit on the back of an ATV in thirty-degree weather, and I'm not prepared. His brown hair was made to curl out from under his beanie, his face sculpted to be a perfect frostbitten pink. He must not have shaved this morning, because a faint shadow of stubble has appeared on his jaw. It does dangerous things to my stomach. When did my best friend become a guy with a five o'clock shadow?

He's never been so achingly, frustratingly, stupidly attractive. He bounces up and down as his body hums with energy. It's similar to the version of Fitz in his baseball uniform at third base, only ramped up one thousand notches.

He fixes me with that same intense and excited stare he had inside, the expression that means he's planning something, the dimple that will break a thousand hearts before he even considers breaking mine. I've waited years and months and days and hours and seconds and eternities for this moment.

Which is why I hate the words that come out of my mouth.

"I'm not coming."

He deflates like the off switch has been triggered on his own personal generator. "Don't do this to me again."

I open my mouth to protest, but nothing comes out. He's right. I've bailed on him before.

Once upon a time, Fitz asked me on a date.

Once upon a time, I ruined everything.

It was the end of sophomore year, Fitz and Ivy were recently uncoupled, and it was already murderously hot. It was the kind of hot that makes you want to lie in front of an industrial fan with your clothes off and never move again. The kind of hot that anchors itself to your bones, weighing you down until it's hard to breathe.

And it was only May.

"I need another snowstorm, stat." I slurped my melting Fudgsicle before it could drip on the trampoline.

"We could go inside. There's air-conditioning inside. I hear good things about it. I think it's gonna catch on," Fitz joked.

"And risk getting handed one of Jane's scripts? No way." Fitz's aspiring playwright sister was already home from college for the summer and liked to force us to run lines with her.

Fitz threw his arm over his eyes to block out the sun. "I'm just saying, there are better places to hang out than this black, heat-sucking canvas."

"Too hot to move." I flipped onto my stomach and placed my cheek against the warm mat. Fitz's arm was still over his eyes, meaning I could gaze at him without feeling awkward and guilty, two emotions I'd felt a lot lately. Awkward for being secretly in love with my best friend (and hoping he wouldn't notice). Guilty because he was dating someone else.

But he'd dumped Ivy last month, and I was full of unexamined emotions about that.

Fitz's arm fell and he squinted into the bright sunlight. When he turned to face me, his forehead was damp with sweat. Last year, it would have grossed me out. Now I had to resist the urge to scoot closer. When did I turn into such a creep?

"If I could conjure a blizzard for you right now"—he snapped his fingers—"you know I'd do it, right?"

Oh yeah. That's when.

The butterflies in my stomach danced, but I didn't trust them. Fitz had never given me a reason to believe he saw me as anything other than a friend. "Don't waste your superpowers on me. Wait for the next girl you need to impress."

"If you say so." He pushed himself to a standing position. "It's too hot. Let's go inside."

"No. Come back." I hooked my foot around his ankle, not caring that I sounded needy and transparent. In the house, I had to share him with his sister or his cell phone or one of a hundred other distractions. Out here, it was only us.

Fitz smiled and lay back on the tramp, close enough that his arm rested against mine. "Do you want to go to the end of the year carnival with me?" he asked.

"What?" I turned, and his face was startlingly close to mine. I was not prepared for the eyelashes or the dimples or the way my cheeks flushed when his eyes found mine. In the span of a single blink, my overactive brain went from zero to fifty. *Why would he ask me that? What does it mean? Is it a date? Is he going to drive? Hold my hand? Pay for my ticket?* "You mean, like—are you going to—are we going to—"

"I'll pick you up and we can drive together. Just the two of us this year. No Clover, no guys from the team. Sound good?"

"Sounds good." I turned so he wouldn't see my grin. I had chocolaty fingers, a hot trampoline below me, a blazing sun above me, and a date with my best friend.

Oh, I realized with a start.

So this is what happiness feels like.

But if happiness is sticky fingers and sunshine, panic is greasy pizza and the sharp tang of nail polish.

"I can't go," I said the next day; Fitz was supposed to pick me up for the carnival any minute.

"Yes. You can." Clover capped the nail polish and leaned over to blow on my toes. The strap of her black swimsuit slipped from under her sundress and fell down her shoulder. It was supposed to be another warm night, and the end of the year carnival always had water slides and dunk tanks.

That morning, I felt fine. Fine-ish. Fine-adjacent. Not terrible, is what I'm saying. By the time Clover arrived to help me get ready, my insides had shifted ever so slightly. Not so much as to be noticeable from the outside, but enough that my whole world felt misaligned. The anxious wrongness I felt in my chest was the sum total of a dozen frustrations. Swimsuit shopping with my mom. A bad grade on my English final. Registering for junior-year classes, and all the choices that came with it. "I don't feel good."

"Mm-hmm. Very convincing," she said.

"No seriously. My stomach hurts. I don't think I can go." I leaned against my bed, legs splayed in front of me on the carpet while my toes dried. I wasn't lying. My stomach *did* hurt. But what I didn't say to Clover was that I was freaking out about going to the carnival with Fitz. Which was stupid. I went with him last year too. Well, him and Clover. His mom drove us, and we met up with the guys from his team. But! The basic elements were the same. Me and him and a couple of snow cones.

Clover sat with her back against the window, frowning at me. "What's wrong?"

"Everything. All of it." I picked at the ruffled hem of my dress. Everything about my appearance was a dead giveaway, from the fresh polish on my toes to my girliest, twirliest dress. It was a floral, off-the-shoulders little thing that displayed the halter straps of my swimsuit. The obvious mistake was in going to so much effort for a silly end of the year carnival with Fitz. When the evening failed to live up to my sky-high expectations, I'd come home and cry two minutes for each one I spent getting ready. So far, that put me at a multi-hour sob fest. "Everything is gonna fall apart."

"How?"

What if I think it's a date, and he doesn't think it's a date, and he realizes how badly I misread the situation, and everything is awkward? Or what if it is a date, and it doesn't go well? Or what if it does go well, but then in a few months he dumps me like he dumped Ivy, and we're not friends anymore?

Instead of explaining the mess in my head, I shrugged. "I don't know. But I know it will."

"What's the *absolute worst* that could happen?"

"A natural disaster."

"This is Gilbert. We don't have tornadoes or hurricanes or forest fires or floods."

"Sometimes we have floods," I countered. "During monsoon season."

Clover reached up and pulled the string to open my window blinds. Outside, the sky was crystal clear.

"A nuclear bomb, then."

"You're impossible!"

The loud rumble of an engine cut through the air. "That's him!" I grabbed Clover's hand and pulled her to the ground with me.

"What are you doing?"

"Hiding!" My room is at the front of the house, where Fitz's truck was idling by the curb.

"You can't ignore him!" Clover whispered.

"I'm not. I'm canceling."

Clover snatched my phone from my fingers. "That's terrible. You can't stand him up."

"He can hang out with the team. He'll be fine."

"You know he'd rather be with you than those guys. When he's with them, he has to act the part of careless heartbreaker. With you, he can be the sappy romantic."

Her words nudge the already tender spot in my chest, but I'm determined. "I don't want to go."

"Liar."

I was desperate to glance out the window. Was Fitz texting me right now? Walking up the front steps? Debating whether or not to step on the gas pedal and get out of here before everything in our relationship turned upside down?

"Fine. I want to go, but I can't. It's not happening." I held my hand out for my phone and she handed it over with a heavy sigh.

I'm sick and won't be able to make it tonight. Sorry.

The sharp ache in my stomach subsided. *Instant relief.*

The air outside my window was silent for a full minute, then the roar of an engine tore straight through my heart. *Instant regret.*

"What's it gonna be, Collins?" Fitz tugs me back to the present, his eyes guarded. I can't help but wonder if he was also strolling down memory lane.

And the thing is, I'm not stupid. I know this plan was for Molly. But with the echo of old regret whistling through the pine trees, I don't care. I don't want an excuse to pick a fight and go back inside, only to lie awake all night regretting another missed evening with Fitz. What I want is to get on the back of the quad. So I do.

I sit behind him and realize immediately that all my touching rules are irrelevant back here. I'm touching him practically everywhere, my legs pressed against his, my chest inches from his back. He seems to understand my hesitation because he picks up my hand and wraps my arm snugly around his waist. "Like this," he instructs. "No such thing as too tight."

I wrap my left arm in a similar fashion and scoot my body so it's flush against his. A thrill of exhilaration snakes through me. He kicks the ATV to life and drives through the forest and into town. As we pass kitschy shops and warmly lit restaurants, biting wind whips my hair into a frenzy and stings my cheeks. I use Fitz as a shield, burying my face in his neck. His woodsy scent surrounds me, and I'm intoxicated enough to slip into a fantasy. Strangely enough, the fantasy is exactly the same as my current reality, with one notable exception.

In my fantasy, he wants me here, and I'm not a replacement for his ex or a distraction from his broken heart. I squeeze my eyes against the ache of being in love with a boy who's so close and still so painfully out of reach.

Fitz slows the ATV to a stop outside the busy train depot. There's a combo gift shop/restaurant and a long, skinny building next to the train tracks. Flocks of families weave in and out of the building, posing in front of vibrant Christmas lights and running after small children. Fitz explains that in a few minutes, a train will arrive to "magically" transport the passengers to the North

Pole. He dismounts the quad and extends his hand to help me down.

"I can't. I think I'm frozen here," I say through chattering teeth.

He laughs and takes my hands in his, rubbing life back into them. "So. What's the verdict on dinner with my family?"

"It was a lot."

"That bad, huh?"

"No! Not at all. But I'm not used to kids and crying and debates about the merits of old romantic comedies. It was a lot to take in—in a really good way. It felt like home. Like one of your movies."

"My movies. My girls. You know none of these things belong to me, right?"

"When you love something, you *love* it. It's like, no one else should even bother liking it because they won't be able to love it nearly half as much as you do. You go all in with everything, and it makes them belong to you, somehow. You're fearless."

His brow wrinkles. "Is that bad?"

"No. It's my favorite thing about you," I confess. My heart pounds hard in my chest. I've never said those words before. They're dangerously close to the truth, to all the things I said in that stupid letter. "I just remembered; Meg thinks the letter might be in your mom's closet with the rest of the Christmas presents."

"Oh. Yeah, maybe." His gaze darts over my shoulder, focusing on something I can't see.

"Where do you think you left it? And isn't it weird that she took it?"

"Sorry." He shrugs. "I don't know."

He's lying. I'd bet every city on my west wall. But I don't know *why* he's lying. For a moment of white-hot panic, I'm scared he read the letter, and that this whole elaborate scenario is his way of letting me down gently, of sparing my feelings.

"Do you remember in freshman year, when I had that panic attack in the science hall after school?"

"Yeah, of course," Fitz says, his eyes finally finding mine.

"And I was so worried about everyone seeing me fall apart that you pulled me into Mr. Irwin's empty classroom and insisted that no one even noticed."

Fitz nods, waiting for me to continue.

"Darren Weatherby and his friends saw me. They teased me for the rest of the year, faking fainting spells and swooning with their arms draped across their foreheads."

"Why didn't you tell me?" His face is murderous.

"Why'd you lie?"

He sighs. "I didn't want you to feel worse than you already did."

"That! Right there!" I place my hand on his chest and immediately think better of it. "You don't have to spare my feelings. Ever."

His eyes blaze into mine, and I'm filled with a frantic desperation to understand what's going on in his head.

"Fair enough," he finally sighs. I wait for him to admit he read the letter. He doesn't. Maybe I'm being paranoid.

A train whistle blares in the distance. "We've got to go," he says, and we both climb back on the ATV. He turns the key, bringing the vehicle to life, and drives parallel to the tracks as a long steam train whooshes by. Fitz drives us away from the lights and the sound and the people, into the cold, black desert mountains.

"Where are we going?" I yell over the growl of the engine. His answer is a quick squeeze above my knee, asking me to be patient. To trust.

The ride is brutal and breathtaking. All my extremities go numb, and the dark hides our surroundings. I close my eyes and instead concentrate on the feeling of being here, trying to pick out what I'd say about Williams, Arizona, if I had the travel career I claim to want.

Cold.

Wow. Brilliant, Paige. Cold weather is cold. Hand me my Pulitzer Prize now, please.

I regretfully loosen my grip on Fitz and sit up, allowing the wind to batter my face.

This is it. This is what I've been waiting for. It's not New York, but it doesn't have to be. New York was never about the city itself. Not really. It's about something new, about leaving the bubble of the only town I've ever known.

I try to summon words for what it feels like to be here, in this place, with this boy.

Alive.

A bone-deep ache has settled into my fingers and toes, but I feel alive in a way I can't remember feeling, maybe ever in my life.

Fitz brings the quad to a stop in a small Christmas village with two-dimensional houses and shops outlined in colorful lights. I stumble off the quad and walk farther into this make-believe winter wonderland until I'm at the center, where Santa Claus is sitting in a giant sleigh, playing poker with a handful of elves.

"Hey, Mike." Fitz nods. Santa returns the nod and folds, tossing his cards facedown with a string of expletives.

"Welcome to the North Pole." Fitz's eyes sparkle as he stuffs his hands into his pockets, watching me.

I'm silent for several more seconds as I take in the outline of the mountains behind the village.

"Well? What do you think?" Fitz tugs on his hat impatiently.

"I think . . ." I take a breath, searching and failing for the words that could describe the warm buzz in my chest. The desert mountains and the dark sky are beautiful, they are. But I can't keep my eyes off the boy who brought me here. "I think it's better than all the pictures on my wall combined."

"High praise."

The train whistle blares in the distance and Fitz grabs my hand. "We have to hide." He pulls me behind the Sweet Shoppe. I peek around the facade and see the train rolling slowly by, the heads of several small children pressed against the windows.

I turn to ask him how long they'll stay and am surprised to see small dots of white on his shoulders. "Is that—?" I look up in amazement.

"Snow flurries," he breathes.

"You kept your promise!" I throw my head back, sticking my tongue out like a six-year-old. When I look back at Fitz, flurries cling to his eyelashes. Painful longing snakes through my body, robbing me of all sense.

I throw my arms around him and squeeze. "Thank you."

He squeezes back, longer and harder and better than he ever has. When he releases me, his broad grin slips sideways off his face. He startles a little, as if I've surprised him. "We have to go." He brushes past me, heading for the quad. I scramble to keep up with his long strides, my feet sliding over slick rocks.

"Wait. Did I do something wrong?" My foot slips out from under me, twisting my ankle. I fall, and my knee slams hard into a large rock.

"Ow!" I roll to my side, clutching both my ankle and my bloody knee.

Fitz is at my side in a second, frowning deeply at the sight of blood. "Can you stand?" He offers me his hand and pulls me gently up. I test my weight on my foot, but my ankle throbs in protest.

"I don't know. It hurts," I hiss.

"Can I—I'm gonna . . . don't make this weird, okay?" he says as he scoops me up into his arms.

The weight of his hands on me makes my brain fuzzy. "What are you doing?"

"I told you not to make it weird, Collins."

Ha. Okay. His face is inches from mine, and I'm supposed to pretend it's not weird? I suppose it's also *not weird* that we hugged for an unprecedented amount of time and then he bolted away from me. Nope. Not weird at all. My gaze snags on my torn leggings and my brain gets even fuzzier. "That's a lot of blood."

"You'll be okay." He places me gingerly on the quad and drives back to the train station. I can tell he wants to go faster, but every bump and jostle causes me to whimper in pain. With his slower pace, we arrive after the train. He stops next to train car J and we watch as people swarm out of it. I press my hand against my knee, but my stomach protests at the sheer amount of slick, warm blood. When the train's empty, Fitz offers me his hand and I gingerly step off the quad. My ankle still aches, but with his hand tight on mine, I'm able to lean my weight against him and limp up the train steps.

"Do you feel okay? Are you light-headed?" he asks.

The blood has soaked through my leggings, pooling at the top of my sock. "I'm a little dizzy," I confess.

Fitz swears under his breath.

To be honest, my mental state is probably half from the blood, half from the fact that Fitz has touched me more tonight than in the last year combined.

"Jane works on this car. She'll have a first aid kit so we can get you cleaned up before we go home," he explains as we board the train. "Hey, sis. We need a first aid kit."

Fitz's twenty-three-year-old sister looks up. Adopted like her older sisters, Jane is half Puerto Rican and half white. Her long, curly black hair is squished under a chef's hat, and she wears an apron over her clothes. She drops her broom and retrieves a first aid kit from the back of the car. "Oh, wow. That's a ton of blood. Is she okay? What do I do?"

"Find crutches. She twisted her ankle."

"I don't need crutches," I say as Jane leaves.

"I know. But I needed to get her out of here. She's bad in a crisis. Tends to panic."

I sit on a bench seat and Fitz sits across the aisle. He picks up my foot and gently places it in his lap. My thick black leggings are already torn at the knee but he rips them further and presses several gauze pads against the cut, applying pressure to stop the bleeding. His brows are drawn, his face serious.

After a minute, he lifts the gauze and checks the cut. "You know, every time you almost kill yourself, my heart nearly explodes." He tilts his activity tracker so I can see the spike in his pulse. I don't know what to make of it.

"The bleeding has mostly stopped." He places a roll of gauze against the pad and wraps my knee securely. His movements are sure and quick, his hands steady. I marvel at them while he works. They're so big. And solid. And calloused. I expect his touch to be rough and clumsy, but his hands are unbearably gentle. "I'll clean it when we get to the cabin, but this should do for now," he says as he finishes up.

I roll my eyes. "I think I can clean my own cut."

"Come on, Paige. Just give me this one."

"Right. I forgot this is part of your whole chivalry shtick."

Fitz scoffs, obviously displeased with my characterization of him.

"It's very charming. I totally get why you do it. Of course all the girls are gonna fall for the white knight who bandages their knee," I tease.

"You think that's why I do all this romance stuff? To get girls to like me?"

"Obviously."

"Well, you're wrong."

"Then why?"

"If I tell you, you'll think I'm an even bigger jerk than you already do." He avoids my eyes as he carefully tapes the gauze down.

"Hey. Wait. I don't think you're a jerk."

He looks up, and *oh*. His eyes are a storm.

"Maybe not, but something feels different between us since we got here, and I can't tell if you're upset . . . or something else." He finishes with the bandage and rests his hand lightly above my knee, precariously close to my thigh. My breath hitches in my chest when he doesn't move. His gaze snags on mine and we hold eye contact for so long it tips into something more. "Tell me you don't feel it too." His hand slips, just an inch or two, sliding up my thigh. I swallow as his pupils dilate, turning his eyes black. I've been waiting my entire life to be looked at like that.

No.

I've been waiting my entire life for *this boy* to look at me like that.

He leans into the aisle, his breath shallow and ragged, but he stops short. If this is gonna happen, I have to meet him halfway.

I'm not sure I can.

Two days ago, Fitz was kissing Molly.

But now he's not.

Does it matter how many girls he's dated or why? What does it mean that he's leaning toward me *now*? What does it mean that he has a history of getting swept away in moments of obvious romance?

I'm starting to spin out.

His eyes search mine, understanding dawning on his features. He gently sets my foot on the floor and scoots to the edge of the train seat. He takes both my hands and looks me square in the eye. "Find the rainbow."

My heart swells painfully in my chest. He always knows exactly what I need, and I love him for it.

I love him.

Of course I love him. I've loved him for so long I don't remember what it's like to exist in a world where I'm not in love with Fitz Wilding. So why am I acting like this is a difficult choice?

"The seats are red," I say, without taking my eyes off him. "Your hair is brown . . . Your eyes are a perfect blue gray."

He fights a smile. "That's not how a rainbow works."

"I don't care." I lean in.

FATE ONE

December 24 | 11:30 a.m. | Manhattan, New York

"First stop, one tourist-trap Christmas tree. This way." Harrison points down the paved path away from the skating rink, and I hurry to keep up with his brisk pace. We come to a fork in the trail and he veers right without missing a beat. I crane my neck to the left, wondering what's at the end of *that* path. The travel-hungry part of me is eager to slow down and take notes on the way the skyline peeks through the empty twisting branches, or how the park feels almost mythical, too pretty to exist in such a bustling city, but Harrison's obviously in a hurry to get this over with. I use my phone to snap as many pictures as possible, text a few of them to Fitz, and promise myself that I'll come back and explore further before the trip is over.

We exit the park too soon and my attention snags on a horse-drawn carriage. It's white with red velvet seats and a retractable red top. The driver is wearing a black suit and top hat, and it's all so ridiculous that I have to ride in it immediately. I put my hand out, stopping Harrison in his agitated tracks. "Can we?"

"No."

"C'mon! I've never been!"

"Not happening."

"I bet you haven't either, have you?"

He sighs through his nose. "Fine. But *only* if we drop something else from your list."

I bite my lip and smooth the list still curled tightly in my fist. What am I willing to give up for a carriage ride through Central Park?

"I suggest nixing the holiday window displays. It's just weird, fancy stuff in the windows of stores neither of us could ever afford."

"Yeah, maybe." I slip my phone out of my pocket and pull up Magic 8, turning to shield the screen from Harrison.

Should I trade holiday window displays for a carriage ride?

Better not tell you now.

"Hello—? Are we doing this?" Harrison calls. He's got one foot on the step of the carriage, waiting for my decision.

"Fine. We'll skip Bergdorf's." I pocket my phone and my list and join Harrison in the back of the carriage.

"Good choice." He nods approvingly while the driver gives us a knowing smile.

"Where would you like to take your lady?" the driver asks slyly.

"She's not—"

"I'm not—"

"We're not—"

We practically trip over ourselves trying to set him right, but I don't think he fully understands, because when Harrison instructs him to "just drive around wherever," the driver tips his hat and looks weirdly smug about it.

"'Drive around wherever'—how romantic." I roll my eyes.

Harrison looks panicked. "Why would you say that?"

"Never mind. Bad joke." I shrink into the corner of the carriage, as far away from Harrison as possible.

The horse pulls us back into the park, the steady clomp of its feet on pavement providing a nice alternative to the heavy silence between Harrison and me. I tip my head back, eyes drawn to the open sky and the tall trees. We pass over a pretty stone bridge and I can't help but sigh softly. Fitz would get such a kick out of the obvious romance and drama of this whole situation.

"How's the guy?" Harrison asks stiffly.

"What? I don't know."

"Please. You've been clutching your phone all morning, and every time I talk to you or ask you a question you do a full one-eighty to stick your nose in your phone."

"It's not the guy. It's the decision-making app I told you about." I cross my arms, pleased to be able to prove him wrong.

"Oh?" His face alights with interest now that we're off the topic of Fitz. "You were serious about that?" He stretches his arm across the seat behind me.

"Afraid so."

"What variables did you enter in? What factors does it take into consideration? Is it, like, AI technology? How does it work?"

"It works exactly like a Magic 8 Ball. 'Cause that's what it is."

"You're joking."

"I'm not."

"Wow. That's . . . Wow." He shakes his head.

"I guess it's 'wow.'" Self-consciousness tears through me. "We don't have to talk about it."

He accepts this. For about ten seconds. When he opens his mouth again, I think he's going to give me a hard time, but his words surprise me. "Last year my ex-girlfriend and I went skating in the park. That's why I didn't want to go. It reminds me of her. The carriage too. Most of the places on your list do, actually. We had just gotten together and we ran around the city like our lives depended on it, doing every festive thing we could think of. We kissed on top of the Empire State Building and had our picture taken with Santa at Macy's and sampled all the sweets at the holiday markets."

His confession hits me where I'm already bruised. There are so many places back home that remind me of Fitz: the water tower, the old farm roads where we cruise on weekend nights when there's nothing to do, every baseball field, the science hall at school. Sometimes it feels like my entire life has been defined by moments with him. If he reads that letter and our friendship inevitably ends, there's not a single place that won't be haunted by his memory.

A stab of sympathy hits my gut. "Let's go back to your house, then. We can check on your dad, watch *Elf*, and I'll bake something festive."

"Here's a question for you. Why these places?" He gestures to the pocket that holds my list. "If you ask me, it looks like you pulled them straight from the pages of a 'ten things to do in New York at Christmas' article."

"Is that such a bad thing?"

"Not bad. Just kind of basic."

Basic.

See also: boring, uninteresting, generic.

Maybe it was silly of me to think that a trip to New York could fundamentally change anything about me, or about my life. In a few days this will all be over, I'll board a plane home, and I won't be any braver than I was before. I was wrong to think this trip would ruin everything. That would imply it had consequences at all.

The only thing this trip ruined is my chance to spend time with Fitz. And when I get home, he'll have set his sights on a new girl, and I'll be forever cemented into the role of best friend. Tears sting the corners of my eyes. I swipe them away before Harrison can mock me.

The carriage pulls to a stop on a street corner. I jump out and push my way into the throng of people crossing the street. He follows me, hand hovering near the small of my back without actually touching me. It's annoying and I hate it. He called me basic. He doesn't get to be thoughtful. We step off the street onto the curb and I tug his jacket hard, pulling him out of the flow of people.

I round on him, years of frustration and angst spilling out of me. "I might be basic to you, but none of this feels basic to me. You had the luxury of growing up here. Down the street from an endless supply of museums and exhibits and festivals and food. I'm from Gilbert, home to churches and schools and not much else. So yeah, Central Park feels special to me. Yeah, I want to see the giant tree at Rockefeller Center. You don't get to make me feel silly or small or *basic* for marveling at this city. This isn't just a trip. This is *the* trip. The thing I've been waiting for my whole life. So excuse me if my list is too basic and boring and pedestrian for your Chaucer-reading-philosophy-textbook-studying-too-cool-for-school snobbery."

I stop for a breath, my lungs burning as I gulp the cold air. Harrison's eyes are wide, and I'm fairly certain I've stunned him into silence.

"What do you have against Chaucer?"

For some reason, this ridiculous response lowers my defenses. *Slightly.* "I don't know anything about Chaucer except that he's a dead white guy that people read when they're trying to impress someone. Who are you trying to impress, Harrison? Your girlfriend already dumped you, so it seems your life is as tragic as mine."

"All right then, let's be tragic together. We'll ask the Macy's Santa for mended hearts, how does that sound?"

"Sounds like a Hallmark movie."

He smirks. "Who does that make me? The big-city jerk she has to dump or the small-town nice guy who gets the girl?"

"You're not that nice of a guy," I muse.

"And this is a big city."

"Your words, not mine."

He laughs. "All right then; we've got a city to see."

And thus begins our grand tour of New York City at Christmas. Harrison was right about the Rockefeller tree; it's big and crowded. And even though it's as amazing as I imagined, we don't stay long. He was pleasant enough on our twenty-minute walk to the tree, but when we arrived, he shoved his hands into his jacket pockets and fell silent. Figuring he was lost in a memory of his ex, I elected to move on.

"What's next?"

"The Grand Central Holiday Fair is less than a mile from here. How're your feet doing?"

"Fine," I say truthfully. My Converse sneakers are well-loved and perfect for a day of wandering the city.

"Okay. Are you cold, though? Do you want to go inside for a bit?" His eyes dart up to the massive skyscraper behind the tree.

"You don't want to go to the fair?"

"What if I told you I had something better?"

"Like what?" I narrow my eyes, suspicious of his motives.

"I want to show you something undeniably New York. You up for it?"

"Watch yourself," I say. He wrinkles his brow in confusion. "You're veering dangerously close to acting like the small-town nice guy who gets the girl." I blush furiously after the words are out of my mouth. I didn't plan it, but when Harrison's lip twitches, I don't regret it either. He doesn't smile freely, and I'm quickly learning that every flicker of a smile is a hard-fought reward.

We enter the 30 Rock building and when I wince at the price, Harrison buys our ridiculously expensive tickets. We're shuttled through security checkpoints and several short lines before stepping onto a large elevator that takes us to the sixty-seventh floor. We step out and walk onto a large, open-air observation deck with 360-degree views of the city.

"Welcome to the Top of the Rock. Best view in the city,"

Harrison says. His eyes flicker with pride. I wander to the edge of the deck and press my forehead against the glass.

I don't know where to look first. Directly in front of us is a swath of green that can only be Central Park. Surrounding the park are miles of skyscrapers wedged together like Lego bricks. I'm struck by an impulse to see what's happening in each one. To ride a million elevators up to a million penthouse suites and inspect the lives of the people inside. I point to landmarks and Harrison patiently names each one, showing me where the Brooklyn Bridge crosses the East River on one side, and where the Statue of Liberty stands in the harbor at the mouth of the Hudson.

"What do you think?"

"It's . . . I don't know." I shake my head. "It's big."

He cocks his head, waiting for me to elaborate.

"It makes me feel big," I clarify.

"It makes me feel small," he muses, eyes lost in another memory.

"No!" I turn back to the city skyline and press my hands on the cool glass. My heart is pounding in my ears in the very best way. When Fitz plays his games with me, I'm forced to focus on my immediate surroundings to keep from spinning out, so that I can't obsess over a million what-ifs. That's how I feel now. I'm 850 feet in the air, but my feet feel solidly tethered to the ground. I'm here, and solely here. It makes me feel alive.

We're quiet while I stare hungrily at the skyline. It's borderline ridiculous, the way I'm living for this view. Harrison can tell too. "For what it's worth, there's this kid down the hall from me—"

"Wait, what?"

"In the dorm. I live on campus. Or at least, I did until my dad's diagnosis. I'm not sure what I'm doing next semester. Anyway, Naveen lives in the dorms now, but he spent the entire last year traveling around the world, living out of a backpack, sleeping in hostels. He did it for something like two dollars a day. You could do something like that."

"Believe me, I've looked. I've tried."

"You've tried?" His voice is sardonic.

"I mean—no. It's not like I've sold all my belongings and hopped on a plane. But that's my point. You can't even get anywhere for that cheap. Let alone food and transportation and shelter." The fact is this. If my family had money, my wanderlust would be charming. As it is, Mom works herself half to death and money is always a factor. Down in the most hidden parts of myself, I'm convinced that I won't make it anywhere at all. I'll live and die in Gilbert, and that thought is so heartbreaking I almost can't breathe.

"Okay. Maybe he's lying. Or maybe you're wrong." His face is indifferent, as if he couldn't be bothered either way.

I keep my hands on the glass as I wander the perimeter of the deck. Harrison doesn't join me. He stays with his hands in his pockets, his face in a near-permanent grimace, and I begin to wonder about the emotional cost for him to be here. "Do you regret dating her?"

His face clears. "What's the point of regret?"

I shrug. Seems easier than explaining how the fear of regret rules almost every aspect of my life.

"There's a philosopher named Kierkegaard. He fell deeply in love with a woman named Regine Olsen, who loved him back. He proposed, and she agreed."

"And the movie adaptation of their love plays every Christmas on the Hallmark Channel," I quip. His tone makes it obvious this isn't that kind of story.

"On Lifetime, maybe. He broke it off a month later. Rings were returned, and they were both devastated. He cried himself to sleep; she threatened suicide."

"Get to the good part, Harrison."

"He did it because he was worried that he couldn't be everything at once: a good husband, a writer, and a faithful Christian. He chose writing over her."

"This story sucks."

"It's said he regretted it for the rest of his life."

"He was disappointed over all the lives he wasn't living," I say, hating how deeply I understand his actions.

"He later wrote, 'If you marry, you will regret it; if you do not marry, you will also regret it; if you marry or do not marry, you will regret both.'"

"So, you're saying no matter what I do, I'll have regrets?"

"Kierkegaard is saying that, not me."

"But you're telling *me* for a reason."

"The way I see it, if all roads lead to regret, you may as well do what you want."

I sigh, fogging the glass with a lifetime of fear and worry and doubt, clouding the city from my view. I swipe my fingers through the haze and turn my back on the skyline.

With Harrison standing in front of me, all dark and brooding, I have no idea *what* I want anymore.

"See?" Harrison nudges me. "I quote Kierkegaard when I'm trying to impress a girl, not Chaucer."

All my focus zeroes in on the spot where the elbow of his coat touched the elbow of mine, and I'm hit with the most ridiculous desire to touch him again. Instead, I lean back against the glass (that hopefully won't crack and send me crashing to my death) and cross my arms over my chest. "Consider me impressed."

Harrison turns his face, hiding the smile I know is there. A bubby, warm feeling starts in my stomach and spreads from there. *Are we flirting?* I haven't flirted with anyone—haven't been interested in flirting with anyone—in so long. It's an injection of fizzy energy straight into my veins. I glance sideways at him, noticing the mole below the corner of his mouth. He's not Fitz. And maybe that's a good thing.

"You hungry?" he asks.

"Starved."

"Lunch and then Santaland at Macy's," he says as we leave the observation deck.

"We don't have to do that," I say, suddenly self-conscious. He already thinks I'm the quaint, hot-chocolate-swigging farm girl who says *freaking* instead of the actual f-word. And if we've moved into the territory of flirting, I don't need him to see me sit on Santa's lap.

"No backing out now. I still need that mended heart." He holds the elevator door open for me with one hand. Inside, we stand closer than the space requires, both of us pretending like we haven't naturally been drifting together since we got off the carriage.

We grab hot dogs from a cart on the street and eat them on our way to Macy's. Santaland is aptly named; it's an explosion of color, fake snow, twinkle lights, Christmas trees, and employees dressed as elves. Too bad the line to see Santa is stupid long.

"This will take hours. Let's leave," I say.

"We walked all this way to cross it off your list," he accuses me with a stare. The line shuffles forward and he snags a place at the end. I sigh and stand next to him, but after a few minutes, I feel incurably foolish for wasting our Christmas Eve this way.

"Let's leave. I'm seventeen, I don't need to—"

"Spare me the angst. Do you want to wait or not?"

I sigh and pull out my phone. I ask Magic 8 for permission to leave, hating that I haven't yet turned into the kind of person who doesn't need it. Two days in New York, and I'm exactly the same as I was.

Permission denied. My shoulders sag. Every thirty seconds, we shuffle forward. By the time we reach the front of the snaking line and I find myself perched lightly on Santa's lap, I'm feeling hopelessly sorry for myself.

"Merry Christmas, young lady!" His twinkly blue eyes shine and I get the feeling that if I tug on his beard it won't budge. "Have you been good this year?"

"Um—"

In the traditional sense, I guess I have. I've gotten good grades and never missed curfew and generally been a "good girl." But sitting here, it suddenly feels like I haven't been *anything* this year. Not especially good, not even a little bit bad. Nonexistent.

"What do you want for Christmas?" Santa prompts, eager to move the line along. "That's a handsome young man waiting for you. Perhaps you want some mistletoe?"

"No." What would I do with mistletoe, when the boy I love is on the other side of the country? But then I turn my eyes to Harrison, and I realize I'm spending Christmas Eve with a boy who doesn't know me at all, who's never seen me have a panic attack, who I've never cried myself to sleep over.

Harrison is a mystery, his hands in his pockets, his eyes trained on me. Everything about him is a surprise. At home with Fitz, every look is full of meaning and buried under a dozen layers of history and feelings and disappointment and expectations.

Maybe Harrison is the adventure I've been looking for.

"I want to be brave." I want to make a decision on my own, without the help of an app. I want to be the type of person who knows what it's like to have a gut feeling and act on it.

"Ho ho ho! I'll do my best." Santa hands me a mini candy cane and signals that it's time for me to leave. Real beard or not, I can't get what I want from him.

"Ready to go?" Harrison holds out his hand to help me up from Santa's lap.

I take a deep breath and exhale it slowly. My phone sits heavy in my pocket, and my fingers itch to reach for the security that lies within the app, but I ignore it. I slip my fingers into Harrison's.

I'm ready.

FATE TWO

Fitz's hand slips off my thigh as I lean across the aisle in the empty train car. His eyes are trained on my lips. My heart thunders as I close the final distance between us, my lips a breath from his, when a voice from the front of the train breaks the heady silence.

"Hide your daughters, Fitz Wilding is in town."

Fitz and I lurch away from each other. A girl our age, maybe a little older, with chin-length brown hair and big round glasses is standing in the middle of the aisle. She puts a hand on her hip, drawing my eyes to her miniskirt and wool tights. "I ran into your sister outside; she told me you were here, but she didn't tell me you were *busy*." Her voice is thick with innuendo as she raises her eyebrows.

The sharp heat of embarrassment burns my cheeks. "No! We're not! It's fine!"

"Bernie. Hey," Fitz says flatly. He slants a pained look at me. "This is Paige."

"Paige? *Ohhh!*" she drawls. "Good for you." She nudges him playfully with her shoulder. "Glad to know you're not still pining over me."

"Bernie . . ." Fitz pinches the bridge of his nose with his fingers. "Now is not a great time."

"Sure. How long are you in town? We should catch up. Oh! Bash and I are throwing a New Year's Eve party at our house. You should come. Both of you!" She smiles brightly. My insides wither.

"Yeah. Maybe," Fitz says shortly.

"Right. Well . . ." Her eyes flick from me to Fitz. "We'll talk later? Say yes."

"Yes," he agrees.

"Perfect!" She bends to hug him, then saunters off the train with a wave.

"Paige—" Fitz turns to me, his hands up in a gesture of surrender as Jane returns empty-handed.

"I couldn't find any crutches."

"It's okay! I don't need them!" I jump to my feet, ignoring the stinging pain in my knee and the dull ache in my ankle. I move quickly down the aisle. Jane steps to the side and allows me to hobble past her.

"Paige! Hold up!" Fitz rushes to follow me.

Outside, the train depot is practically empty. The passengers are gone and the lights inside are shut off. Employees sweep trash in the dark. The snow has stopped falling, leaving behind slick surfaces, bitter cold, and nowhere to sit. Just like that, the magic is gone.

Fitz catches up to me on the wet sidewalk outside the train. "I've never seen you run so fast."

I can't hold it in any longer, not after coming face-to-face with another girl from Fitz's past. "You wanted it to be Molly on that train. You invited her first, and you're stuck with me."

"No. Inviting you here had nothing to do with her."

I've been his best friend for long enough to know when he's lying to me. This time, he's not. But only because he doesn't know the truth.

"She regrets breaking up with you."

"What?" His spine straightens. "How do you know that?"

"She told me."

He blinks, processing this information.

"Knowing that, do you still want me here?"

Fitz hesitates for the length of a single heartbeat. "Obviously. I always want you where I am," he says quietly.

And this time? I *want* to believe him, but that moment of hesitation still hangs in the air like a hand grenade.

"Tell me this night wasn't planned for Molly."

He sighs. "What do you want me to say?"

"The truth."

"Fine. Yes. I planned it for her—"

I turn to leave.

"Wait, wait, wait, hold up," he says in a desperate rush. "I'm glad it's not Molly here with me."

"Why?" I breathe, not daring to hope for a specific answer.

"Because—" He sighs, rubbing his hands over his face. "Because—" he tries again, and my insides shrivel with humiliation at the fact that he can't even come up with *one* reason he wants me here.

"Because we're best friends?" I supply, just to end the agony.

He pauses, his face inscrutable. "Sure," he says derisively. "Best friends."

I cannot believe I almost kissed him. I'll never not be a fool for him, and I hate it. When I'm feeling wounded like this, I have two modes: teary or bitchy. I choose the latter. "So where does Bernie fall in the lineup? Before Molly, obviously. But after Ruby? Or between Ivy and Ruby? Or, I don't know, maybe there was some overlap," I say, sounding every inch the jealous girlfriend.

"I've never cheated on anyone." Fitz's voice is colder than ice.

I raise my eyebrows and shrug.

His jaw strains. "If you've got something to say, why don't you come out and say it?"

I swallow, already hating the words I'm about to say. "Come on, Fitz. It's no secret that you . . ."

"That I *what*?"

"You know. You date around. Like, a lot." I choke on the words. I'm such a coward, putting him down for his fearless heart.

He turns to leave.

"That's it? Fight over?" I call after him.

He spins and stalks toward me. "Fight definitely not over. We're going to figure this out, but we're going to do it inside because it's freezing out here." He takes me above the elbow and steers me into the gift shop. My ankle loosens up with every step, the pain receding quickly. As soon as the warm air hits my face, I wrench out of his grip, breathing hard.

He backs me up against a shelf of snow globes. My eyes dart to the exit, but he puts his arm on the shelf, blocking my path. "I know every instinct in your body is telling you to run from this conversation, but there are obviously things that need to be said. Bernie and I—"

"You don't owe me an explanation."

"Interesting apology. Kinda sucked, actually. But I'm going to forgive you, because I'm operating under a theory right now."

"I have a theory too. It goes like this: Every decision I make is wrong. There is no end to the ways I have and can and will screw up my life." The venom in my voice is gone. I sag against the shelf behind me, too tired to keep sparring. Fitz and I almost kissed, and now we're fighting. That's not a coincidence. All of SIM's lists, all my what-if scenarios, all my painstaking decision analysis out the window—for what? To be his next heartbreak? If he really had feelings for me, it wouldn't have taken a romantic winter wonderland for him to figure it out.

"When have you ever screwed up your life?" he asks in a sharp voice.

"Do you know what the butterfly effect is?"

"You know I don't, because you are much smarter than I am."

"It's a scientific theory that says a butterfly flapping its wings in China can cause a hurricane in Texas."

"Forgive me for being slow, but what does this have to do with you ruining your life?"

"I'm terrified that the decision I make today will be the reason I'm unhappy tomorrow, or next week, or next year."

His face softens. "I suppose it won't make a difference if I tell you that won't happen?"

"Maybe it will, maybe it won't. But what matters is that it *feels* true. That fear is the reason for my panic attacks, and it's why I've literally put my destiny in the hands of some cheesy Magic 8 Ball app."

"What?"

"The only reason I'm here in Williams is because some app told me to come."

"Oh." He stuffs his hands into his pockets and rocks back on his heels, blowing out a long breath. "Answer this: If you had kissed me on that train, would you lie awake at night regretting it, wishing you could turn back time?"

"Probably," I whisper. We were both swept up in the moment, but the fact is that it would have meant more to me than it did to him, and it's not a stretch to imagine that a month or two from now, he'll move on to someone else and I'll be worse off than I am now.

"We don't talk about the night of the carnival, but I always wondered if you lied about being sick. Do I trigger some kind of panic button in you?" His eyes are trained on our shoes.

"I guess so."

"I don't ever want you to feel terrible because of me," he whispers.

"I know. That's why it's better that we were interrupted."

Hurt flashes across his features, gone in an instant. I want to say something, *do* something, to make sure he never looks that unhappy again. But before I can figure out what to say, he squares his shoulders and clears his throat. "It's getting late; we should head back to the cabin."

He turns without a word, and I'm left trailing behind.

On the morning of Christmas Eve, I wake up warm. I snuggle deeper into the covers, drawing the cozy quilt to my chin, unwilling to open my heavy eyelids.

And then I remember.

Last night rushes in like a nightmare. I tried to kiss my best friend. I leaned in and practically threw myself at him, only to be interrupted by one of his exes. I'm frustrated at myself and angry at him and sad about the whole situation.

But I didn't do anything I can't take back, didn't say anything I can't apologize for. And for that, at least, I'm grateful. Another day of maintaining the status quo means another day of Fitz and me. And that's not nothing.

I dress in leggings and a sweater and wander out of my room. The fire is roaring, but Fitz's blanket is folded neatly on the end of his couch. I climb the dark stairs and pause at the top, watching him crack eggs in the kitchen with his mom and Meg.

Pretend with me, I think. *Pretend that nothing happened.* He looks up and sees me, and I realize too late that I'm directly under the mistletoe.

"I hear those things are poisonous." He grins as he cracks another egg against the side of the mixing bowl. I breathe a sigh of relief, because that's exactly the joke he would have made yesterday. *Status quo: maintained.* But relief isn't the same thing as happiness, I realize as I watch him show off by cracking an egg one-handed. He fails spectacularly, and his laugh fills the cabin as yellow yolk runs down his hand. I wanted him to pretend like nothing happened, but now that he has, the sharp knife of disappointment twinges deep in my gut.

I sit across the table from Darcy and watch her work on a thousand-piece jigsaw puzzle. "Want to help?" she asks.

"No thanks."

"Are you sure?" She holds out a piece of all knobs, offering it to me. "It's totally addictive."

I accept the piece and spin it in my fingers. "Who's to say that putting this piece right there"—I gesture to the spot where it belongs, near the top corner—"won't cause a cyclone in Japan?"

Fitz scoffs loudly from the kitchen.

"It'd be a mistake to make your decision based on that," she muses.

"Why?"

"If you're trying to avoid a cyclone in Japan, who's to say making *me* place the puzzle piece won't do the same thing?" She raises an eyebrow. I hand her the piece anyway. The outcome might be the same, but I'd rather her be the cause of it. Avoiding responsibility for anything and everything is basically my MO.

With my head in my hand, I watch her assemble the puzzle. Every so often Fitz wanders over and places a piece before returning to breakfast.

"You miss your mom?" Darcy asks casually as she tries and fails to find a spot for an all-white piece.

"I guess so," I say, even though I do miss her. We texted a bit this morning, and it sounds like she's having a good time with her friend. "She usually works the morning of Christmas Eve so that she can have Christmas with me. Do you miss your wife?"

"Ugh. So much," Darcy says. "She's working today too, and tomorrow. She's a firefighter."

Fitz sets a large platter of baked eggs next to the puzzle and the family swarms the table, leaving me with no time to find out more about Darcy, April, or their spontaneous wedding.

The rest of the day is spent lazing around the cabin: working on the puzzle, watching the cheesiest, fluffiest holiday romance movies, lively debates about the merits of each one, and pulling Gray away from the roaring fireplace every thirty seconds. Starting in the early afternoon, Mrs. Wilding spends most of her time in the kitchen. Fitz and I offer to help, and they teach me to make homemade tamales. It's not as meditative as baking, but it's still enjoyable. By the time we drop the tamales in the steamer, I'm openly grinning at Fitz as he sets the table. It's so different than Mom's and my tradition of Chinese takeout on Christmas Eve, but I could get used to this easy routine with his family. Even Whit isn't so bad once he calms down with all the teasing.

Shortly before dinner, my phone rings.

"Hey, Clover! What's up?"

"I feel terrible for asking, I know it's Christmas Eve and you're probably snuggled up under a blanket next to the fire playing footsie with Fitz—"

"I'm watching him set the table. He keeps forgetting which utensil goes on the left and which goes on the right."

Fitz lets the rest of the silverware drop to the table with a clatter and raises his arm in a giant shrug, making me laugh.

"Fork on the left, knife and spoon on the right. Anyway, Jay and I need help. We served lunch at the shelter today, and then he surprised me with Polar Express tickets. You know how many nieces and nephews he has—"

"Like a hundred."

"Exactly. They're all coming. It's a huge thing. We're right outside Williams now with a flat tire. We have a spare but no jack."

"Where are you? We'll bring one." I don't need to ask to know Fitz will want to help.

"Thank you, thank you, thank you. I owe you big. We're on the highway, at the ten miles to Williams sign. We were behind his family and we don't want to call them back in case they miss the train. The kids are all so excited."

"No problem. See you in a few minutes." I hang up the phone and explain the situation. Fitz leaves the silverware in a pile and we pull on coats and gloves as we dash out to his truck. Inside the freezing cab, I'm all too aware that this is the first time we've been alone together since last night. He drove me to the cabin in silence (me touching him as little as possible, him grumbling when I refused to put my arms around his waist). Inside, I trekked to the basement, where I locked myself in the bathroom and took a steaming shower that turned my skin red. When I returned to my room, a first aid kit was on my bed, and while I disinfected my cut alone, I wished Fitz were there to do it for me.

"Look at you," I muse as I hold my cold hands to the vent, willing the heat to kick in more quickly. "Being all charming and chivalrous even though you have no hope of winning Clover's heart," I say to lighten the mood. I glance sideways at him to see his reaction, to get some sort of clue as to where his head's at.

"Maybe I do, maybe I don't," he says flatly.

Well. That's the opposite of helpful.

We ride in silence for a few minutes. The streets are deserted, all the shops and restaurants closed for the holiday. Only the train station is bustling with life, but the road is too far from the depot for me to spot Jay's family.

"Can you tell me more about Magic 8?" Fitz asks, his hand flexing around the steering wheel.

"I'm bad at making choices. This makes them for me."

"So, coming here was a choice you didn't want to make?"

"Coming here was a choice I didn't know how to make."

He glances at me sideways, and I think he wants to say more, but we spot Clover's Prius pushed to the side of the road. Fitz cuts across the empty road and pulls to a stop in front of it. Clover and Jay both hop out as Fitz pulls out a car jack and carries it to them. He and Jay crouch to pull the old tire off while Clover sprints to the truck and takes Fitz's vacant seat.

"Heat!" She peels off her gloves and lets her fingers thaw in the warm air.

"I can't believe you're here! How long are you staying?" I ask.

"Jay's family is staying overnight in the hotel next to the railroad station, but my parents wouldn't agree to that, so Jay and I are driving back home tonight."

"What? That's, like, seven hours of driving in one day."

"I know. I feel terrible, but it's the only way my parents would let me come. And Jay's family is driving home first thing in the morning, so it's okay. Besides," she muses, "I'm not going to complain about seven hours of alone time with Jay." A dreamy smile crosses her lips before she turns to me and says, "So. Fitz hasn't read the letter?"

"Nope."

"How are you feeling about everything?"

"Seeing him first thing in the morning, all rumpled hair and cooking breakfast for his family . . ." I groan at the memory. Fitz is so attractive it hurts.

"You have to tell him."

"I almost kissed him last night." I cover my face with my hands as my cheeks flush.

"Tell me everything. Now."

I tell her the story and when I'm done, she looks horrified. "Why didn't you kiss him?"

"Because I'm in love with him."

"Seems like all the more reason to, you know, smash your faces together."

"Lovely. But I can't. We had a *moment* because he's a hopeless romantic and there was snow and twinkle lights and I slipped and he got to dramatically save me like we were in our own personal movie. He was in love with the moment, and I'm in love with him." I bite my lip so I don't cry. If my life has taught me anything, it's that I always screw things up. One way or another, I'll definitely mess up this thing with Fitz, and I might as well get used to it now.

Clover wrinkles her nose. "I don't think you're giving him enough credit."

"Maybe not."

"I'm confused. If you're in love with this boy, why are you so scared of getting close to him?"

I lean my head back with a sigh. If only there was an easy answer to her question. "I think loving someone and trusting them might be two different things."

The following silence is disrupted by my stomach growling.

"I have snacks in the car," Clover says. "Pretty please be the one to get them so I can thaw out before going back to that icebox?"

I dash to Clover's car, but don't see any food. I check under the seats and in the center console and then stretch across it to open the glove compartment.

I unlatch it, and a small black ring box tumbles out.

FATE ONE

December 24 | 5:58 p.m. | Manhattan, New York

My pulse thrums happily as we walk through Macy's. If I thought Harrison nudging me with his elbow was exciting, that's nothing compared to the feeling of his fingers threaded through mine. I expect him to drop them, but he doesn't. He holds on like he means it until we reach the gold-and-glass doors at the front of the store. And then, because I don't want him to do it first, I slip my hand out of his and shoulder the heavy door open. We spill from the brightly lit store into the glistening night. My mouth waters at the scent of candied nuts from a street vendor.

I shiver against the cold and bring my hands in front of my face, breathing into them. "Subway? Or walk?" I look down the street in the direction I think is Harrison's apartment, trying to estimate how far we are from his building.

"Let's walk," he says. And even though it's dark and cold and my feet are starting to hurt, I'm utterly delighted by his answer. He motions to the left (I was looking right) and we fall in rhythm next to each other.

"Who takes their kid to see Santa on Christmas Eve? What if the kid asks for something that's not under the tree? Seems like a big gamble," Harrison says. The back of his hand brushes against mine, sending sparks all the way up my arm.

"I don't know. Santa seemed kind of magical to me. He could make it happen."

"As in, the real Santa Claus?" He narrows his eyes.

I shrug and smile. "Maybe." He doesn't answer, but I don't mind. I feel floaty and fizzy inside, light and happy. I want to stamp this moment in my brain. The whole city seems to sparkle. It's the twinkle lights and the streetlamps, obviously, but it's also the steam rising from the manhole covers, casting a backlit glow on the streets.

"This city is a little bit magic. I bet it's even better with snow."

"It's not. The traffic is terrible, bus routes are canceled, trains are delayed, and it's a matter of hours before all that sparkling white snow turns to disgusting sludge."

"You are way too young to be so cynical."

"You're not wrong," he says lightly as his fingers thread through mine again. It's the best kind of surprise, a shock to my already overloaded system. My heart skips in my chest as I walk down a dark NYC street with a cute stranger who represents possibilities I never dared to dream of.

Several blocks later, we pass the place where the vendor was selling Christmas trees yesterday. He's gone, but a few trees lean against the side of an alley, looking lonely and sad. "We have to take one home."

Harrison sighs, heavy and long-suffering.

"C'mon! We have to! Tomorrow is Christmas, and your apartment, no offense, is dark and depressing and hopelessly sad."

He laughs. "No offense?"

"I'm taking it." I pick the tree closest to us and reach through the branches to get a good grip on the trunk.

"Isn't this stealing?"

"No, it's charity. One less tree to deal with in the morning."

He grumbles but eventually bends to help me lift the heavy tree; as he does, his dragon book slips unnoticed out of his jacket pocket.

"You dropped this!" I set the tree down and reach for the book. My eyes snag on a familiar-looking symbol. It's swirly and black and— "Your tattoo! This is on your chest!"

Harrison props the tree trunk against his shoulder and takes the book, sliding it into his pocket. "Yep."

"What is it? You have to tell me now. I'll look it up, I'll figure it out, I'll—"

"*Reaper in the Stars.* It's my favorite book. I've reread it every winter since I was fifteen."

"What's it about?"

He lifts the tree again. "I'll tell you as we walk." He nods to the front of the tree, which I lift eagerly. "It's about—"

"Speak louder!" I call over my shoulder.

I can feel Harrison roll his eyes, but he raises his voice. "It's about dragons and warring kingdoms and found family and fighting for what you believe in."

"And the symbol?"

"Is the seal of the dragon warriors."

At this, I drop the tree again. I turn to him with a grin. "You tattooed a symbol for a fictional dragon warrior on your chest?"

"Yeah . . ." He shifts the tree on his shoulder, looking uneasy.

"You're a closet nerd!" I clap my hands together in excitement. This is the best discovery I've made all day.

"There's nothing closeted about it." He sets the tree back down and pulls his phone out of his pocket. He unlocks it and scrolls for a couple of seconds before turning the screen to face me. I gasp in happy surprise. Judging by the shorter hair and softer features, it's an old picture, and Harrison is dressed in full fantasy garb, standing in front of a giant *Reaper in the Stars* poster.

"You cosplay!"

"Less now, but I used to dress up and go to all the local conventions."

"Why did you stop?" I ask, eyes returning to the picture of young Harrison. Behind him, a man is standing on the hem of his cloak, and Harrison's brows are drawn in annoyance. Same old Harrison, even in medieval trappings. I find it a little too endearing.

"Not any specific reason. I grew up. Got a girlfriend. Mom left. Dad got sick. Life got in the way." He holds his hand out for the phone and I give it back, letting my cold fingers brush against his.

"Then why get that tattoo?"

He hesitates.

"Come on, it's just you, me, and New York City. Who am I going to tell?"

He takes a deep breath. "I got the tattoo to remind myself of what it's like to be fifteen. It was an attempt to take myself less seriously, but joke's on me 'cause every morning I look in the mirror and feel like I'm off to fight my demons." He juts out his chin, daring me to make fun of him, but I would never. Not for this.

"I'm sorry you have demons" is all I can think to say. I grab his hand, wrapping my freezing fingers around it.

"I'm not the only one who does," he says. We're close enough that I can see the small puffs of air as he breathes. He surveys me with dark, unreadable eyes. We stand like that for several seconds, eyes locked, before he clears his throat and shakes off my touch.

"Your hands are freezing. We should go," he says. We lug the heavy tree the rest of the way to his apartment and up five flights of stairs. Needles drop to the ground, leaving an incriminating trail behind us. By the time we get to his door, my hands are covered in sap, needles are in my hair, and all the muscles in my body are burning.

Tyson and Mom are once again in the kitchen with takeout, and as starved as I am, we have to deal with the tree first. "I think I have a stand somewhere," Tyson says. Ten minutes later he emerges from his closet with a small, rusty tree stand, a box of tangled lights, and a handful of mismatched ornaments. Harrison twists large bolts into the trunk while I hold the tree upright and Mom directs me which way to push it so that it's standing straight.

"The Christmas tree was always Jenna's doing," Tyson says quietly to Mom as they untangle an old strand of lights. She lays her hand gently on his arm. I follow Harrison to the kitchen for bowls of Thai food. His hair is a dark curtain over his face as he dishes himself a plate of yellow curry.

"You've got needles in your hair," I say. He brushes them away, then thinks better of it and ties his hair up in a high bun. "Do you want to talk about your mom?"

Harrison rears his head back. "No."

"Okay. We can if you want to, though. I heard your dad say that she used to be in charge of all this Christmas stuff, so I understand if you're feeling weird about it or whatever."

"She's not dead. She lives in Vermont with her boyfriend. I'll see her next week."

My cheeks burn in embarrassment. "Oh—okay," I stammer. "Sorry I brought it up."

"And before you get any other ideas, I don't want to talk about my dad and his MS or my ex either."

"Understood," I lie.

The silence is tense between us as we eat. I keep my eyes on my plate, blinking away tears. When he mentioned his demons, I thought he might want to talk to me. I thought I might want to talk to him. To be shut down so completely is humiliating. And to be humiliated makes me feel panicky, wishing I could retrace my steps until I find a spot where I didn't feel this way.

When Harrison leaves the kitchen, I call Fitz. More than anything, I need to hear his reassuring voice, telling me that everything will be okay. That my demons aren't so big. The phone rings and rings and rings, eventually sending me to the dreaded voicemail. I hang up without leaving a message.

I join the festivities in the living room and watch Mom and Tyson laugh and dance and decorate the tree. When they say good night, I'm not tired, so I sit in the glow of the twinkle lights with my arms wrapped around my knees.

"My dad was diagnosed just before Thanksgiving," Harrison says, his voice low. He slips off the couch and joins me on the floor. "It seemed frivolous to spend time and energy on things like Christmas decorations when our entire lives have been turned upside down."

"You don't have to talk about it." The memory of Harrison's censure is still fresh. I had no idea he was going to react that way to a comment about his mom, which is a stark reminder that I've only known him for a day. For an hour or so earlier this evening, I thought he could be my adventure. Shows what I know.

He sighs and unties his bun, dragging his fingers through his hair. "I'm bad with emotions. Like, really bad. If you want to talk about feelings, I'm not the guy you want around."

"Who says I want to talk about feelings?"

He raises an eyebrow.

"I was trying to be nice," I say.

"I know. I shouldn't have snapped."

"It's fine." I keep my eyes on the lights of the tree, but I can feel him watching me.

"We thought a tree wouldn't matter, but it does." He puts his hand on my knee, and I finally look at him as the heat from his hand sears through my leggings. Shadows fall across his face. "My dad looked so happy tonight, stringing these crappy old lights and dancing with your mom. I'm glad you made me drag this thing half a mile and up five flights of stairs."

"This is a thank-you speech?" I ask, eyes straying to the hand still resting on my knee. It's unfamiliar and unexpected, but I don't want him to move it. I think back to how giddy I felt walking to the apartment tonight, and am pretty sure it had less to do with the city or the tree and more to do with the fact that surly, brooding Harrison keeps a philosophy textbook by his bed, a dragon book in his pocket, and a warrior tattoo close to his heart. It's a Mad Libs combination of traits that makes him more intriguing than he has any right to be. I inch closer, and for a moment I'm so nervous I can't breathe, wondering if he's going to kiss me. But instead of leaning in, he repositions himself and lies on his back, looking up at the Christmas tree. "The view is great down here," he says, raising his eyebrows.

"Me, or the tree?" I say, leaning back on my arms.

He gently knocks the inside of my elbow so my arm collapses and I fall next to him; nerve endings come alive from my leg up to my shoulder, lighting a flame along every inch of skin that is pressed to my clothes to his clothes to his skin. My stomach clenches and I let my head fall to the side, facing him. I'm begging him to kiss me, and he sees it; he leans in at the same moment my phone beeps.

"I should check that," I blurt. He pauses, then nods. "Could be my dad." I sit up and grab my phone from the coffee table. He sits up too and places his hands on my knees, his fingers dancing idly.

"Or your love letter guy," he muses.

Mention of Fitz sends my heart into my throat, but thankfully it's a text from Clover. I open the message to see a picture of her hand with a diamond ring on the fourth finger.

?? I reply.

"Is everything okay?" Harrison asks as I frown at my phone.

I tilt the screen so he can see it. "From my friend Clover."

"Hot damn, that's a diamond ring! How old is she?" he asks.

"Eighteen last month."

He whistles under his breath. "Do they put something in that desert water?"

"What do you mean?"

"You're in love with this best friend guy, and now this chick has run off and gotten engaged."

"What? No! She wouldn't."

"She did."

When my phone rings, I answer immediately. "What happened?"

"Jay proposed! We're engaged!" Clover squeals so loudly that even Harrison winces.

I run my hand over my face as all the worries I keep stored in my brain on a daily basis squish tightly together, making room for this new thing. SIM licks his fingers, flips to a blank page, and starts a new list.

All the ways Clover will ruin her life if she gets married at eighteen:

- higher risk of divorce (statistically proven fact, I'm pretty sure)
- more likely she'll drop out of college—if she even *goes*
- no college = no job = no place to live = she'll be homeless and destitute

I'm not proud of the fact that my mind takes Clover from engaged to homeless in approximately 2.2 seconds, but my brain is an expert at worst-case scenarios. My tongue sticks in my throat. *What can I say? How do you tell your best friend that she's about to make the biggest mistake of her life?*

"Paige? You there?"

"Yeah." I try to force my voice to sound happy, but it comes out strangled and forced. "Tell me everything."

Clover seems blissfully oblivious to my hesitation and launches into the story. "Well, it started with him surprising me with tickets to ride the Polar Express train with his family. On the way up there, we got a flat tire and didn't have a spare so we called Fitz and he came to help us—"

"You saw Fitz?" I blurt without thinking. Harrison's fingers stop waltzing and he sits back. I cringe, hating myself for being so desperate to know about Fitz, for almost kissing Harrison when I'm in love with someone else, and for getting distracted when this moment is about Clover. "Never mind. Keep going."

She describes the train ride in perfect detail, down to the hot chocolate and the cookies and the twinkle lights at the depot. Because my mind is a dirty traitor and my heart is hopelessly predictable, my mind wanders while Clover talks, placing Fitz in the scene she describes. It's too easy to imagine him amid the white lights, his hands clasped around a warm drink. The picture tilts my entire world on its axis, making this moment with Harrison feel cheesy and wrong. I force myself to focus on Clover's story, because I can tell by her voice that she's getting to the important part.

"—Jay drove me home and dropped me off at my house. We sat in my car and talked for a long time, and he told me he couldn't wait another second to give me my present. Then he showed me the ring and told me how much he loves me and that he cannot wait to spend the rest of his life with me, and asked me to marry him! Isn't that the most romantic thing you've ever heard?"

"Uh—" My heart hammers in my chest. I wipe my sweaty palms on my pajama pants, suddenly sweltering.

"Paige?" Clover's voice falters. "Why aren't you saying anything?"

"What do you want me to say?"

"That you're happy for me," she says flatly.

"I—I'm . . ." I clear my throat. Harrison cocks his head to the side questioningly. "Is this because you want to have sex?" I blurt. Harrison shakes with silent laughter. I angle my body away from him.

"No!"

I don't believe her. She and Jay are both intent on waiting until marriage. "What other reason is there to get married *now*?"

"What reason is there to wait?"

"The obvious one."

"Age is just—"

"—a number? Maybe. But in this case, it's a *really* important one."

"Jay's the one. I know it more than I know anything else in this world. If the only reason to wait is to make other people more comfortable, then that's stupid. My life has never been about making *other* people comfortable." Clover sounds like she's on the verge of tears.

"You're still in high school!"

Silence. I think the call has dropped. When she finally speaks, her voice is frosty around the edges, hard and brittle and danger-ous. "The wedding will be after graduation."

"But you're still so young! What if you change your mind about him?"

"I know what I want. Just because you're afraid of making big choices doesn't mean the rest of us are." Her brittle voice breaks into thousands of icy shards that tear at my heart.

"Hey," I say. I glance up, meeting Harrison's eyes. My voice sounds wounded and I hate it. "I just want you to be happy. I don't want you to ruin your life—"

"Message received. And thank *you*, for ruining the happiest moment of my life." She ends the call.

My stomach swims as my forehead breaks out in a sweat. I lean forward, head in hands, and try to stave off the coming nausea.

I messed up.

I lift my head. Harrison's still here, waiting for me to say some-thing. "I should have lied and said I was happy for her, right?"

"Are you kidding? She's *freaking* crazy."

"Don't talk about her like that."

"I'm agreeing with you! She's nuts and you were right to tell her that."

My heart pounds furiously in my chest as the slimy snake of unease coils through my stomach. That moment was all wrong. I need to fix it. "She's not crazy. Don't say that. But—what about college? What about her life? What about—"

He places his hands on my knees again. "She's not getting married tonight. So you can calm down for now."

Calm down? I shake my head. He doesn't get it.

I've never missed Fitz more in my life.

"I wish I could." I drop my head into my hands again. What I need is a way to time travel out of this, not a guy telling me to calm down. "I screwed up. I should have asked the app. I shouldn't have—"

"Reacted? You're allowed to have a reaction. Don't be so hard on yourself." He reaches a hand out to comfort me.

"Stop talking, please!" I snap. His hand drops. "I need to go." Except it's after midnight on Christmas morning and it's twenty degrees outside and I have nowhere to go and no way to get there. "Bed. I need to go to bed."

"Paige, hang on—" Harrison's exasperated. But I can't care about him right now. I leave him in the shadow of the Christmas tree, crawl into his bed, and stare at the dark ceiling for the rest of the night.

FATE TWO

**December 24 | 5:22 p.m. | Ten Miles Outside
Williams, Arizona**

My stomach plummets.

No.

It can't be what it looks like.

No no no no no no no.

This is not happening. I refuse to believe that my best friend's eighteen-year-old boyfriend bought an engagement ring. I open the box with trembling fingers. A white-gold ring with a small princess-cut diamond is nestled in a bed of black velvet. Fitz's shadow falls across me as he stands up, blocking the fading daylight from the window. I snap the box shut and shove it back in the glove compartment. Fitz sees me stretched across the front of Clover's car and gives two thumbs-up. They're done.

I have to do something to stop this coming train wreck. I crack the door open. "Distract Clover for a few minutes, okay? I need to talk to Jay about a surprise. A Christmas thing."

"Sure thing." Fitz jogs back to his car and sits in the passenger seat. Clover laughs at something he says. I crawl backward over the center console and sit in the driver's seat as Jay opens the door. His broad shoulders fill the car as he climbs in.

"Hey, Paige. What's up?"

"Don't propose to Clover." My statement comes out easily, because this isn't a hard decision to make. This is me saving Clover from herself.

He looks stricken. "She found the ring?"

"I did. She doesn't know, but I promise you, it's a bad idea."

His face visibly relaxes. "We've talked about this. We want to spend our lives together."

"You've talked about this? Now? You told her you're going to propose to her while she's halfway through her senior year of high school?"

"We're in love."

"Then be in love! Spend your lives together! You don't have to start now. At least let her graduate before you tie her down forever."

Jay's confidence falters. "I thought Clover and I were on the same page. We wanted a summer wedding."

"Trust me, Jay, I'm her best friend. I know what she wants. She needs more time, or you'll scare her away." I'm rambling, talking without thinking, saying words I don't even believe.

He nods, still looking uncertain. "I'll think about it."

"Thank you." A nagging guilt tugs at my stomach as we look through the windshield at Fitz and Clover, who are singing loudly in his car. Fitz catches my eye and winks.

What if this situation was reversed? What if Clover was making decisions about my life, about the boy I love?

I shake the ridiculous thought away. I may be an anxious, paralyzed disaster of a human, but I'm not stupid. I would never dream of marrying Fitz, or anyone, now or even five years from now. There's nothing romantic about being eighteen-year-old newlyweds who don't know the first thing about how to adult.

I'll tell her the truth someday, and she'll thank me for saving her from a huge mistake.

Clover climbs out of Fitz's car as I approach.

"What was that all about?" She bounces on the balls of her feet.

"Nothing important." I shrug, hoping she won't read into it. But she nods and smiles knowingly, her face glowing with anticipation.

"I'm excited about tonight."

"Why?"

She takes a deep breath, preparing to tell me something. *Does she know?* She can't. She wouldn't actually agree to marry Jay, would she? Her face lights up as she looks over my shoulder at Jay in her van, and a boulder drops in my stomach.

Yes.

She would.

I knew it as soon as I saw the ring, which is why I intervened.

I did the right thing.

I'm positive I did.

I'm, like, 95 percent sure.

"We'll talk later. Thanks again for saving us. You're the best, and that boy of yours is pretty great too. Cut him some slack. He might surprise you." She squeezes my hands and joins Jay in the

Prius. They wave as they pull out onto the road. I trudge slowly back to Fitz's truck as SIM whispers terrible things in my ear about how I destroyed my friendship with Clover.

My stomach squirms with unwelcome guilt as Fitz drives us back through town. He frowns, darting sideways glances at me, but it takes him half the drive before he says anything.

"You look miserable."

"I might have done something bad, but if I did it for the right reason, it's okay, right?"

"Depends. What'd you do?"

"I lied to someone."

Fitz mulls this over. "Last night you made me promise not to lie to spare your feelings."

"What about . . . lying to save someone from making a decision that has the potential to ruin their life?"

"Who decided that this thing would ruin their life? Are you stopping them from committing a crime?"

"No. But it's something they'll regret eventually."

Fitz narrows his eyes. "What'd you do?"

"Jay has an engagement ring, and I told him not to propose to Clover."

"Because you think she'll say yes." Fitz slowly pulls the car into the long driveway and shuts it off.

I nod once, because I don't want to hear how it sounds out loud, and I don't particularly want to hear Fitz's rosy-tinted view of the situation.

"I'm not gonna lie, Paige. That's pretty messed up."

"I shouldn't have asked you." I lean against the window, toward the cold and away from the warmth radiating off him in waves. "Of course you would think it's a good idea. What's more romantic than graduation slash wedding?"

"That's not fair."

I roll my eyes. "Don't pretend like you don't think a Christmas Eve proposal is wildly romantic. You'd have probably proposed to Molly if she hadn't dumped you."

"And don't pretend like you're not projecting *your* fear of commitment onto Clover. Did you ever stop to think that some people like living in Gilbert, and that staying there isn't the punishment you make it out to be?"

"This isn't about me."

"Get real. Clover and Jay are in love. And maybe getting married at eighteen and nineteen is the stupidest thing they'll ever do. Or maybe they'll be happily married for seventy years and they'll die together in their nursing home, *The Notebook* style. It's their life. They can do whatever they want."

"I didn't break them up. I told him to put the brakes on, to wait until after graduation." *Or one or two or five more years.*

"It's not your decision to make!" he yells. His chest heaves as he shoves the sleeves of his sweater up to his forearms. I've seen him upset like this. The time Ruby broke up with him for Bryson Black, and then a week later Bryson sent a picture of her in her bra to all the guys at school. Or when Jane was moving away for college and Fitz picked a stupid fight with her over a game of Scrabble (*yowza* was not an acceptable word, it turns out) because he was sad that she was leaving. You don't spend five years of your life as someone's best friend without seeing him lose his cool, is what I'm saying. But his anger isn't usually directed at me, and it makes me feel sad and furious. I'm torn between the desire to apologize and the urge to tell him to go to hell.

In the end I do the thing I'm best at, which is nothing at all.

An awful silence follows his outburst. We make timid, miserable eye contact a couple of times, but mostly he fidgets with the radio and the heater while I stare out the window, wishing I'd never found that ring. My head and heart are full of regret, which is ironic, because all I really want in life is to avoid regrets at all costs.

We stay in the car until my stomach growls loudly. We're both sullen as we head inside for dinner, and no matter how many times I try to catch Fitz's eye between bites, he keeps his gaze steadily on everything and everyone but me.

It's four a.m. on Christmas morning, and I'm out of time.

Mrs. Wilding shooed everyone to bed early last night, once again denying my offer to help with presents, thereby thwarting my opportunity to find and destroy the letter. I tossed and turned for the rest of the night.

If I let Fitz read it, he'll know exactly how much I love him and how much I hate him and I'll be left to salvage what I can from the wreckage of our friendship. If I don't let him read it, well. I can try to fix things, at the very least. Stop acting like a jealous ex-girlfriend and start acting like a normal human.

What do I do?

What

Do

I

Do?

What do I do what do I do what do I do what do I do?

I'm paralyzed by indecision. And I hate that about myself. I open Magic 8 and ask the question I've been too afraid to ask this whole time.

Should I let Fitz read the letter?

The ball on the screen lights up the dark as it spins. My emotions are dangerously close to the surface this morning. I'm confused about what happened on the train and guilty about meddling in Clover and Jay's relationship. I'm still convinced—at least 90 percent—I did the right thing but everything feels just out of my grasp. Beyond my control in a way I've never been comfortable with. I curl into a ball, arms wrapped around my aching stomach.

Reply hazy, try again.

Should I tell Fitz that I'm in love with him?

Better not tell you now.

Is this a joke?

Is Fitz in love with me?

Don't count on it.

Well, obviously. At least it can get something right.

Tears spill over my cheeks. I drag myself out of bed, pulling the warm blanket around my shoulders.

I have a letter to steal.

And look, I know it's stupid to base my decision on this random app. But the random app told me Fitz is not in love with me, and I'm crying actual tears. If this hypothetical situation makes me cry, there's no way I'll survive him reading my letter, finally understanding how I've felt all these years, seeing my heart spilled across the page.

He's sleeping deeply as I walk past his couch. I'm tempted to reach out and brush the hair off his forehead, but I can't go down that route. I'm not sure I'd be able to stop myself from crawling under the blanket next to him and burrowing my head in his chest.

The house is quiet as I tiptoe up the dark steps. The white lights from the Christmas tree cast a hazy, magical glow over everything. I pause, alone under the mistletoe, and appreciate how enchanted the room looks at this hour. The porcelain Christmas village is aglow, tiny yellow lights streaming from tiny windows. It makes my tender heart ache.

I scan the packages under the tree, searching for an envelope with Fitz's name.

"Paige?"

I startle, nearly falling down the stairs as Fitz's mom approaches from the hall where her bedroom is. In one hand is a mug, in the other, a book.

"What are you doing up so early?"

I open my mouth—to say what?

The truth?

"What are you doing up?" I deflect.

She smiles and takes a seat in the recliner, facing the tree. "I love this holiday. The quiet magic of Christmas morning. All the hopes and wishes and possibilities. I like to sit here and savor that feeling before the chaos begins."

I glance at the stack of presents under the tree. It's sprawling and deep and I'm hit by a wave of embarrassment over having nothing for anyone in Fitz's family.

"I wrote Fitz a letter and I need it back."

Her face scrunches in obvious confusion. I rush to explain. "It's not a big deal, it's just kind of embarrassing. Please don't tell him. Not that I'm asking you to keep secrets from your son, but we got into this fight and—"

"Paige." She stops my inane rambling. "It's not a big deal. I won't tell him. But I haven't seen a letter."

My heart stutters. "Are you sure?" I scan the presents again.

She shakes her head with a sympathetic smile. "I'm sorry. I can ask Whit. Maybe Gray grabbed it."

"No!" I don't need even more attention drawn to this disaster. "It's okay."

It'll be fine, I lie to myself.

You won't be, SIM whispers.

Crushing panic spreads quickly and easily. I take a breath, feeling like I just swam a mile. *I can't breathe.* Sharp pangs tear through my stomach and tears build behind my eyes. *I can't breathe.*

"Can you check your closet for the letter?" I don't register what she says, but she leaves the room.

What I *want* to do is tear apart every present under the tree, in case the letter got trapped under the pile—or worse, *inside* one of the perfectly wrapped packages.

What I *actually* do is shake the angsty energy from my hands as I pace the room, because I have just enough presence of mind to realize that tearing wildly through the presents will only make this bad situation worse.

He'll find the letter. Or maybe not him, but someone will find it. Maybe they'll read it; maybe they'll give it to him. Either way, he's going to find out.

And that's when I lose him.

Once he realizes I've been pining for him the whole time, secretly hoping for all his relationships to fail so he'll realize he's in love with me, he won't even want to be friends with me. Even being in the same room with him will be awkward and terrible and I'll have to change all my routes at school to avoid him. And Clover is going to marry Jay and move on to an adult life with her husband and leave me behind.

I wasted my one chance to get out of Gilbert, and it'll never come around again.

I'll be friendless and alone in the same small town for the rest of my life.

"I couldn't find it," Mrs. Wilding says. "But I'll look again when everyone is awake and I can turn the lights on."

"Thanks," I say shrilly. "I'm gonna go back to bed."

"I'll tell everyone to be on the lookout for it today." Her voice stops me at the top of the stairs.

"No! Please don't. I'd rather no one else know." I take the stairs two at a time, a plan forming in my mind.

I'll stay in my room today.

I'll tell Fitz I'm sick and don't want to infect his family, and I'll hide. They'll find the letter, and Fitz's dad will read it out loud around the fire, the kids gathered at his knee like he's Santa

Claus. When they get to the part about how Fitz is the only person in my life who makes me feel like I'm not out-of-my-mind crazy, they'll all laugh. Especially Whit. He'll never let Fitz live this down. But I won't hear it, because I'll be in the basement with my head under a blanket. And that's the whole point. They'll feel so bad for me that they'll let me hide out until it's time to go home, and then I'll never have to see th—

I run smack into someone outside the bathroom. "Sorry!" It's Darcy. Beautiful, Christmas-mouse Darcy, in expensive leggings and a soft sweater.

"My fault," I whisper back.

"Merry Christmas! I should be sleeping, but Jane snores. Why are you awake?" She frowns. "Are you okay?"

I furiously blink away the tears. What is it about that question? When I *am* okay, the words are weightless. When things are going sideways, it's the fastest way to get me to break down. A lump rises in my throat. I almost choke on it. "I don't feel good."

"Oh no! Is it the flu?" She leans away, holding her breath.

I don't want to add unnecessary stress to her life, so I say, "It's something I ate."

She steps aside, clearing a path for me to the bathroom. I ignore the implication and dart inside my room, slamming the door behind me. I lean against it and slide to the floor, taking giant gulps of air that don't feel like nearly enough. My chest is tight and a wave of nausea rolls through me. Bile rises in my throat and I choke it down.

I need to move. Need to get out—*now.*

The room is too small. I can't breathe in here. I push myself to my feet and pace across the worn carpet.

Air. I need air or I'm going to die in this room.

I open the door and stumble into the main room. I put my hands on my knees and gasp for air.

Why is there no air in this place?

Fitz startles awake. "Paige—"

"I can't breathe," I gasp. My lips are numb. My fingers tingling. Fitz leaps over the back of the couch to stand by me.

"It's a panic attack. You're not dying," he says.

But it feels like I'm dying.

It's too hot in here. Maybe I am sick. Cold sweat slicks down my neck as my heart pounds in my chest. There has to be a way out of this, but I can't think what it is.

Fitz threads his warm fingers through mine and squeezes three times.

I close my eyes and sink to my knees, pressing my forehead to the cool wooden floor. Fitz comes with me, his hand never wavering. "I feel sick I can't breathe I think I need to lie down."

"Name five things—"

"I can't do that right now," I snap.

"This is going to end. I promise. You won't feel like this forever." His free hand rubs calming circles on my back.

He's right. This has happened before.

I feel like I'm dying but I'm not.

I sit like that, curled in a trembling ball on my knees in my best friend's basement, until my heart slows. My gasping breaths slowly even out. Feeling returns to my lips and my fingers. And when the worst of the attack is over, the embarrassment settles in its place. I pull my fingers from Fitz's grasp and turn away as hot, prickly shame crawls over my skin like a rash.

"It's okay. Talk to me," Fitz pleads.

I quickly wipe tears off my cheeks. I probably look like a wreck: unbrushed hair, unbrushed teeth, still in my pajamas. I can't believe Fitz is seeing me like this.

Why can't I ever be normal?

"I'm sorry, I can't right now." I glance over my shoulder at Fitz, whose face is a mix of sadness and frustration and worry. I hate that I'm making him look like that. I hate that I'm such a disaster, but I don't know how to be anything else. I escape to his room, climb in bed, pull the covers over my head, and make plans to stay there for the rest of my life.

FATE ONE

December 25 | 9:30 a.m. | Manhattan, New York

SIM starts a new list, titled How I could have avoided this disaster with Clover. (He can be so wordy.)

This list isn't as quick or as easy to compose as the one about Clover ruining her life, believe it or not.

Option one: The phone call (and what I could have done differently).

I consider this while I sit on the couch in my pajamas, watching (and occasionally participating in) the requisite giving and receiving and unwrapping and thanking. Tyson gives my mom a No Doubt record. It seems sort of generic and whatever, because Mom doesn't strike me as a huge Gwen Stefani fan, but she tears up when she opens it. So apparently, he knows something about her that I don't. Tyson has a present for me too, and I'm all sorts of awkward when he hands it to me. It's a Nat Geo *50 States, 5,000 Ideas* book. Mom must have told him about my bedroom. It's about ten times more thoughtful than I expected, and I wonder why he went to the trouble.

Once the attention is off me, my mind goes back to the phone call. First, I convince myself I could have lied, forced myself to sound excited for her, and hung up ASAP. I've never been that good of an actor, but maybe I could have gotten through it. She was determined to be happy, and I wouldn't have had to say much at all.

However.

Blindly lying about my feelings would only have taken me so far. There's no way I could keep that attitude up for the next five months, and presumably, for the rest of their marriage. Best-case scenario is I lie and lie and lie and lie some more and bottle up all my emotions until they come exploding out on her wedding day, true rom com style, when the priest says, "Are there any objections" and I'm like, "Uh. Yeah. Me?" Except that's not the plot of a rom-com, because I'm not the ex-boyfriend that she's still in love with.

The phone call was doomed from the start. Which brings me to option two: Williams instead of New York.

This daydream is very seductive, because it starts exactly like it sounds. I'm in Williams, and it's snowing, and Fitz is snuggling me in front of a fire and he's realizing that (surprise!) he's *loved me the whole time*! How convenient, right? I get sidetracked with this all through breakfast, and it takes me nearly an hour to remember this exercise is supposed to be about Clover. Avoiding the disaster with Clover. And it turns out that me being in Williams doesn't fix that at all. Unfortunately.

I move on to option three: Stay in Gilbert. This one is tricky, because Clover still gets engaged, and my mom is in New York, and Fitz is in Williams, and my dad is in Tucson, so what am I even doing alone on Christmas Day in Gilbert? The logic isn't there, but the thing about time traveling and the secretary in my brain who keeps a list of all my worries is that he doesn't rely on logic. In this scenario, Clover accepts Jay's proposal and then immediately drives to my house. She wakes me up to tell me the news, and I'm able to delicately, gently explain why it's such a bad decision. And because we're face-to-face, I get my point across without offending her and she cries but realizes that I'm right. Our friendship is still solid, and there is no fight. She gently tells Jay that they have to wait, and he agrees.

It's a solid, foolproof plan, with the very small exception that time travel doesn't exist and it'll never happen.

But still. I obsess over it all day, until I'm absolutely positive that coming to New York was a huge mistake. What I should have done was shut myself alone in my bedroom and waited for Clover to get engaged so I could talk her out of it.

"Paige?" Mom's voice snaps me out of my imaginary world and brings me back to New York. "Are you okay?"

"Huh? Yeah. I'm fine." I'm on the couch, ostensibly watching another Christmas movie.

"We're going for a walk. Do you want to come?"

"Who's we?"

"All of us." She points to herself, Tyson, and Harrison.

Harrison, who hasn't made eye contact with me since I snapped at him last night. Harrison, who watched my brain implode and who now refuses to talk to me. It only took two days for him to realize that dealing with me is more trouble than it's worth. What guy wants to kiss a girl who's always on the verge of losing it? None that I've ever met. And even though I was frustrated with him too, I can't pretend like I didn't enjoy the weight of his hand on my knee and all the possibilities implicit in that gesture. It might have been a bad idea to kiss him, but that doesn't mean I didn't want to do it.

I tell them I want to stay home and bake. They leave, and I decide on a yeast bread. Correctly getting a loaf of yeast bread to rise never fails to make me feel like a magician. And my life could use a little magic right now. I drag my feet around the kitchen as I mix the water, yeast, and a pinch of sugar in the stand mixer. I cover it with a towel, wait for the mixture to bubble, and sink back into a daydream of regret.

"Hey."

I yelp at the sound of Harrison's voice, startled to discover I'm not alone in the kitchen.

"What are you doing here?" I stayed behind so I could avoid potentially awkward conversations.

He shrugs. "Changed my mind about the walk. What are you cooking?"

"Baking," I correct him. "French bread."

"No kidding?" He unwraps a scarf from his neck, lifting the towel to peer in the bowl. His arm brushes against mine, and the proximity to him, the scent of him, perks up all my senses. I feel like I've been sleepwalking through the whole day, and I'm only now waking up.

My growing crush on Harrison is lightning fast and electric. It's also a new experience, because it's the opposite of the way my feelings for Fitz developed. One day, Fitz was that kid who was a head shorter than me with a Boy Scout haircut who whispered jokes into my ear while our teacher read Shakespeare. A month later, I bossed him into partnering with me in the PE "Dance Unit," an awkward and stumbling encounter that paved the way for the friendship that eventually formed during those afternoons on the curb, waiting for a ride home. It would be a few more years before he shot up twelve inches, grew his hair out, hit the weight room with the baseball team, and transformed into Fitz Wilding, certified Dream Boy. By the start of sophomore year, everyone wanted to be friends with Fitz, but by then, I'd already claimed him as my own.

I wanted him first, and I wanted him the most. When he chose Ivy, I knew it had been a mistake to laugh at his jokes and orient my life around him. But it was too late, and I was too far gone.

And now my insides are all electric because of a boy who isn't Fitz. I can't decide how I feel about that.

Relieved.

Excited.

Unexpectedly sad.

"Is it supposed to be all frothy like that?" Harrison wrinkles his nose, pointing to the bubbly mixture in front of us.

"Yes. That means the yeast is alive." I remove the towel and add more sugar, along with flour, salt, and oil. "I'm sorry about last night." I keep my eyes on the dough, afraid of the potential scorn in his expression.

"You were upset. And I shouldn't have said what I did about your friend," he says. Only then do I dare a glance, and it seems like he means it. "Where have you been today?" He raps lightly on my head with his knuckles. "It's like you're here but not here."

My heart flutters in my chest at the gesture. It's not romantic, not in the over-the-top way that Fitz specializes in, but it's silly and sweet and genuine, and not at all what I expected from a surly bookworm like Harrison. "You're different than I thought you'd be," I muse.

"Yeah—" He rubs his hand over his jaw. "You met me on a bad day. My ex and I had this argument because I found out that she's already moved on to a new guy, less than two weeks after we broke up."

"Ouch."

He makes a face in agreement.

"Is that why you broke up, do you think?"

He leans back, his palms resting behind him on the kitchen counter. "It has taken every ounce of self-control not to go down that particular rabbit hole," he says. "If she was cheating on me . . ." He sighs. "I don't want to know."

"You're better with self-control than I am. Rabbit holes are my specialty. I live and breathe in them. That's why I've been out of it all day."

"What happened? Did the Cabin Kid read your not-so-secret declaration of love?"

"No, thank heavens. But I have spent the better part of the day trying to figure out how my fight with Clover could have been avoided."

"The whole day?"

I nod as I flip off the mixer and drop the dough into a greased bowl, spinning it to grease all sides.

"No offense, but what's there to think about? You said something that hurt her feelings. If you apologize, she'll forgive you."

"It's not that simple."

"Do tell."

I sigh, not sure how to put my truly warped way of thinking into words. But I'll try, because he looks like he sincerely wants to know, and because I'm leaving in a few days and I'll probably never see him again, so what do I have to lose? "First of all, I'm sorry for the way I said it, but not for what I said. So, right now, this problem feels very unfixable, as so many mistakes are. But if I figure out how the situation could have been avoided, that means I'll be able to avoid it next time."

He's looking at me like I've lost my mind. Which maybe I have. I shrug. "It makes sense to me."

He drags his fingers through his hair. "What do you mean when you say so many mistakes are unfixable?"

"Exactly what it sounds like."

"Do you really believe that?"

"Of course." It sounds like my voice, but it's SIM's too. If I didn't believe that mistakes are unfixable, SIM wouldn't exist, and my brain wouldn't be a veritable catalog of all the things that could go wrong. "At any second, I'm one bad decision away from ruining my life. We all are."

"That's—" Harrison sputters, looking baffled.

My stomach twists in shame and my cheeks flame. Maybe I should have kept my strange philosophy to myself.

"—that's not how life works," he finishes.

I shrug, not sure how to argue with him, or if I even want to. I cover the bread dough with a towel and set it near the heater vent to aid the rising.

"What now?" Harrison asks. I'm not sure if he's talking about our conversation or the bread, but I pretend it's the latter.

"Now we wait. An hour to an hour and a half, depending on how quickly the dough rises."

We move into the other room and sit on opposite ends of the couch. He has a book on his lap, and offers to lend me something, but my brain is wrung out from the day of obsessive worrying. I don't know if I can handle anything other than a mindless social media binge. I absently scroll through Instagram, sliding quickly past endless tree and present selfies, until Molly's profile shows up and the picture stops my heart.

It's her and Fitz, under the mistletoe, her arms thrown around his neck while he smooches her soundly on the cheek. She's grinning, her eyes sparkling, her cheeks flushed, like she ran a marathon or was kissed absolutely senseless.

I feel every emotion at once: sadness, regret, jealousy, heartbreak, and anger. They surge through my veins, mingling to create a sickening poison. I jump up. "Let's get out of here."

"And go where?"

"Anywhere. I don't care." I only have a few more days in New York. Fitz is obviously enjoying his vacation. I should too.

"Not much is going to be open on Christmas," Harrison says.

"Then we'll wander."

"In thirty-five degrees?"

I throw my phone across the couch. It lands with a thud on Harrison's book. "This is what I mean about unfixable mistakes."

His brows crease as he studies the picture. "Is that your guy?"

"Not anymore."

His gaze rises to meet mine. "Let's go."

We grab our coats, leave the bread dough rising on the counter, and head into the city without a destination or plan. But as much as I wish I were in the mood for adventure, my mind keeps wandering back to the photo. I open it on my phone again, just to torture myself.

"It doesn't look all that romantic, if you ask me," Harrison says. "The dude's under mistletoe and he's kissing her cheek? They could be brother and sister."

I hate how much I wish his words were the truth. "He said she was '*the one*.'"

"Then this would have happened even if you were at the cabin, and it would have sucked a hundred times worse seeing it in person."

"Or maybe I would have given him the letter and it would have been us under the mistletoe. Now I'll never know, and that's what I hate the most. All the missed opportunities, all the lives I'll never have."

"That's what you're scared of?"

"To simplify it, yeah. I wish I could have a hundred lives. One where I come here and see New York and meet—" I cut myself off, and then decide, screw it. "One life where I meet you, one where I'm Fitz's girlfriend, one where I travel the world for a living. I want them all."

"You're Kierkegaard."

I nod. "Do you ever feel like you're wandering around in the dark, with no idea what you're doing or where you're going?"

"Pretty much every day."

"How do you deal with it?"

"I read."

"Must be some book," I mutter, thinking that none of the books I've been assigned in English prepared me for what it would feel like to have my heart repeatedly stomped on by my best friend.

He looks at me sideways, his lips pressed together. After a beat, he says, "C'mon, we're going to Columbia." He picks up the pace, and I increase my speed to match his.

"What's at Columbia?"

"The meaning of life."

FATE TWO

December 25 | 9:47 a.m. | Williams, Arizona

A knock on the door pulls me out of a heavy, dreamless sleep. Watery sunlight streams through the lacy white curtains on the window. I pull the blankets tight around me and try not to think about who in Fitz's family saw/heard/knows about my panic attack. "I don't feel good," I call.

"I know. I'm coming in anyway." Fitz opens the door and sees me curled in his bed. Our eyes meet, and for an endless breath, neither of us says a thing. He sets a plate of cinnamon rolls on the nightstand. "They're from a can. You could do better."

"I've never made cinnamon rolls."

"Trust me on this one. You have the intuition."

"Baking isn't intuition. It's science."

"If you say so. Mind if I . . . ?" He gestures to the bed.

I scoot to the edge so he has room to climb in. He pulls the covers over his lap and slouches down so his head is on the pillow next to mine. Fitz is in bed, next to me, and I forget how to breathe. I sync my breaths with his, but his are deeper and slower than I'm used to, and I have to give up before I'm left gasping for air.

He curls an arm behind his head. "Do you remember the game against Highland two years ago? We were down by two, bottom of the ninth, two outs?"

I remember, but I don't say anything because I could listen to the low rumble of his voice forever. I glance up at him, knowing that even if I miraculously live to be one hundred, I'll remember him exactly like this: long eyelashes, stubble on his chin, hair unruly.

"The pitcher threw a perfect ball. Hard, fast, straight down the middle. My dream pitch. And I struck out looking. Didn't even swing." He laughs a little, his eyes still on the wooden beams above us.

"What made you think about that?"

"A couple of things, I guess. I told myself that I'd never again strike out looking. Given the opportunity, I'm gonna swing. Every time. Drives my coach crazy. He's always telling me I need more patience."

"Oh."

"Yeah. And I was embarrassed. Couldn't even look any of the guys in the eye in the locker room after the game. I was determined to bolt out of there and spend the rest of the weekend hiding in my room."

"I know the feeling."

"Yeah, except you were waiting for me outside the locker room with our bikes. We rode to Val Vista Lakes, scaled the wall, and swam in the clubhouse pool until the security guard chased us away."

I grin at the memory. It was after Ivy but before Ruby, only a couple of weeks before the carnival. He splashed and tackled me into the pool, his hands on my waist without a second thought. I thought I'd die from the contact. It was the perfect spring night, and I was still drunk off the heady rush of first love. I hadn't yet grown to resent him for loving everyone but me.

"That was a good night."

"The best," he agrees. "You saved me from a lonely night in my room. I'm here to do the same for you."

"I can't." *No way.* I cannot face his family. It's late enough that they must know *something's* wrong with me. The thought of Fitz explaining my panic attack is too awful and embarrassing.

"You can." He places a finger under my chin and nudges my eyes up. My gaze halts on his mouth before finally finding his eyes. They're unreadable.

I slouch deeper under the covers. Fitz grabs the blankets with his hand and whisks them off the bed. "Stay if you want, but I revoke your blanket privileges."

"That's not fair!"

"My house. My rules."

"Fine. I don't need blankets anyway," I grumble as I reach for the plate of cinnamon rolls.

"On second thought—" He snatches them out of my grasp and holds them above his head. "Your cinnamon roll privileges have also been revoked."

I kick my heels against the bed. "I'm starving."

"Good. Come upstairs."

We scowl at each other for a full ten seconds before I give in. I groan and crawl off the bed. "Fine. You win."

"Merry Christmas, indeed." He chucks the blankets down the hall with a wide grin and bounds up the stairs three at a time.

Mom and I do Christmas like this: We wake up and immediately open our presents. Because it's just the two of us and we have no money, this takes approximately four minutes. We spend the rest of the day lying around with Christmas movies playing in the background and enjoying our presents.

Fitz's family is not like my family. First, they eat a giant breakfast including eggs, bacon, hash browns, and canned cinnamon rolls. After breakfast is the annual reading of the Christmas story from the Bible. They did these things while I hid and slept, and by the time Fitz and I make our grand entrance, Gray is lying on his stomach, chin on his hands, practically salivating at the giant pile of presents.

"Hey, buddy!" Fitz scoops him up and tosses him in the air. "You excited?"

"Santa came!" Gray cheers.

"Where are the Santa presents?" I look around the room, searching for a toy for Gray.

"Right here. I'm gonna open this one first! Can I, Mom? Please can I now? Fitz's friend is done barfing now."

"All right, all right. You've been patient. You can start."

"That's from Santa?" I whisper to Fitz. "Why is it wrapped?"

"What do you mean? Santa always wraps presents."

"Not at my house."

"No offense, but your Santa is wrong."

We stare at each other in disbelief until Gray shrieks with

delight when he sees the toy garbage truck, complete with trash cans and a working lift. Everyone in the family oohs and aahs and comments on it, and I assume it's because Gray is three and they're humoring him, but no. This is how they do Christmas. They take turns opening presents, and *every* member of the family watches. It makes the whole thing last forever.

"Thanks, Fitz; thanks, Paige!" Jane says as she pulls on a pair of black-and-white fingerless gloves. "These will be perfect for when I'm writing!"

After multiple family members thank me for gifts that I didn't purchase, it's clear that Fitz included my name on all his gifts. And if I wasn't so distracted by the shrinking pile of presents under the tree, I'd be touched by his thoughtfulness. As it is, I'm freaking out. I glance under the tree approximately every five seconds, but nothing. Noelle catches my eye and shakes her head, confirming that she hasn't found the letter either. I refuse to accept that it's gone. It *has* to be here. Except the pile under the tree continues to dwindle, and the letter never materializes.

Structure breaks down eventually. Whit helps Gray assemble his new Hot Wheels track from Santa while Meg tries to soothe an extremely fussy baby. Darcy and Mr. Wilding are involved in a lively debate about health care and Mrs. Wilding cleans up stray wrapping paper while Jane lies on the couch with a new book.

"Ready to open your present?" Fitz says, drawing my attention back to him. I turn so we're facing each other, both sitting cross-legged on the ground, knees touching. My automatic response is to inch back, but I don't. I let my knees rest against his as my entire focus zeroes in on that contact.

"You first." I thrust his present into his hands.

He tears the small box open. "A baseball?"

"My turn for a story. Do you remember the district championship game last year?"

"Yeah."

"You made that out at third and won the game."

A slow smile appears as he looks back at the ball in his hands. "This is the ball?"

"That's the ball."

"But how'd you get it? They told me I couldn't have it!"

"I know." I can't help but match his grin.

"Do I want to know what you did?"

"Don't ask," I laugh. After the game, I heard him ask if he could keep it. The district's official stance is that they don't give balls to the players for funding reasons. So, I waited until the coach wasn't looking, and I took it. Technically it's not stealing because I left a five-dollar bill in its place.

"It's perfect. Thank you. Now it's your turn." He hands me the last present under the tree.

I break the gold ribbon with my finger and gently tear the green paper. Inside is a small black box, the kind used to hold a diamond bracelet in Fitz's rom-coms.

My breath catches.

He wouldn't. *Would he?*

One month after he created the snowstorm to woo Ivy, he dragged me to the mall to help him buy her birthday present. "How should I know what she wants?" I asked, one part annoyed and one part hoping the errand would never end.

"You're a girl. She's a girl."

"Women are not a monolith, Fitz." It's something I heard Clover's mom say.

In the end he'd picked a bedazzled necklace from Claire's, Ivy wore it to school every day for two months, and I hated how much I wished he'd given that tacky piece of costume jewelry to me instead.

Fitz's tastes have improved significantly since then, but he hasn't outgrown the desire to buy presents that are shiny and flashy and scream "*This is my girlfriend!*" to the world.

Which is why I'm scared of what's in this box. Would he recycle a Christmas gift meant for his ex-girlfriend? My fingers tremble as I lift the lid, and as soon as I see that it's not jewelry, my muscles relax. Nestled against a bed of satin that certainly housed a pretty bracelet at some point is a small slip of paper.

TrekkingwithCollins.com

"You bought me a website?"

"And secured all the proper social media handles. Now you're ready to go out and conquer the world."

I stare at him, speechless. "I can't believe you did that for me."

"It was selfishly motivated, really. I want to be able to keep up with you when you're gone."

I shake my head as I reverently place the slip of paper back inside the box. "There goes my theory that you regifted Molly's present."

He abruptly freezes, and I know it was the wrong thing to say.

Really, super, stupid wrong. The wrongest.

"Do you honestly think I'd do that?"

"No! I mean, when I saw the jewelry box, I wondered for a second, but—"

"Here we go again." He stands, rubbing his hands over his face in frustration.

"Wait. What's going on?"

"Not here. Downstairs." He stomps down the dark stairwell. I follow, because what else am I going to do? The room is ablaze with the orange glow of the fire. I move toward it, drawn by the warmth it's radiating through the cold basement. Fitz follows me, not bothering to flip on the lights.

He crosses his arms over his chest and faces me, taking a deep breath. "Have I ever treated you like you didn't matter?"

I stop breathing. His question hangs in the air, challenged only by the crackling and hissing logs.

"No." Of course he hasn't. I wouldn't be in love with him if he had. "But there have been so many other girls—"

"*Girl*friends." His heavy emphasis on the first syllable causes my stomach to squirm in embarrassment.

"Right."

"And you are my *friend*."

"I know that." I cross my arms, defensive.

"And yet . . ." He pauses. "It feels like you're punishing me for dating other people."

"That's not what I'm doing!"

"Are you sure? Because the way you've been acting this weekend makes it seem like I've kicked you to the curb every time I had a girlfriend. Did I ever forget your birthday? Or Christmas? Did I ever ignore the phone when you needed to talk about family stuff?" He closes the gap between us until we're inches apart. My heart pounds wildly as I look up to meet his stormy eyes. "Answer the question."

"No."

"If I didn't know any better, I'd think you were—" He cuts himself off, searching my eyes in the dark.

"What?"

"Jealous."

Jealous.

The word is a clap of thunder on his lips.

To acknowledge my jealousy, and by default, my feelings for Fitz, feels even more daring than a kiss. Kisses are frightfully easy to explain away.

I got caught up in the moment.

I was lonely.

You chivalrously rode a quad across a frozen desert landscape and carried me onto a train like a rom-com hero.

"What would I be jealous of?"

His eyes never leave mine. "I don't know, Collins. You tell me."

"I'm not jealous."

He nods slowly. Then he steps back and passes his hand over the back of his neck. My hands and heart are jittery, making me feel scattered and out of control. I'm overcome with an intense desire to hunt down the pieces of myself that I lost during this conversation, but I don't know where to look, or even what to look for.

"What are you so scared of?" he demands.

"Missing out. Screwing up. Choosing wrong. Take your pick."

"You think you're the only person on this planet who knows what it's like to want something? To have impossible dreams? You think I'm not terrified out of my mind at the possibility of a future that doesn't involve me playing third base for the rest of my life? You think I don't know how small those odds are? We're all scared shitless about our futures all the time. All of us. Me and Clover and Jay and Molly and my sisters and everyone. But the difference between us and you is that we don't walk around making other people feel expendable. Like the cost of being with you is some great loss we're mourning."

"I don't do that."

"What about 'I should have gone to New York, Fitz,' and 'I don't want to be here, Fitz,' and your perennial favorite, 'I'd rather die than spend one second longer than necessary in Gilbert, the town where you live, Fitz.' How am I supposed to react to that?"

"That's not what I meant. I'm not trying to get away from you."

"No?"

"No!"

"Then why won't you tell me the truth?"

"About what?"

"What's in the letter, Paige?"

I'm too shocked to speak. This conversation has veered way too far out of my control. He accused me of being jealous, and then of not caring about him enough, and now? Now he's demanding answers about the letter he claims he lost? "What does any of this have to do with anything?"

He takes one long stride to me, the tips of his feet bumping into mine. His eyes are all smoke and ash, blazing into mine until I can't breathe.

"Bread!"

Fitz crooks an eyebrow. "I need to bake bread!" I slip away from him and sprint up the stairs. I need the soothing, methodical kneading of dough between my fingers. I need measured ingredients and exact recipes and a start and a middle and an end. I bound quickly up the stairs and call for attention. "Who's in the mood for homemade bread?"

A beat of confused silence passes, and then the baby starts to wail.

"You're our guest," Mrs. Wilding begins. "You don't have to—"

"I want to. Please. It's the thing I'm best at, and it's the only way I have to say thank you for taking me in."

"It's her superpower," Fitz says from behind me. Forearm against the stairwell, alone under the mistletoe. "You want to say yes."

They say yes, and I raid the kitchen. It's pretty well stocked, with the notable exception of yeast. Not surprising, considering the tragic canned cinnamon rolls and the even worse freezer rolls from our first night here. "Are any of the stores in town open?"

Fitz is sitting on the kitchen counter, eating cheese and crackers and nuts and watching me assemble ingredients on the counter. "I doubt it."

"But maybe?"

"Maybe." He tosses an almond in the air and catches it with his mouth.

It's amazing, bordering on astonishing, the way he's able to resume normal programming. As if that weird scene in the basement never happened. But maybe that's the point. He accused me of being the petty, jealous best friend I am, I assured him that I'm not, and that's all he needed to put me back in my proper box. The one labeled BEST FRIEND and not GIRLFRIEND.

"Good enough for me." Without yeast, this is a lost cause, and I'm not ready to give up, not even with the thick blanket of clouds building in the sky, or the outside thermometer that says eight degrees. Baking puts me in a calm, meditative space, and I need that to forget Fitz's eyes on mine or the hard edge to his voice when he said I was his "friend." Emphasis on *not-girl*. I throw on my jacket and gloves.

"Where are you going?" Whit asks as he bounces the baby around the room with a worried frown. Meg hovers nervously beside him.

"On a yeast-finding expedition."

"Will you grab fever medicine for the baby?"

Meg puts her hands on the baby's cheeks, her face growing grim. "She's getting worse." As Fitz and I step outside, they whisk the baby down the hall, whispering frantically to each other.

The brutal cold sucks the air from my lungs and stings against my face. The air feels different today. Like the whole world is holding its breath in anticipation, and Fitz and I are the only souls who dared to disturb the universe.

Fitz first drives to the Dollar General. Closed. Family Dollar. Locked and dark and no getting inside. The only activity in town is near the train station.

"Maybe the gift shop is open," I say.

"They won't have yeast there."

"But they might have baby Tylenol."

Nope. Another strike. Back in the car, Fitz tells me he has one last idea and drives into town, scanning the driveways and streets for signs of life. "I don't want to randomly knock on doors on Christmas, but if I see someone outside—bingo." He pulls the car to the side of the road, where an old man is shaking a box of salt over his front walk. Fitz rolls down the passenger window and leans across the console, his face perilously close to mine. "Merry Christmas! Can I ask for a favor?"

The man ambles slowly to the car. "What can I do for you?"

"We need baby Tylenol and every store in town is closed."

"You have a baby back there?" He peers through the back window.

"No, sir. We're on an errand for her parents. Do you have any we could borrow? I'll buy you a new bottle when the store's open tomorrow and drop it by."

"It's been a long while since we've had a baby in this house, but I'll check."

"And yeast!" Fitz calls as the man turns back to the house. "If we could borrow yeast, we'd owe you forever."

He returns a few minutes later with a jar of yeast, the same brand I use at home, and no medicine. "Sorry about that." He hands me the jar.

"I'll bring you a loaf of bread as a thank-you," I reply.

"Don't." He draws a deep inhale. "The snow's comin' and the TV says it's gonna be nasty."

I sit up in my seat and grip the jar of yeast. "When?"

He squints into the sky, his eyes full of the wisdom that comes with a life spent in the mountains. Or maybe he's trying to remember what the meteorologist said. Probably the latter. "A couple of hours," he says, his voice gravelly and low and filled with premonitions of bad things to come. Or maybe he needs to clear his throat.

The cabin is quiet. Jane's at the train depot, because apparently the train doesn't stop for impending snowstorms. I asked Fitz why anyone would want to visit the North Pole on Christmas Day, when the presents have been delivered and surely Santa is too tired to stand in the middle of town waving at a train of incoming children, but he said it's tradition. The train runs well into January, which is stretching the limits of believability, if you ask me. Gray is conked out on the couch next to Mr. Wilding, their stomachs rising and falling in a steady rhythm.

I start with a simple artisan loaf. It couldn't be easier to bake, but it always impresses. Not that I need to worry about impressing Fitz's family. He made that painfully clear. I'm waiting for the yeast to bubble when Meg finally appears. "Did you find the medicine?"

I shake my head. "I'm sorry. We looked everywhere. How's she doing?"

"She's miserable and her fever keeps climbing."

"How high is it?" Since Mom works at the ER, I hear plenty of stories about panicked parents bringing in their babies, claiming fever as soon as the thermometer hits ninety-nine. I can't help but hope Meg and Whit are those kinds of parents, and that the baby doesn't even need medicine.

"One hundred and three." She looks out the window behind me. "It's snowing."

"It is?" I turn quickly, almost knocking my mixing bowl to the floor. Fat, puffy snowflakes drift past the window, already sticking to the deck and the car and the trees.

"I don't want to get stuck here with a sick baby."

"*Stuck?*"

"Snowed in. Whit's going to freak. He's probably already packing."

"Fitz didn't mention anything about getting snowed in."

"It's always a possibility. Especially with these mountain roads. It can take days to clear them. I have to go talk to Whit and check on the baby. Good luck with your bread."

The next hour is a flurry of excitement and chaos as the snow builds steadily on the ground. I glance out the window every thirty seconds, anticipation building low in my gut. Jane calls, reporting that Santa Claus is sick and they need a replacement. Mr. Wilding rises quickly, if begrudgingly, from his chair. I get the feeling this is not the first time this has happened. He and Noelle leave first, because apparently, he's a terrible driver and she doesn't trust him, even in a few inches of snow. Meg and Whit take the kids next, hastily packing their minivan with luggage and Christmas presents, shouting apologies for leaving so suddenly.

By the time Fitz, Darcy, and I are alone in the house, the artisan bread is rising on the counter, a loaf of gingerbread is in the oven, and I'm rolling out buttery crescent rolls. Darcy and Fitz are at the table in the kitchen, working quietly on the puzzle. I gaze at the pans of rising dough, my heartbeat and hands steady, my head clear for the first time all day.

With the rolls rising, I begin to mix the dough for a braided cinnamon loaf. I pulled up the recipe on my phone and followed it exactly, but the dough is too sticky. It clings to my fingers in a way that will make it impossible to work with. I measure another tablespoon of flour and add it to the mixer. And then I add another.

"What are you doing?" Fitz asks. I explain how elevation and climate affect baking. The higher you are, the more flour you need. "Huh." Fitz smirks as he tries to shove a puzzle piece where it doesn't belong.

"What?"

"You're not following the recipe?"

"Not exactly."

"Then how do you know when to stop adding flour?"

"The feel of the dough."

"How do you know what it should feel like?"

I shrug. "Practice."

"Have you made this recipe before?" He clasps his hand behind his head and my eyes snag on the curve of his bicep. *No, Paige. Bad, Paige.* I'm not noticing things like that anymore, because I'm the *friend*.

"No."

"Then *how* do you know?"

"I don't know. It's, like, a gut thing. I just know."

"Sounds less like science and more like intuition, if you ask me." He leans back, his smile triumphant.

"Ha. Ha. Fine. You win. I have baking intuition."

"You have more than that." His eyes are back on the puzzle, his voice quiet. "You need to learn to trust your gut."

Darcy, who has been listening to our conversation with interest, rises. She points to the window. "That's six inches at least. We should put chains on the tires, in case we have to get out of here." She and Fitz layer up and head outside to add snow chains to the tires of his truck and her rental. From the cozy, yeasty warmth of the kitchen I keep one eye on the window and the other on the oven. Before I know it, Darcy is back inside, pounding snow off her boots.

"I found your letter."

My heart spikes. "Where?"

"In the side cubby thing in Fitz's truck door. By the driver's seat."

"He said he lost it."

She shrugs. "Maybe he forgot."

"Where is it now? Was it opened?" I'm already walking to the door.

She sits in front of the fire and holds her palms out to warm them. "I don't think so."

I rush outside without a coat or gloves or a hat, hands still dusted in flour. The snow blinds me as the wind nearly blows me over.

"I need my letter!" I yell.

Fitz cocks his head toward me, not hearing.

"I need my letter!" I yell louder.

He finishes the last chain and grabs my hand, trying to pull me inside. I dig my heels into the snow, refusing to be moved. I'm not about to have this conversation with Darcy standing by. I hold out my hand, palm up. Fitz takes the letter out of his pocket and spins it between his fingers, his eyes thoughtful. "Why do you need it?"

"I can't tell you."

"What does it say?"

"I can't tell you."

"Paige." His eyes soften and he steps close to me.

"No." I back away, refusing to be swayed by his puppy dog expression. "You knew it was there, didn't you? You didn't lose it."

"I can explain."

"Give it to me."

His expression turns wolfish. He holds the letter above his head. I jump for it, my fingers grasping uselessly for the envelope still several inches above me. Fitz wraps his other arm around my waist, trapping my body flush against his, the envelope high in the air.

I stop breathing, the length of my body snug against his.

"Paige," he says again, my name barely more than a breath. He tilts his head toward mine, and pauses. Waiting.

"What are you doing?" I whisper.

"Taking a swing." He leans in, and—

"Fitz?" Molly emerges from her car, eyes wary.

FATE ONE

**December 25 | 7:45 p.m. | John Jay Hall,
Columbia University**

John Jay Hall takes my breath away. Harrison's dorm is less than
two miles from his apartment, nestled in the center of campus at
Columbia University. It's a massive redbrick building with fancy
white arches and solid black doors that are heavy with impor-
tance. The imposing residence hall sits next to Butler Library,
which Harrison points out as we approach the dorm.

"See that?" He gestures to the names inscribed above the clas-
sical columns on the library's facade. Plato, Aristotle, Cicero.

Not a bad view for a budding philosopher. "So did you choose
John Jay Hall, or did John Jay Hall choose you?" I tease.

"What can I say? I was a highly impressionable, starry-eyed
freshman once upon a time."

"You? Starry-eyed?" I scoff.

"A lot can change in four months," he says, and I'm unsure if
he's joking or not. Either way, I can't help but admire the sheer
magnitude of it all, although a small part of me twinges with
regret that I could never afford an experience like this. "Is that
where I'm supposed to find the meaning of life?"

"Not today. C'mon, we're going this way." He opens the door to his residence hall, and we step inside a large welcome lounge. I hardly have time to take in the squashy armchairs and the grand piano before Harrison leads me away. I move toward the elevator, but he tugs me gently in the opposite direction. "The elevator is complete garbage, getting stuck all the time." He opens the door to the stairwell. "Naveen takes it every time he's on his way to a test, on the off chance he gets stuck and misses the exam. His success rate is about fifty-fifty."

I pause before entering the stairwell. "We're going to your room?" I don't know why it's only *now* hitting me that I'm going to a dorm room with a college guy I barely know, but it is. My palms sweat.

"Well, yeah." He hesitates, eyes flicking over my face. "There's a few things I want to grab, but you can wait here, if you want?"

I bite my lip in embarrassment. Nothing says quaint, small-town girl like being afraid to go near his room. "No, it's fine. I'll come."

We exit the stairwell on the sixth floor, passing wooden doors decorated with names, stickers, and whiteboards scrawled with swear words and dirty pictures. We stop in front of a blank door. "You should wait out here," Harrison says.

"Why? Is your roommate here?"

"I don't have a roommate. Most of the rooms here are singles."

"Oh." My cheeks flush.

"Yeah." He looks at his shoes. "I don't want you to think I brought you here to . . . you know—" It's his turn to go red, which is so endearing it makes my throat dry.

"Seduce me?" I tease in a husky voice, earning a wry smile from him. His smiles are so rare I'm collecting them, mentally hanging them like charms on a bracelet.

He opens the door. "Just wait here, okay?"

I peek inside. His room is medium messy, books and clothes and notebooks strewn about, but not in a disgusting way. I'm relieved that there are no half-eaten pizza crusts on the floor or sweaty socks under the bed. We both notice a pair of boxers at the same time, and Harrison frantically kicks them under his desk. "Is there a bathroom around here?" I ask, saving us both from discussing his underwear. He points the way.

I expect the bathroom to be empty, because we haven't seen another person in the building. So I'm startled to see a girl with a chaotic swirl of teal-and-purple mermaid-length hair washing her hands at the sink. She's in sweats and a graphic tee that reads CENTRE OF THE MULTIVERSE.

Something in my brain snags on the word *multiverse*. I've heard it before. "What's a multiverse?"

"A hypothetical group of multiple universes," she replies in a British accent.

I flash back to Clover, the day she downloaded Magic 8. "How does that work?"

Mermaid girl tilts her head, studying me. "Do you live here? I haven't seen you around." She dries her hands and I follow her out the door.

"I'm visiting Harrison."

"Is Harry back?" Her face lights up in an expression I know well. I'd bet a plane ticket to Madrid she's in love with him.

"He's in his room. We're not staying long." I don't plan on emphasizing *we*, but it sure comes out that way. "I'm waiting for him out here," I add.

She smiles brightly. "C'mon then. I'll explain the multiverse while you wait. I'm Kate, by the way."

"I'm Paige. But really, you don't have to do that. It's Christmas."

"Nonsense." She waves off my objection. "Any friend of Harry's, yeah? Besides, I've been with my family all week and needed a break, so I snuck back here to get away from the toxic drama that is my mum and granddad arguing about politics," she explains as she leads me to a room a few doors down from Harrison's. She pushes aside the clothes and books on her bed and pulls the quilt up, creating a space for us to sit. I toe off my shoes and sit cross-legged next to her pillow while she unearths a giant textbook from under her desk and places it on the bed between us. "If you're interested in string theory, you've got to take Wallace's class. She's the best."

"I'll keep that in mind," I say. It's easier than explaining that I'm still in high school.

She claps her hands together, eyes bright. "In order to understand the multiverse, we have to start at the beginning. In quantum mechanics, there are four fundamental interactions that particles go through: gravitation, electromagnetism, strong nuclear force, and weak nuclear force."

"Four interactions. Understood."

"String theory is a set of mathematical models that attempt to explain all those interactions in the same theory. Currently, gravity is explained by the theory of relativity, and the other three interactions are explained by quantum physics. The problem is that these two theories occasionally come into conflict, which means there has to be something else out there that explains everything."

"That's string theory?"

"Yes! String theory explains all elementary particles and all their interactions in terms of tiny, vibrating strings of energy."

"How tiny?" I ask, because Kate is looking at me expectantly and I still don't know why I'm here and what else am I supposed to say?

"A millionth of a billionth of a billionth of a billionth of a centimeter."

"Wow. Yeah, that's small." It sounds even sillier out loud than it did in my head. *Brilliant, Paige.* I'm so out of my depth.

"So, that's string theory at its most basic level, and one theory *within* string theory is the multiverse, which is a hypothetical group of parallel universes. According to this theory, there are an infinite number of other universes, in which every possibility is played out."

"Every possibility about what?"

"About everything."

Everything. Every wrong move, every missed opportunity. If that's true, there could be another version of myself that's with Fitz in the cabin in Williams right this second. I can't help but smile.

"You look pleased."

"Harrison brought me here to show me the 'meaning of life,' but this is better."

"That sounds like him." She picks up a purple plush pillow and runs her fingers across the soft fabric. "What's your major?"

"I don't have one."

"Can I interest you in quantum mechanics?" She does jazz hands around her textbook.

"I don't think so. What I really want to do is travel, but I can't afford it."

She grabs her phone off her desk. "You need to talk to Naveen. He can help you. He's always talking about how he's gonna get out of here again. Teaching English in China or serving on a cruise ship or being a social media influencer intern or some rubbish like that. I'll ask him. It won't take a minute." Her fingers fly over her phone, and thirty seconds later she's scrambling through her desk for a blue sticky note and a pen. She scrawls a website on it and hands it to me proudly. "He says to check here. Travel jobs for college students. The pay isn't good, but they'll get you out of town."

I accept the paper and slip it into my pocket as she says, "So, you and Harry, huh?" She raises her eyebrows meaningfully.

"I'm sorry if it's weird that I'm here. I don't know what's going on between you two, but I—"

"Don't worry about that." She waves away my concern.

I sink back against the wall, fighting a smile. "Good."

She raises her eyebrows. "Oh?"

My cheeks flush. I tell myself it's too soon to be thinking about Harrison *that* way. But my brain's never been all that good at taking instructions from me, and I'm thinking about him anyway. "Nothing's happened, yet. But maybe." I shrug, no longer fighting the smile.

"You like him?"

"We don't know each other that well."

"That's a yes." Her fingers quickly dance over her phone, tapping out another text.

I smile. "It's not a no."

Kate presses her lips together. "Well! I'm glad to hear that he's okay. Our breakup was hard for him, especially with everything going on with his dad."

All the happy, bubbly energy inside me whooshes out like a popped balloon. "You're his ex-girlfriend?"

"What'd you think?" she asks as a knock sounds on the door.

"It's Harry," he calls from the hall. Kate lets him in, and his eyes are full of questions when they find me.

"We got sidetracked talking string theory."

He takes in Kate's shirt, and understanding lights his eyes. "All you needed was a science lesson from our resident genius." The two of them share a long look, and my stomach sinks. Her phone is still in her hand. Did she text Harrison about what I said?

"Thanks again, Kate. I should go." I pick up my coat and brush past Harrison into the hall.

He follows me, but I'm too fast, making a beeline for the elevator. I don't have a plan, other than to get out of this building as quickly as possible. I'm not sure what I feel about Harrison, and I'm definitely not ready to discuss it with either of them.

"Paige! Wait up! What's wrong?"

I step into the elevator as he catches up to me, sticking out his arm to keep it from closing. He squeezes inside and lets the door shut behind him.

FATE TWO

December 25 | 3:45 p.m. | Williams, Arizona

"Molly!" Fitz drops the arm around my waist and steps toward his ex-girlfriend. His arm falls to his side, and I use the moment of distraction to snatch the letter from his hand. His eyes flit to me for only a second before falling back to her. Guess he doesn't care about the letter now that she's here.

"What's going on?" Molly wavers uncertainly by the door of her car as snow gathers in her hair. She looks like a princess in a snow globe.

"He stole something of mine," I explain. She doesn't look convinced. Which, fair enough. His arm *was* around my waist.

"Let's get inside." Fitz reaches easily for Molly's hand and leads her up the porch. A small flicker of something that felt suspiciously like hope is extinguished. I follow them, feeling small and stupid and frozen.

Inside the cabin, Darcy is frowning at the oven. "The timer went off, but I wasn't sure if—" She turns, taking in the new addition to our snow-pocalypse party. "Oh! Are you Molly?" Molly nods as Darcy's eyes dart to mine. "I didn't realize you were coming. Especially on Christmas . . ."

I look away, afraid she'll see my embarrassment, and hurry into the kitchen to take the gingerbread loaf out of the oven. I transfer the artisan loaf to the oven rack, shut the door, and get back to work braiding the cinnamon loaf while the rolls continue to rise. I keep my eyes down, hands busy, and pretend not to listen to their conversation, but it's impossible not to hear since we're all technically in the same room.

"I wasn't planning to come. It was a surprise for Fitz. A good one, I hope." Molly smiles shyly. I turn away, pounding the dough with as much force as I can. I'll have to start the braid over.

"I'm glad you're safe," Fitz says. "Give it another hour and these roads will be undriveable."

"That's why I came today. My family's big celebration was last night, so I'm not missing much . . ." She trails off, and the room fills with awkward silence. "I hope it's okay that I'm intruding on your family's Christmas." Doubt creeps into her voice. Good. She should feel awkward for showing up unannounced.

"Of course!" Darcy says in a rush. "Although there's not a lot of family time happening now." She explains where everyone is while Fitz runs back to Molly's car to get her bags.

"You can have Meg and Whit's old room, but I'll have to change the sheets first. The baby is sick, so there might be germs."

"Oh, please don't go out of your way for me! You can stick me wherever, really. Any old couch will do."

"Well—" Fitz starts, and my heart stutters.

This is my nightmare. I'm quite possibly about to be trapped in a snowy mountain cabin while the boy I love and his soon-to-be ex-ex-girlfriend snuggle together on the couch for warmth.

"You can sleep in my room!" I blurt. "The bed is big enough for both of us." *Right, Fitz?* I bite my lip as my cheeks flame at the memory of Fitz's body next to mine, the curve of his bicep tugging against his shirt, the spark in his eyes while he talked about that night at the pool. The kind but insistent way he dragged me out of bed by depriving me of food and warmth. And then I groan inwardly, because Fitz is never going to fall in love with the girl who requires so much help. If Molly was fortunate enough to be alone in that bedroom with Fitz, she wouldn't ruin everything by freaking out, and he wouldn't have to spend his Christmas morning talking her down from a humiliating panic attack.

"Thanks, Paige!" Molly smiles warmly, and the two of them take her things to the basement. Her eyes tip toward the mistletoe briefly, a small smile tugging at her lips.

"That was awfully nice of you," Darcy says.

"I'm an awfully nice person."

"Mm-hmm."

"Molly's great. Fitz's lucky to have her."

Darcy hooks her hair behind her ear as she looks at the puzzle pieces in front of her. "I thought they broke up."

"Give it ten minutes. He won't be able to resist her."

"Why do you say that?"

"She drove through a snowstorm for him and showed up unannounced. On Christmas Day. Does that sound like something your brother would be able to resist?"

"The funny thing about the grand gesture is that it doesn't mean anything if it's performed by the wrong person. I used to have this rule: If a girl texted me within an hour after our date, I dropped her for being too clingy. But it turns out that they were the wrong girls, because when April texted me four minutes after our first date, I couldn't have been happier."

"Fitz said Molly is *the one*."

"Did his actions say that?" She arches a perfect eyebrow.

Whatever Fitz and Molly are doing down there, it takes a lot longer than ten minutes. The artisan bread comes out of the oven, two dozen rolls go in, come out, two dozen more go in. I clean as I go, so by the time I'm sliding the braided cinnamon loaf in, the counters are sparkling clean. I pull out my phone and text Clover.

Crazy blizzard happening right now. Fitz and I may have almost kissed again. Oh, and did I mention Molly's here? And we're sleeping in the same bed?

Darcy pulls a fourth crescent roll from the pan and moans. "What did you put in these?"

"Butter."

"Yeah, but what else? They're amazing."

"Butter in the dough. Butter on the bottom of the pan. Butter slathered across the dough before I rolled them up, and melted butter brushed on top, right out of the oven."

Darcy pauses mid-bite, then shrugs and pops the last bite in her mouth. She licks the tips of her fingers. "Oh well, April's stuck with me for good now, even if I do gain ten pounds this weekend."

The lights go off at once, plunging the cabin into darkness, with the exception of a dying fire. "Power's out," Darcy says.

Excuse me?

I grab my phone.

"Don't!" Darcy says. "Save the battery in case we really need it."

"Oh. Okay." But I send a quick text anyway to my mom, telling her about the power outage but assuring her that I'm safe. Then I turn to Darcy and try to keep my voice calm. "Does this happen a lot? How long will it last? What do we do?"

"Not a lot. No telling how long. We hunker down and try not to freeze," she says.

"You two okay?" Fitz's voice comes from the stairs, followed by two sets of footsteps. He begins to revive the fire while Darcy, Molly, and I rummage through cupboards looking for flashlights and candles. We find a couple of each and an old case of bottled water. As Fitz finishes the fire, Darcy piles a bunch of blankets into the main room. We sit on the couch, our dying cell phones on the coffee table, and watch the front door.

"I'm glad Meg and Whit left," I say.

"No kidding," Fitz agrees. "Especially with Sienna's fever. They'd both be freaking out right now. Jane too. I hope she doesn't try to drive back here in this weather."

"She wouldn't," Darcy says. "She's probably with Mom and Dad."

My phone buzzes. A text from Clover.

Jay and I broke up.

Wait. What? Guilt buries me like an avalanche.

Why?! What happened?

Is this my fault? No way. It can't be. I'm absolutely positive this has nothing to do with me. They're having a normal couple fight and soon enough everything will be fine. Except Clover and Jay *never* fight.

What if they're not okay?

Well, that proves that I was right about their relationship. They're in no place to be considering marriage. At least, that's what I tell myself as minutes pass and Clover doesn't respond.

Heavy, wet snow continues to stream past the window as the sun sets, piling up higher and higher against the house. Darcy and Fitz talk about their parents and Jane, guessing which people in town would offer up their homes.

"Are you okay?" I whisper to Molly, who hasn't said a word since the power went out.

"I'm fine," she replies, in one of those voices that so clearly screams I AM NOT FINE.

"We'll be okay. I'm sure the power will be on again by morning," I lie.

She pulls the blanket tighter around her legs. "The problem is Fitz . . ." She trails off in that way that invites questions.

"What happened? Didn't you get back together?"

"Not yet. I can't tell what he wants."

That's shocking. Fitz, the boy with his heart on his sleeve, didn't make his feelings obvious?

Maybe I have a chance, the traitorous part of my brain whispers. And then I feel guilty for conspiring against her, so I say this: "I'm sure he wants to. Just give him some time."

"I need to do something big to win him back."

"Like what?"

"I thought driving up here would be enough, but I should have known better. When we were dating, he was always giving me stuff and writing me love letters and planning surprises and—"

"I get it. What do you want to do?"

"I don't know yet. That's why I need your help. You know him better than anyone. If you were in love with him, how would you tell him?"

A sharp pounding on the door interrupts us. I jump up, desperate to get away from this conversation. Wind pushes the door open, bringing in heavy swirls of snow and two figures buried deep under layers of coats and scarves. The layers peel off, and it's the girl from the train station and a boy with blond hair and wiry glasses.

"Your parents are at Beatrice's house. They helped her get home, and then decided to stay to make sure she'll be okay through the night," Bernie explains as she stomps snow off her boots.

"Who's Beatrice?" I ask.

"Mrs. Claus," Fitz says.

Bernie surveys the room, eyes landing on Molly. "I'm Bernadette. This is my brother, Sebastian. Bernie and Bash, much to my mother's dismay. We're in the next cabin over." Bernie collapses onto the couch next to Fitz. Her brother stands back, his nose wrinkled in displeasure. "So, what's the plan? We're obviously staying the night. No way are we going back out in that."

"Oh. Uh—" Fitz hesitates.

"It'll be fun. Who wants to play a game of Never Have I Ever?" Bernie slips her hand into her cardigan and retrieves a bottle of peppermint schnapps.

"As the adult in the room, I'm going to have to take that,"

Darcy says. "Cold weather plus alcohol is the worst of all the bad ideas."

"I thought you were Fitz's cool sister," Bernie mutters as she hands over the bottle.

"That would be Meg," Darcy says. "But there's sparkling cider in the fridge if you still want to play." She gives us two big thumbs-up before retreating downstairs.

Bernie rolls her eyes at the suggestion. "What else do you have?" she asks Fitz.

He shrugs, and she takes that as an invitation to comb through the kitchen. She comes back a minute later with an armful of supplies. She dumps them on the floor, and we all circle around. She found half a dozen jalapeño peppers, a bottle of vinegar, a jar of cinnamon, and a box of soda crackers.

"Well! This has been fun but I'd prefer the blizzard," Bash deadpans.

"Sit down!" Bernie orders him, and surprisingly, he does. "It'll be a mashup of Never Have I Ever and all those viral internet challenges," Bernie says as she fills plastic cups with vinegar. She hands them out and then divvies up the peppers and the saltines. "When it's your turn, you say something you've never done. And if other people have done that thing, they have to eat something here. But if no one's done it, then *you* have to eat it. Got it?"

Nods all around. "What's wrong with saltines?" Molly asks.

"You won't be asking that question once you've tried to eat six of them in under a minute," Bernie explains.

I sniff the cup of vinegar in front of me. My eyes water. Fitz's eyes find mine across the circle. He's sitting between Bernie and Molly. "You don't have to play."

"I know." And it's true. I know I don't have to play. But I'm not sure if I *should* play. I eye the assembled ingredients and have to admit, it all seems pretty harmless. I'll steer clear of the cinnamon, though.

"Of course she does! We're all playing!" Bernie says.

"I think I'm gonna—" I point to my phone by way of explanation. My fingers fumble over the screen but I manage to ask the question.

Should I play Never Have I Ever?

"What are you doing?" Bash asks.

"None of your business."

He reaches out and snatches the phone from my hand. "Should I play Never Have I . . ." His eyes widen as he reads my question. "This is the saddest thing I've ever seen."

Bernie smacks his shoulder. "Rude." She turns to me. "Ignore him. What's it going to be?"

"It told me to play."

"The Magic 8 Ball has more positive answers than negative. If you don't want to do something, you should rephrase the question," Bash says.

"I never said I didn't want to play."

"Well, do you?"

"What does that matter?"

"That's how most people make decisions. You do what you want, you skip everything else. Right?" He looks around the circle for confirmation.

"This is boring. Let's play already," Bernie says loudly. "Never have I ever gotten a speeding ticket."

Fitz and Molly both swallow a shot of vinegar. When they're done coughing and wincing, Fitz tells us about the time he got busted for going eighty-five on the freeway in an attempt to meet curfew after dropping Ruby off at her farm on the far end of town. His turn is next. "Never have I ever flirted my way out of a speeding ticket."

Bernie's laugh is loud and abrupt. "Well played." She raises her cups to her lips and drinks. "Whew! That's worse than I thought!" She seems delighted by this fact.

Molly says she's never stayed up all night.

"This is so immature," Bash grumbles, but he takes a giant bite of jalapeño pepper anyway. Fitz and Bernie do the same, and soon they're all breathing heavily and wiping tears from their eyes.

I'm up next, and I realize with a start that I'm the only one who hasn't had to eat or drink anything. Hopelessly Boring, party of one! "Never have I ever skipped school." I stare at the cup in my hands, avoiding Fitz's gaze. He showed up at my house last year on senior ditch day, arguing that if the seniors didn't have to be in class, we shouldn't either. He wanted to rent tubes, float down the Salt River, and laugh at all the drunk seniors. I didn't go, because—*shockingly*—I couldn't decide what to do. I was too nervous to skip, but I hated the idea of Fitz going without me. Eventually, he did, though. He came home from that trip with a sunburned nose and a date with Molly.

The jar of cinnamon is passed around. In unison, they all lift the spoons to their mouths. "Wait!" I say, and all eyes turn to me. "Don't do it. My mom works in the ER; she saw this kid who did this and ended up with a collapsed lung."

"Is she serious?" Bash looks around the circle for confirmation. Fitz sets his spoon down and drinks the vinegar instead; Molly and Bernie do the same.

"Thank you." I mouth the words to Fitz. He winks in response as Bash defiantly tips the cinnamon into his mouth. When Bash spends the next five minutes sputtering and wheezing for breath, it's hard for Fitz and me to smother our smug grins.

Bash is up next. He narrows his eyes at me. "Never have I ever kissed a guy."

Molly and Bernie drink. When I don't, Bash's eyes widen. "You're a real party, aren't you?"

I shrink into myself, thankful for the dark for covering my flaming cheeks.

Bernie: "Never have I ever been stuck in an elevator." Molly and Bash race through a stack of soda crackers. He taps out at three, but she manages to down four in a minute.

The later it gets, the more personal the admissions become. We might not have alcohol, but they're laughing like they're drunk anyway. The vinegar or the hour or the cold has gone straight to their heads. My cup stays full, my chest hollow with the suffocating realization that I've never done anything. Even if half these things seem like a really bad idea, at least they're something. All I've ever done is sit in my house and bake bread.

"Never have I ever lied to my significant other," Molly says, her eyes flicking to Fitz. He drinks, his eyes on the floor. She grimaces.

Watching this exchange with undisguised interest, Bernie swirls the liquid in her cup. "Never have I ever been in love."

Molly takes the smallest sip known to man. Ugh. Poor girl. It's like looking in a mirror. Fitz and I lock eyes across the circle as my face burns red hot.

"Just get on with it already," I say flippantly. Keeping me steady in his gaze, he raises the cup to his lips and drinks.

"A guy like you should take six drinks," Bernie quips, but Fitz's eyes don't leave mine. He's waiting for me. One quick gulp, then. Down the hatch. I'm caught between coughing and gagging as the sour liquid burns my throat, eyes, and nose.

"Interesting," Bash muses. I'm really starting to hate him.

We play several more rounds; I eat half a pepper and drink one more time. Fitz, Bernie, and Bash all require refills while my cup is a pathetically full testament to my cowardice. Bernie moans as she tries to pour more, sloshing it across her blanket. She doubles over and dissolves in a fit of giggles. When she finally stops laughing, she stretches across the pillows and blankets like a cat. "My stomach hates me. I'm gonna puke."

The others groan in agreement, and since no one wants to move, we decide to sleep on the floor. Bodies shuffle and crawl over one another, snagging pillows and calling dibs on blankets. Bernie and Bash are on my left, Fitz and Molly to my right, with Fitz in the middle.

"I don't wanna sleep by you," Bernie slurs at her brother.

"Ow. Get off me!" he grumbles as she climbs over him. Her

knee lands heavily in my stomach. She drags herself over Fitz and collapses between him and Molly. Fitz shifts slightly toward me to make room for her. Silence falls over the group. I'm already so cold I'm shaking. I pull the blanket up to my chin and swirl another one around my feet until I'm in a perfect cocoon of cozy. I better not have to pee, because I'd rather die than move again.

To my left, Bash snores and rolls over, his shoulder resting against mine. "Gross. Move, Bash." I shove him off, but he's heavier than expected. He hardly moves.

"Switch spots with me," Fitz says. His low voice raises all the hair on my arms.

"It's fine." My blankets are all exactly right and only my nose is cold. It's not worth the risk.

Another minute passes, and Bash rolls toward me again. His hand lands on my stomach.

"Ugh." I push him away again.

"Switch me," Fitz insists.

"No."

"Do it."

"No! I'm finally warm!"

"I'm not going to be able to sleep if I'm thinking about him touching you," he says so quietly I'm half-sure I imagined it.

Without waiting for an answer, he crawls between Bash and me while I scoot-slide my pile of blankets toward Bernie.

Fitz is quiet, but to me, the steady in and out of his breathing is the loudest thing in the room. That's another consequence of being in love with him; he's my North Star. My back to the door, I know when he enters any room. At school, I easily pick his laugh out in a crowd of hundreds. My heart tugs me toward him, no matter the situation. It's been that way for a while now, but I've never been so aware of his body, and of mine, as I am in this moment. I'm 98 percent nerve endings and 2 percent everything else that makes a human.

A minute later Molly is in my ear. "Move over," she whispers. And probably she means for me to make room between Fitz and me, but I scoot toward him, allowing her to slip in between Bernie and me.

"So what do you think?" she whispers. "Can you help me win Fitz back?"

I glance over my shoulder at Fitz, expecting him to be asleep, but by the flicker of firelight I see him watching us, his face openly curious. He quirks an eyebrow at me, then nods at Molly. He's dying to know what we're talking about, because no matter what Darcy thinks, he's in love with Molly. He admitted that much when he took that drink tonight. And now he's getting the romantic cabin trip he planned. And what kind of friend would I be if I took that away from him?

I ignore the ache in my chest and turn back to Molly. "I'll help."

FATE ONE

December 25 | 8:55 p.m. | John Jay Hall,
Columbia University

It's only as the door is sliding shut, Harrison and me decidedly *inside* the elevator, that I remember his warning about faulty wiring. Is that what he said? I'm not sure. Definitely something about it breaking down. Cords snapping. Elevator plunging to the basement.

SIM is going to have a field day with this one. I can see the list now. It's very apocalyptic, because we get stuck between floors and no one is on duty to help and we have no food and it's cold and what are the chances this box gets cell service, anyway?

Harrison turns, and something stirs in the pit of my stomach. He seems to read my mind. "If we get stuck, at least we'll have time to talk about whatever happened back there," he says dryly.

This is a very bad idea.

And yet, it's not the things on SIM's list that terrify me. It's the erratic thump of my heart and the fact that every sense in my body is coiled tightly in Harrison's presence. For someone I've only known a few days, I'm too aware of him by half.

Without taking his eyes off me, he pushes the button to take us to the ground floor, and the machine groans to life with a jerky shudder. I grab on to the railing, just for something to do with my hands. I take small comfort in the fact that in a parallel universe, there is a much smarter version of me who remembered to take the stairs.

"You're mad at me," Harrison says.

"Nope."

"You're mad at Kate?" he guesses.

"Wrong again."

He frowns. "Did you talk about the multiverse?"

"We did." I can't keep my eyes off the jacket pocket where he keeps his phone. There must be a text from Kate, because he knew to find me in her room. I try to remember what exactly I said to her. *That nothing had happened, but it might? And when she asked if I liked him, I didn't say no.* It's not as horrifying as the love letter confession, but it's not great either.

He retrieves a book called *The Meaning of Life: An Overview of the Different Branches of Philosophy* from his messenger bag and hands it to me. "I wanted to show you the campus, but I also thought this might be of interest to you, given our conversation about stumbling around in the dark."

"Can I see your phone?"

He cocks an eyebrow. "No?"

"Did Kate send you a text?"

"Are we having the same conversation?"

The elevator halts, sending me stumbling sideways. Harrison reaches out to steady me, his hand on my hip. He removes it after a breath, and part of me wishes he hadn't. I expect the elevator to start moving again, but it doesn't. He jams his finger into the door-open button. Nothing happens.

"Is now a bad time to say I told you so?" He casts an amused look in my direction.

"Kate thinks I like you," I blurt. Better to get it out of the way now, before it turns into this huge, awkward, unspoken thing.

His eyes spark. He crosses his arms and steps closer to me. "Why does she think that?"

I shrug.

"Is she right?" A smile plays at his lips.

"You could have told me I might run into her," I huff.

The glint in his eyes dims and he steps away. "Hang on." He holds up a finger and calls a nonemergency line for help, detailing our situation. SIM was wrong about at least one thing: We do get service in here. He hangs up. "Sounds like we've got some time to kill."

"Peachy." *Peachy?* Never in my entire life have I uttered the word *peachy*. There's not enough oxygen in here. Harrison's too close. His hair hangs in his face and I can smell his spicy shampoo.

"Why didn't you tell me that your gorgeous ex-girlfriend lives two doors down and is conveniently in town on Christmas Day?" I ask again.

"Because I don't like talking about it. I told you I'm bad with feelings."

I bite my lips, unsure how to put words to the nagging feeling in my stomach. "Was bringing me here an excuse to see her again?"

"Are you kidding me right now? You think I wanted to know how much she doesn't miss me? To see the bedsheets and imagine how they were rumpled by her new boyfriend?" He shakes his head and makes a disgusted sound. "You're way off. Don't forget that *you* wanted to go out tonight."

"Were you using me to make her jealous? To prove that you're over her?"

He narrows his eyes. "Listen to me now, because I'm only going to say this once. I had no idea Kate would be here tonight. We were out, with nothing to do, and you seemed mildly interested in philosophy and generally confused about life, so I figured I'd lend you this book and show you around campus. End of story."

I search his eyes, surprised by how honest they appear. "Okay," I say at last.

"Do you believe me?"

I nod, and he breathes a sigh of relief, stepping closer to me. I hold up both hands, maintaining the sliver of space between us. *Bible width*. That's what they say at Clover's church. I'm already feeling flustered and if he takes another step, there's no telling how my traitorous body will react.

"How much longer until help gets here? What exactly did they say?" I ask.

"Don't change the subject."

"Back up. Two steps," I order. He rolls his eyes but obeys. I cross my arms, feigning a bravado I don't feel. The corner of his lip twitches. He knows I'm bluffing. I know he knows.

"Why does Kate think you like me? And why are you bothered by the fact that we used to date?"

My skin prickles uncomfortably. For a guy who hates feelings, he's certainly asking for a lot of mine.

"I'll wait," he says.

"How charitable." I wasn't jealous, although that's clearly what he's implying. No, I would have recognized that emotion. I wear jealousy like a perma-sunburn: hot, painful, and impossible to ignore. Kate isn't Molly, or Ruby, or Ivy; she's just some beautiful, genius girl who used to date a guy I barely know.

Not jealousy.

Then what?

He takes a step closer, so there's hardly any space between us, making it supremely difficult to think.

"I don't—I don't know," I stammer. The nearness of him is impossible to ignore.

"I think you do."

He doesn't know me as well as he thinks he does. I close my eyes against the sight of his lips and concentrate. *When I thought the trip was about Kate, instead of about him doing something nice for me, I felt . . . disappointed.* The word lands in my head with a deafening thud.

It's so plain and obvious and baffling.

Mere hours after that picture of Molly and Fitz, why would I be disappointed about Harrison?

He rests a hand lightly on my waist. When I don't object, he pulls me in. My brain is frozen. My body isn't. I lean into him, too scared to make any other moves. His free hand tucks my hair behind my ear.

"You're still in love with her," I say.

"There is always some madness in love. But there is also always some reason in madness."

"Don't distract me with quotes from obscure philosophers."

"Friedrich Nietzsche isn't obscure." Harrison pulls away in mock offense. I miss his body close to mine and pull him back.

He makes a sound low in his throat. "Don't act possessive," he admonishes with a smirk. "Besides, you're still in love with Cabin Boy." His eyes carry a challenge. He brushes my hair away from my face again, running his fingers through it.

"Yes. But—" *But what?* My thoughts are all mixed up as every ounce of focus narrows to the feel of his fingers in my hair. In another life, this decision would have been paralyzing. But now, even with all this chaos in my head, I don't need Magic 8 to tell me what to do. Maybe because Harrison is impossible to resist. Or maybe because I'm calmed by the notion of infinity, of the fact that different versions of me are playing out different versions of this same scenario in every space and time imaginable.

Or maybe I finally know what I want.

Yes, I'm in love with Fitz. ". . . But I want to kiss you anyway."

His lips crush against mine.

It's fifteen more minutes before help arrives to pry the elevator doors open, and in those fifteen minutes, I don't think about Fitz at all. But when Harrison and I spring apart, our lips swollen and our hair mussed, I do.

I close my eyes, and Fitz is inescapable. I open them and am disappointed when he doesn't appear. I'm awash in a combo of guilt and lust and homesickness and fear and confusion and relief.

They swirl together like the worst kind of emotion smoothie. I'll chug until my stomach is sloshy and I can't separate one thing from the next. I'll drink until I'm sick.

I'll kiss Harrison until the thought of Fitz kissing Molly doesn't make me want to cry.

After we climb out of the elevator and tumble breathlessly into the stairwell, Harrison pushes me against the closed door and kisses me again. We stumble home this way, pausing every ten feet, stopping under streetlights, choosing empty subway cars. He tangles his hands in my hair and I feel all the lean muscles beneath his shirt, our hands shaky and fumbling and fast. We're both breathless and filled with desperate wanting. Whether we want each other or someone else, it's hard to tell.

All I know for sure is that we kiss until my lips are chapped and my head swims.

We kiss until I no longer think about Fitz at all.

FATE TWO

December 26 | 2:13 a.m. | Williams, Arizona

I wake up freezing. Literally freezing. Possibly to death.

I pull the blanket to my chin, only to have my feet stick out the bottom. My cocoon has dissolved. I curl my legs into my shaking body and am startled by a noise. Fitz is adding wood to the dying fire.

"Hey," I whisper through chattering teeth.

"Hey," he whispers back, adding another log. "You looked cold."

I'm shaking too hard to reply.

The flames flicker brighter, enveloping the new logs hungrily. Looking at Fitz in the dark, something stirs low in the pit of my stomach. He dusts off his hands and returns to his spot, facing me. There's at least eighteen inches between us and I'm still shaking uncontrollably.

"I feel partially responsible for this blizzard," he whispers.

"W-wh-why?"

"I asked Clover to pray for snow."

My laugh forms a cloud of icy breath in front of me. "If I die of hypothermia, do I blame y-you or C-Clover or G-G-God?"

"I was prepared to take the credit for your first snowstorm, so I guess I'll take the blame too."

I laugh again, but it's muffled behind chattering teeth.

"This is stupid. Take my blanket," he says.

I shake my head. I can't leave him with *nothing*.

"You could get under my blanket with me. Unless—unless that's weird."

Well, it's weird now that he mentioned it could be weird. But I'm honestly too cold to care. "I co-could make an ex-exception to my rule."

"What rule?"

"Never mind. If there was ever a situation that ne-ne-necessitated touching, it's now." I crawl under his blanket with him and flip over so my back is against his chest. He wraps an arm around my waist and pulls me tight to him. Heat bursts across my skin.

"Are you a little drunk on vinegar right now?" he jokes, his voice low, his breath tickling the back of my neck.

"Are *you*?"

He cinches me tighter. "It would explain a few things."

It's obviously a joke, but I don't love the implication that he needs an excuse to put his arms around me, so I squirm out of his grasp and turn to my other side so we're still under the same blanket, but facing each other instead of touching.

I regret it immediately.

Bad idea.

Super bad idea.

The worst idea.

The thing is, my face is inches from Fitz's and all I can think about is his lips. The firelight casts a glow on his face, and the shadow of his lashes on his cheeks does dangerous things to my stomach.

"I haven't done anything." I don't know *why* I say that, or even what I mean by it. Except maybe what I mean is that for every drink I took, Bernie had six. And now I'm in the dark next to the boy I've loved for years, and I can't do anything about it. Just like every other day of my sad, boring life. "Bernie's more exciting than I am," I add. I glance at her over my shoulder, remembering the way she chose to sleep next to him. "I think she's still into you." Again, I'm not sure if I mean it, or if I want to hear him deny it.

"She's not." His warm breath feels too good on my cheeks. "It's not what you're thinking."

"What am I thinking?"

"That I'm a slut. You said as much after the train."

I cringe. I did say that, more or less. "Can boys even be sluts?"

"If girls can be, guys should too."

"In a perfect world," I joke as I slip my socks off with my toes. I nudge up the bottom of his sweatpants and press my icy toes against his calf. It's something I would never, ever do in my normal life, but I'm beginning to think we left normal back in Gilbert and entered some bizarre dreamworld where it's okay to snuggle under a blanket next to your best friend.

He hisses at the contact and grabs my waist, his face threatening. "I'll tickle you." His fingers sear the skin under my shirt.

"Only if you want me to wake up—everyone." I almost said

Molly. But then I didn't. Because I don't want him thinking about her when he's under a blanket with me.

He narrows his eyes and slowly relaxes his grip, but he doesn't move his hands.

His hands.

My waist.

I can't think about anything else.

Bash snores loudly. Fitz's expression clears and his hands fall away from my skin. "You surprised me tonight," he says.

"Because I'm so boring?"

"Because you've been in love," he says, less accusation than invitation. "Why don't I know about this guy?"

"Why didn't I know about Bernie?"

Fitz's brow creases. "Because I wasn't in love with her. She was an older girl who I kissed *one* time. It was years ago, and it meant literally nothing."

"Was Bash right?" I ask quickly in an effort to defuse the tension. "When you're making a decision, is it as simple as deciding what you want and then doing it?"

He's quiet for a long time. Too long. I'm worried I've said the wrong thing. When he finally speaks, he chooses his words carefully. "Sometimes yes. Sometimes no."

"But it's easy for you to decide, right? You don't struggle the way I do?"

Fitz goes very still. "Not usually," he whispers.

"Does that mean something is wrong with me? Like, with my brain?" If I had a dollar for every time I wondered that, I'd have enough to spend the rest of my life flying around the world.

"There's nothing wrong with you. But maybe—" He hesitates.

I fill in the blank for him. "Maybe I'm crazy, right? Don't pretend you haven't thought it."

"Don't put words in my mouth. You've been doing that all weekend, and it's not fair."

He's right and I know it. I swallow the iceberg-sized lump in my throat and try not to cry.

"Are you warm enough?" Fitz asks finally, his voice sad and tired and exasperated.

I've mostly stopped shivering, my thumping heart and deep regret heating me through. But I don't want that to be the truth, so I lie.

"No," I whisper. At first, I don't think he hears me. But then he closes his eyes with a sigh and loops his arm around my waist again. I flip over and let him pull me to his chest, resting my head on his other arm. His body is warm and steady and solid against mine. A few feet away, Molly sleeps peacefully, her hair fanned out across her pillow, her skin smooth and worry free. My promise to her comes rushing back to me, and I know that when the sun comes up, I'll have to help the two of them get back together.

"Fitz?" I whisper. His breathing is deep and steady, and he doesn't respond. I slip out from under his arm and pull the letter out of my pocket. I toss it into the fireplace and watch the flames turn my words to ash. When the evidence is gone, I slip back under our shared blanket. I wrap one arm around my waist and use his other as my pillow again, already nostalgic for this moment that I'll never get again. A tear slips down my cheek and lands on his skin, and I'm grateful when it doesn't wake him up.

* * *

The power's still out in the morning. I can tell because my toes feel like they're about to snap off. I wiggle them, and I think they move. I hope they move. I'm going to assume they move.

Fitz is gone, and so are Molly and Bash. Bernie is still asleep, despite the fact that most of her blankets slipped off in the night. Voices float in from the kitchen, but I snuggle deeper below my blanket. I'm not ready to face Fitz yet. Not after spending the night in his arms. And Molly! What if she saw us snuggled up together?

I check my phone. It's at 3 percent. Because of course it is. Stupid, crappy battery. I have a handful of texts from Mom checking in, and one message from Clover.

I thought he loved me. I don't know what happened. Followed by a dozen sobbing face emojis.

My friend is hurting, and it's my fault. I screwed up, and I need to fix it.

I have to tell her, but my fingers don't move.

Tell her the truth?

Don't tell her the truth?

I open Magic 8, and my battery dies. With a groan and an enormous shiver, I pull a blanket over Bernie's bare feet and then join Fitz, Molly, Bash, and Darcy in the kitchen. They're sitting around the table eating all the different breads I made yesterday. Stress baking for the win! They're wrapped in blankets and coats, their breaths coming out in puffs, and discussing our options. I quickly gather that the only real option is to wait. This doesn't sound so bad. I'm good at waiting. Sometimes it feels like my whole life is waiting. Waiting for Fitz to fall in love with me. Waiting for a plane ticket to be dropped in my lap. Waiting for a better, more exciting life. So yeah, I can wait for someone to dig me out of this cabin.

Fitz's eyes flick up and he sees me hovering, an unreadable expression on his face. "Hey."

"Yeah. You too. Hey, I mean, good morning."

Before this week, I didn't think there was a Fitz expression I wouldn't recognize. But something changed around the time we got here, and now I find myself confused more often than not. He quickly averts his gaze and my stomach lurches as I remember last night. I grab two slices of cinnamon bread and smooth my tangled hair with my fingers.

"Bernie still asleep?" He frowns slightly, a worried crease appearing in his forehead.

It's not what you think, Fitz said last night.

What do I think? They had a fling, obviously. If I had to put money on it, I'd say he saw her standing in the gift shop at the train depot, flurries stuck to her hair, miniskirt and wool tights on her legs, and fell madly, devastatingly in love. He bought her the Christmas tree ornament she was admiring, put his coat around her shoulder, and threaded his fingers through hers while they walked along the tracks. After an hour, he kissed her. After two hours, he took her home to meet his parents. By the end of the trip, the relationship was over, and he never cared enough to even tell me her name.

Which says, what? What does that say about Fitz Wilding, like, *as a person*?

I used to think it meant he had a fearless heart, but maybe he's just reckless.

I glance at Fitz out of the corner of my eye, but his head is down, his eyes on the puzzle. My cheeks heat at the memory of last night, his arm around my waist, my body curled into his. Every inch of me felt wired, alive in a way I'm not used to. Last night, I acted without thinking. It didn't feel wrong or scary in the moment, but standing in this tiny, frozen kitchen, with Fitz refusing to meet my eyes, everything feels flipped upside down.

"How much longer do you think it'll be until the power comes back?" Molly asks Fitz. Her hand is resting on the bench next to his in a position that's heartbreakingly familiar in its faux casualness.

"I don't know," Fitz says. "Hopefully soon. I'm worried about water."

I glance out the window. The storm is over, but more than a foot and a half of snow is piled up on the deck. I bite the inside of my cheek. Even if the power does come back, we could be here awhile.

"Can I borrow your phone?" I ask Fitz as I sit next to him on the bench. Molly's on his other side, slowly tearing a crescent roll to bits.

"Sure, but I can't guarantee it'll work. What's up?"

I lower my voice so only he can hear. "I want to check on Clover, make sure she's okay."

"She didn't get caught in the blizzard, did she?"

"No." I bite my lip, trying to figure out how to delicately word this. Actually, screw it. "You were right, okay? I meddled in her and Jay's relationship and they broke up and she's devastated and I already feel like trash, so don't lecture me, okay?"

Fitz shakes his hair from his eyes and gives me a hard stare. It's not a lecture, but it feels like one. "I turned off my phone last night to preserve the battery." He turns it on and tilts the screen so I can see. "Nineteen percent."

"Better than nothing. I need to make this right."

"Wait." Fitz puts his hand out to stop me. His fingers brush mine, but he immediately pulls them back. "You can't tell her that Jay was going to propose. What if he doesn't want her to know?"

"Good point. Do you have Jay's number saved?"

"I think so. From that time we surprised you and Clover with concert tickets."

"I'll call him, then." On my way to the fireplace hearth, I trip over the empty bottle of vinegar by Bernie's feet and stumble over her.

"Oops! Sorry!" Now that I'm up close, I gasp at her appearance. Her skin is snow white, her lips deep blue. Her eyelids are heavy and her whole body is trembling.

"Bernie! Are you okay?" I wrap the nearest blanket around her shoulders, but her hands are shaking too hard to keep it in place as the others rush from the kitchen to get to us.

"Bernie!" Bash takes her hand. "You're freezing."

Bernie squints at him with sleepy eyes, like she's not sure who he is or how she got here.

"She's hypothermic," Darcy says. "Did she drink last night?" she asks Fitz sharply, looking around the room for the bottle of schnapps.

"No! I mean, just vinegar." Fitz pushes his hands through his hair with wide eyes.

"She might be dehydrated," Darcy says before turning to Bash. "Does she take any medications? Have any medical conditions?"

"She has a thyroid thing," Bash says.

"Hypothyroidism?"

Bash nods and Darcy swears under her breath as she turns back to Bernie. "Bernie, honey, can you get up on this couch here?" She and Bash gently help Bernie onto the couch, and then Fitz and I push it across the room to the fireplace.

"Molly, find mittens and a hat for her. Make sure they're dry. Nothing wet from the snow. Paige, she needs warm water to drink."

"What can I do?" Fitz asks.

"You should have given her water instead of letting her get dehydrated. You better hope nothing happens to her."

"Wha's gonna happen to me?" Bernie mumbles. Her words are heavy, slipping across her tongue like ice.

"I'm sorry," Fitz says. "Tell me what to do."

"I don't know, Romeo. Help your girlfriend," Darcy snaps.

Fitz freezes. My eyes dart to Molly, but she's already grabbing mittens and a hat from the pile by the door. And Bash is next to Bernie on the small sofa that only has room for two. Which means . . . when I glance at Fitz, he's looking at me, having come to the same conclusion. I'm door number three. "Warm drink," he says.

"Oh. Um . . ." Do they think I'm the type of person you turn to in a crisis? News flash: I'm really, really not. "I don't know."

"The stove—"

"Is electric. It won't work." I search the room frantically. "The fire!"

In the kitchen, he grabs a bottle of water while I search the cupboards for a cast iron skillet. I empty the bottle inside and place it over the fire. Darcy and Bash talk to Bernie, asking her questions and keeping her conscious. My heart relaxes with each question she answers correctly. When the water is warm but not scalding, we carefully pour it into a mug and hand it off to Bash, who holds it to Bernie's lips and helps her drink.

Molly, Fitz, and I sit on the other couch, not saying a word, hardly daring to breathe. I pull a blanket over my lap, and Fitz drags half of it over him, scooting closer so we both fit.

"Do we need to call 911?" Fitz asks.

"No, she's warming up. She's going to be okay." Darcy sits back on her heels, looking every bit as relieved as I feel.

Fitz leans back against the couch, his head lolling to the side so he's looking at me. "I'm such an idiot."

"It's not your fault," I say. His thigh is pressed against mine and I have to fight every urge in me to take his hand, to touch his knee, to get closer.

Darcy stands. "She's stable, but we should get her checked out as soon as we can. I'll try to get in touch with her parents while you all dig the cars out of the snow." She takes her phone from her pocket and wanders off to look for decent reception.

"Someone should stay with my sister and make sure she's okay," Bash says. He nods to me. "Have you ever shoveled snow before?" When I shake my head, he appoints me as Bernie's babysitter.

Bash, Molly, and Fitz gear up for the snow. When Molly's coat is too puffy to get her boots on, Fitz bends and helps her step into them.

Well then. I guess I'm staying.

I take Bash's place next to Bernie on the couch. When the door closes behind them, she takes another sip of the warm water and smiles weakly. "They're gone?"

I nod.

"Perfect. Now we can gossip about Fitz."

FATE ONE

December 26 | 9:11 a.m. | Upper West Side, Manhattan, New York

Some days, I wake up with a black pit of doom in my stomach. This is not one of those days. I wake up smiling, the memories of last night so vivid I blush.

The sounds of morning float down the hall and through the crack under the door. Footsteps putter around the kitchen, overlaid with soft laughter and sizzling bacon. My stomach growls but I snuggle deeper under the covers anyway. Streams of sunlight—the first I've seen in days—fall across the floor of Harrison's room.

Harrison.

I grin wider, pulling the covers up to my chin. I stay there for a long time, staring at the ceiling and listening to the sound of my heartbeat.

The thing about my life is this: It's safe. It's predictable.

Please note: Predictable does not equal boring.

I love goat yoga with Clover and baking bread in my own kitchen and daydreaming about trips around the world and everything with Fitz.

I love *everything* with Fitz. All the movies and the aimless drives around town and the sour-gummy-worm binges and late-night talks about broken hearts and impossible dreams. Being in love with Fitz is a lot of things: scary and heartbreaking and disappointing and exhilarating. But it is never boring. And that's kind of the point, isn't it? Even on the days when my future is the scariest, maybe even especially on those days, Fitz is the Technicolor in my black-and-white world.

But the predictability of it might kill me. The way I dissect his every look and touch and glance makes me frustrated and angry with myself. Angry for being so hopeful and desperate and scared.

Last night was anything but predictable, and as I count the beats of my heart in a warm bed the day after Christmas, I feel raw. Human. Surprised.

I revel in the feeling. For about ten minutes. And then I'm brimming with the need to tell someone. I spend so much of my life listening to Clover's stories about Jay and Fitz's stories about whomever, and I never have any juicy secrets of my own. Now I finally do. And if I don't tell someone what happened, I might explode.

I want to tell Fitz. The thought comes as a surprise, although it shouldn't, because I always want to tell Fitz everything. That's the way it is with a best friend, and even more with a best friend you're in love with. Sometimes it's hard to know my opinion about a thing until I've talked it through with him, because he knows me better than I know myself. I unlock my phone and my fingers fly over the keys. **Last night, I made out with a boy in an elevator. And on the subway. And up and down the**

streets of New York City. I did it until I stopped thinking about you, until I stopped wondering how his kisses are different than yours.

Delete.

Obviously.

This is a story for Clover, which is why it's too bad I was such a thoughtless jerk last time I talked to her.

I write a new message, and this one I do send.

Can we talk?

It's not good enough. I know that. But I can't bring myself to type the apology she deserves. Because what if she marries him, and her life goes to hell, and I didn't try to stop it?

On its heels, another thought comes barreling toward me:

What if she marries him, and we're not friends anymore?

Please. I send. It's not great, but it's not nothing.

Hunger pulls me from bed. I duck into the bathroom to brush my teeth and my hair, and then step into the kitchen, not knowing what to expect from Harrison.

He looks up from his bowl of oatmeal. "Hey," he breathes, and I'm bombarded with a million thoughts at once: his hand on my waist, his breath on my neck, his lips on mine. And then he tucks his hair behind his ear, and all those vivid memories are washed in a bittersweet haze. Because the way he tucks his hair behind his ear is not the way Fitz shakes his out of his eyes, and the difference between those two moments, and the visceral reaction my body has to one and not the other, is a canyon so wide I might never be able to cross it.

Will I ever get to the side of the canyon where I'm allowed to be in love with Harrison? In this universe, with this version of myself?

"Hey," I say back.

A beat, and then we break out in matching smiles.

I'm not yet in love with this boy, but according to string theory, anything is possible.

"I was thinking we could go to the High Line this morning."

"That sounds great."

I expect I'll have to sell Mom on the idea, but she seems distracted. She agrees quickly and doesn't ask for specifics.

"That was weird," I tell Harrison as we step into the bright, cold sunshine an hour later. "Our first day here, Mom was intensely worried about me. Now it's like she couldn't care less."

"Maybe because she trusts me," Harrison says.

"It's probably because she remembered she trusts me. I'm not the trouble-making type."

"Really?" He raises an eyebrow. "You could have fooled me." He takes a casual sip of his coffee as my cheeks turn pink.

"Did you really bring me to your dorm just to lend me a philosophy book?"

"That and *On the Road*. Kerouac hits the spot when I'm feeling confused about life."

"You have that book in your room in the apartment."

"I can neither confirm nor deny this fact," Harrison says lightly.

"I knew it! You *were* trying to seduce me!"

"Only until I saw the apprehension in your eyes outside my room. Then I called it off. You were the one who mauled me in the elevator, if you remember."

"Oh, I remember," I say, surprising myself.

The High Line, it turns out, is an elevated concrete trail built on an abandoned railway. In warmer months, Harrison tells me it's surrounded by wildflowers and overgrown grasses. Today, it's flanked by skeleton trees. The view changes quickly as we walk. One second I'll be looking at crumbling, graffiti-stained buildings, only to turn a corner and see an imposing skyscraper. It's the whole of New York at once, old and new, dirty and expensive, planned and chaotic. And after the crush of people at Rockefeller Center and then in Santaland, it feels positively abandoned. Harrison takes my hand and we stroll slowly to the soundtrack of warbling winter birds, stopping every now and then for a quick kiss.

It's a movie-ready scene, and for the first time in the history of ever, I'm the heroine. Too bad I can't fully enjoy it. I check my phone repeatedly, hoping for a message from Clover, but there never is.

"Either Clover's furious with me for telling her not to get married, or she's so blissfully happy in her newly engaged life that she can't be bothered to respond. I don't know which is worse."

"Let me see your phone."

"What? No!" I clutch it tighter.

"Relax. I want to look at her Instagram. What's her full name?"

"Clover James."

He types on his phone. "Got it." He's silent for several seconds as he examines her pictures. "She's pissed at you, which is good, because it means you can apologize."

"How can you tell?" I grab the phone from his hands and inspect the stream of happy selfies. "Six disgustingly adorable pictures in two days. She's hardly sitting around missing me."

"It's not like you joined a convent to mourn her," Harrison deadpans.

"You know what I mean." I nudge him with my shoulder. He responds by dropping his arm around me and pulling me into his side.

"She misses you. No one who is actually this happy works so hard to prove it. Right before Mom cheated on Dad, her Facebook page was practically a tribute to him. She was trying way too hard to convince herself that she was happy. Same as Clover."

"I don't know—"

"Look at this hashtag: #engagedandunderaged. She's trying to get under your skin, to prove to you that she's making the right decision. She cares about your opinion, and you two will work it out."

I look back at the pictures and the hashtags. They could be directed at me, but they could just as easily be a dig at her mom, who is undoubtedly less happy about the engagement than I am. Which is why she needs a best friend right now.

My stomach sinks. I really messed up.

I continue to scroll, coming across another picture from Molly's feed. This one is a selfie in a snow-covered forest.

"Is that him?" Harrison takes my phone, clicks on Fitz's profile, and scrolls through the pictures. I lean over his shoulder as he zooms past several images of Fitz and me together. He goes back a full year, pausing on the homecoming-to-Halloween transition from Priya to Fiona. "That's a lot of different girls."

I bristle against the insinuation, but for once, I don't leap to defend Fitz, because I can't deny what Harrison is seeing. "I know."

"Most guys do a profile purge after a breakup."

"He's not like that. He doesn't erase people from his life like they never mattered to him."

"So what's so special about him?" he asks, his voice tinged with something very near jealousy.

What's so special about Fitz? A fair question.

I cast about for a concrete example. Something to hold up in the sunlight and say, "This! Right here! This is why Fitz Wilding is my favorite person." But it's impossible to untangle five years of memories. It's the snowstorm and the jumbo-sized bag of sour gummy worms in his truck console and the way he holds his breath when he introduces me to a new movie, waiting to see my reaction. It's the way he clasped my hand in that cold science classroom and talked me through my panic attack. He saved me that day, and he's been saving me every day since, pulling me from the scary black place that tries to pull me under.

"He knows me," I say, answering Harrison's impossible question. *And he likes me anyway*, I add in my head.

"Hmm."

"Just say it." I try to play it cool, like I'm not desperate to know what he thinks about me and Fitz.

"I bet all these other girls think he knows *them* too." His tone is marked by his chronic cynicism.

"Probably." They'd be wrong, though. He didn't even know Molly's afraid of heights.

"When you wrote that letter, you hoped he'd read it and pick you over this Instagram girl. Over any of these Instagram girls, really."

"No. It was a breakup letter, telling him all the reasons I can't be in his life anymore."

Harrison presses his lips into a thin line. "Be serious."

"I am."

"But deep down, you hoped he'd see it for what it was and pick you."

I want to tell Harrison he's wrong, but the honest part of myself knows that he's not. "That's not a question."

"Let's say he does read it, and he does pick you. How would you know that you were any different than any of these other girls?"

His words are broken AC in the dead of summer, a drink sucked down the wrong pipe, an impossible decision I don't want to make. They are every bad thing in this world. I stop walking, and with his arm around me, he stops too.

Every part of me wants to defend Fitz's honor. But the words that once came so easily are gone. In their place is a horrible realization. "You're right," I whisper. It feels like a confession and a betrayal.

Even if Fitz did read my letter, even if he did kiss me or date me or plan one of his grand gestures, then what? It stands to reason that eventually I'd become one of those Instagram girls too.

"I'm always right," Harrison whispers in my ear. He tucks me tighter into his side. It's so couple-y, so possessive, that it startles me. But I lean into him anyway, because what do I have to lose?

I gaze at the New York City skyline, breathtaking in the morning sunlight. We get plenty of sunshine in Gilbert, but I swear the light here is different. The tall buildings create long shadows and sharp angles and small, unexpected pockets of sunshine. Back home, we have a big open sky that unfurls over a flat desert landscape. "I can't believe I've been so stupid for so long. I almost missed this view, for what? A few extra days with the same boy who didn't love me yesterday and won't love me tomorrow."

"'Life must be understood backward. But it must be lived forward.' Kierkegaard."

"Say that again." I'm entranced by today's Philosophy 101 quip.

"Life must be—"

"Lived forward," I finish for him.

"That's right. After all, what's the point in wishing for a fate that's surely happening in a parallel universe?"

I take Harrison's hand and pull it tighter across my shoulders, keeping my fingers entwined with his. It feels bolder than our shadowy sidewalk kisses. We walk like that for the length of the High Line, and people look at us like we're an adorably in love couple. And for a split second, I wish we *were* in a parallel universe. Because some girl is going to fall madly in love with this surly boy and his philosophical one-liners, and why shouldn't it be me?

I never made the choice to fall in love with my best friend. But maybe I could make the choice to fall in love with Harrison. Stranger things have happened, right?

There's a bench near the end of the High Line where we sit and make out until my stomach growls. We decide to return to his apartment for lunch, and although we don't kiss like we did last night, we keep our hands clasped together, our shoulders bumping into each other, grinning like fools.

In his apartment building, Harrison backs me up against the front door and kisses me again.

"Stop! What if our parents see!" I swat him on the shoulder and try to make myself presentable as he unlocks the door. We're both fighting grins as the door opens and we spill into the quiet foyer. I shrug out of my jacket and hang it on one of the hooks by the door.

"See, they're not even here," Harrison says as he bends to kiss my nose. "No need to worry. What are you in the mood for? Ramen?"

We walk into the kitchen, where my mom is sitting on the counter, her legs wrapped around Tyson's waist, her arms around his neck, engaged in a make-out session that puts Harrison and me to shame.

FATE TWO

"So, what's Molly's deal?" Bernie stretches her feet out so they're inches from the fire and wiggles her toes. "She seems nice enough, but mopey. Quiet."

"I thought you wanted to talk about Fitz."

Bernie gives me A Look. "We are."

I sigh. She's not wrong. "She has a Fitz hangover."

"Ahh!" Bernie's eyes light up. "I know the feeling well. It's intense for, like, three days, but then it goes away."

Three days. If that were true, I should have been over him approximately seven hundred and twenty-seven days ago. Give or take. "What happened between you two?" It feels nosy to ask, but judging by the look on her face, she doesn't mind. Color is coming back into her cheeks and she's obviously in the mood to chat.

"It was a few summers ago. I live in Williams, and I was sneaking around with this guy in town. But he was a jerk, always giving me backhanded compliments, implying that I was lucky he was willing to spend time with me."

"Ew."

"Exactly. It really messed with my confidence. But then

there was Fitz. He's younger than me, kind of dopey in his eagerness, but he was nice and thoughtful. Taught me how to skip rocks by the lake and then kissed me on his last day in town. I saw him again six months later, and we were both dating other people."

I'm stunned speechless by this barrage of information. First off—dopey? Never in his life has Fitz been dopey. Second, this must have been the summer after I bailed on the carnival. I wonder if things would have been different had I been brave enough to go.

"I was heartbroken for three days after he left. And then on day four I woke up and the thought popped into my head: Did he even like me? Did he even *know* me? And I snapped out of it."

"You think he didn't like you?"

"I think he thought he did, but at the end of the day, what we had was a week hanging out because I was depressed about someone else. And look, I didn't know him either. It was a thing that happened, because summers are hot and this town is small and when a boy who looks like Fitz teaches you how to skip rocks by the lake, it makes you want to kiss him. Once your friend Molly figures that out, she'll be fine."

"It's not like that with Molly. She's in love with him. She came here to win him back."

Bernie raises an eyebrow. "Do you think he'll go back to her?"

"I don't know." I think of tennis-prodigy Priya from junior year, and how less than two weeks after the homecoming dance, Fitz had moved on to Fiona. And then after Halloween, when he told Fiona they should just be friends, she texted him every day during November, but he didn't seem at all tempted to try again. "He never has before."

"See? That's what I mean. He moves on quickly. I know his type. Fall hard and fast and then it fizzles. Boys like that are good for a weekend, but there's no point in getting attached."

Darcy walks back into the room. "How're you feeling?"

"Like my insides have been scooped out and replaced with cement," Bernie says.

"I finally got a text through to your parents. The roads closer to town have been plowed, so they're on their way to get you. If Fitz can get you and Bash to the end of the driveway, they should be able to pick you up."

Darcy suits up and joins the crew outside to help dig out the truck. Bernie and I sit in silence on the couch. Her words slosh around my brain, making me feel even worse than last night's vinegar.

Good for a weekend.

Didn't even know her, didn't even like her.

They're the same accusations I've been lobbing at him all weekend, but coming from her mouth, they feel wrong. The Fitz I know, third-base Fitz and rom-com-loving Fitz and behind-the-wheel Fitz and brokenhearted-on-the-water-tower Fitz, doesn't use people. If he were that person, wouldn't I have been able to tell? He might not be in love with me, but he's never made me feel anything other than wanted. And that has to be worth something.

I've never had intuition. Or if I did, I scared it away with all my pro-con lists and my what-ifs and SIM's incessant nagging.

But right now, I feel the whisper of *something* nudging my heart, refusing to believe Bernie's characterization of Fitz. He's not the guy she says he is.

Right?

I groan and prop my feet next to Bernie's.

"What's wrong?" Bernie asks.

I deflect. "You could have died." I'm not positive this is true, but it feels true. SIM has already made a very long list of all the other ways this morning could have gone. In several of them, it's me with the blue lips instead of her. In others, it's Fitz. In all of them, I'm an endless well of regret.

She laughs. "Can you believe it? Almost killed because I have a lousy thyroid and an aversion to sleeping in socks."

"Why aren't you more upset?"

"What do you want me to do? Cry? Yell? Swear off vinegar-based games for the rest of my life?"

"That last thing for sure," I say.

"It was stupid. I'll try not to be so stupid next time. But I'm not dead, so . . . ?" She shrugs. Like, *that's that.* Like she's not going to spend the rest of her life second-guessing every decision she's ever made. *Ugh.* The jealousy is strong today.

Outside, they've dug out Fitz's truck and cleared a semi-drivable path to the main road. Everyone comes back inside for snacks and water, and then Molly and Fitz prepare to drive Bernie and Bash to meet up with their parents.

"Do you want to come?" Molly asks.

She's too nice. I hate her for it. Why does she have to be so nice? I glance behind her, out the window. Sunlight shines off the snow. The world is white, tree branches heavy with snow. I'm longing to touch it, taste it, throw a snowball.

"My phone is dead." That's my actual answer, if you can believe it. My stomach pangs again and suddenly I want to cry.

"Oh . . . Um . . . Is that a no?"

"I can't make any decisions because my phone is dead."

"Okay. That's fine. And, um . . ." She bites her lip. "I'm sorry. We'll talk later, though, right?"

"Yeah."

Later, when I have to repair her relationship with Fitz. I hate later. They leave. Darcy stays. I drag myself to the table, feeling shaky and nauseated, wishing the power would come back on for the sole meditative purpose of baking bread. I need to bake. I need to do *something*. I settle for working on the puzzle.

Darcy wanders in and out of the room with her phone in her hand, frustration mounting. "This is useless; nothing is getting through to April," she moans as she sits across from me and stuffs a piece of gingerbread in her mouth.

"Will she be worried?"

"She'll assume I'm okay until she hears otherwise. I miss her, but she's not a worrier."

"That must be nice," I say drolly as I place another piece in the puzzle. It's almost finished, only a few spots left in the middle.

"Do you worry a lot?" she asks.

"Constantly."

"Do you always use that phone app to help you with decisions?"

My head snaps up, and she looks sheepish. "They were talking about you at breakfast."

"Who?"

"Bash."

I roll my eyes. Of course it was Bash. "The app is new."

"Is it helping?"

"Mostly not. I'm at least as big of a disaster as I was before. Maybe more." I think of all the things it led me to do, and all the times I didn't ask it when I should have. So, does that mean the app is to blame for my current mess, or the times I didn't use the app? I don't know. That sentence made my brain hurt.

"What happens when you try to make a decision?"

"I get this overwhelming feeling of panic. Every bad outcome that could possibly happen races through my head. I can't stop the what-ifs. What if I get into an accident and die? What if I start a chain of events that leaves me feeling miserable? What if—"

"What if you're happy?" Darcy cuts me off. "What if life turns out even better than you imagined?"

"I—" I close my mouth. That's not how the what-if game works. It trades exclusively in bad shit.

"Next time you find yourself in a what-if spiral, stop yourself and ask a *positive* what-if."

"Maybe."

"If you want, I could give you some techniques for dealing with that worry."

"No offense, but how do you have 'techniques'?"

Darcy blinks away her surprise. "Oh. I thought Fitz would have told you. I'm a psychiatrist who deals with mood disorders."

Oh. Right. "Yeah, no, he did tell me. I forgot."

Darcy waves it off. "A lot of my patients with anxiety disorders find grounding techniques helpful. One thing you can do is find the rainbow, naming objects that are red, orange, yellow—"

"I do that!" When Fitz reminds me. I have to be better at remembering for myself. "Did you teach Fitz?"

"I did." Darcy nods.

"But Fitz doesn't have anxiety."

"Not—not that I know of." Darcy's eyes shift and she suddenly looks uncomfortable, and the truth hits me. My cheeks burn in shame as I realize Fitz was talking to his sister about me.

Anxiety *disorder.* I hate that word. It makes me feel broken. Wrong.

It's not as if seeking help has never been suggested. Mom gave me the phone number for a therapist, gently explaining that talking to someone might be beneficial to my mental health. I appreciated the effort, but it seemed like an overreaction. Therapy is probably really expensive, meaning if I *can* manage on my own, I should. I'm supportive of therapy and/or medication for people who *really* need it, but it feels silly to ask for those kinds of interventions when so many people are worse off than I am.

"I'm not that bad."

"What do you mean by that?" Darcy asks.

"There's nothing actually wrong with my life. I have no tragic backstory or sick relatives or dead parents." *Poor me, I don't know how to choose my class schedule.* I'd probably be laughed out of therapy.

"There's no Olympics of suffering, some threshold of pain you have to meet. Everyone deserves help."

"I get anxious, but that doesn't mean I have a disorder."

"I wasn't trying to—" Darcy takes a breath. "A lot of people find it helpful. I do it sometimes. Maybe Fitz does too. I honestly haven't asked him."

Prickly tears form behind my eyes. I push the bench back from the table and stand. The edge of the puzzle catches on the arm of my sweatshirt, dragging the whole thing off the table. I watch in horror as pieces scatter across the floor. "Sorry! I'm so sorry. I have to go!"

I grab my heavy coat, pull open the door, and stumble into the snow. The sun glares off the white powder, blinding me. I throw my hands up to block my face and squint until I adjust to the new world.

That's not an exaggeration. This is a new world, completely unlike anything I've ever seen. In the aftermath of the storm, the world is still. I bend to drag my fingers through the snow; it's wetter, heavier than I imagined. I scoop a handful, roll it into a little ball, and drop it on my tongue. I grin and lean over for another handful when a stinging clump of snow hits my ear. It slides down my neck, into the back of my shirt, all the way down to the waist of my pants. I gasp and look up. Fitz is standing outside his truck, a wicked grin on his face. He tosses another snowball in the air and catches it, his eyes sparkling brighter than the snow. He tosses it again, taunting me.

I duck behind the porch railing, scoop two snowballs, and run down the porch. He releases at the same time I do, but we both miss. A snowball sails from behind a nearby tree and hits Fitz in the shoulder. We turn and see Molly whip around the trunk, trying to hide. I throw my second snowball at the back of Fitz's head, cheer at the contact, and make a beeline for Molly.

"Alliance?" I ask as I grab the large tree trunk and swing my body around it, hiding next to her. We make an arsenal of snowballs to attack Fitz. He laughs and dishes it right back, although I swear he throws three snowballs at me for every one he levels at Molly. But I guess it's normal to spare the girl you love from getting a face full of frozen slush.

After several minutes, Molly and I collapse on the porch in a fit of laughter. I'm soaking wet, frozen to the core, and panting from effort. My lungs burn and my heart is racing, each thump pumping blood through my veins with a frantic beat. *Alive alive alive.*

"That was fun," Molly laughs as she helps me brush chunks of snow and ice from my hair. A trail of snow slides down my spine. It feels awful, but I deserve it. Molly would hate me if she knew I allowed Fitz to tuck me by his side last night, and it doesn't seem fair to laugh and joke with her like nothing happened.

"Go away, we're going to talk about you," Molly says to Fitz. His eyes dart between us, but he nods his head and retrieves a shovel to dig out Darcy's rental car. For a traitorous second, my heart skips a beat the way it does whenever I get to talk about Fitz. I'm always looking for excuses to bring him up with Clover, but with Molly, I don't need to invent a reason.

Too bad this reason sucks.

"So, what do you think?" she whispers to me when he's out of earshot. "What's the best way to win him back?"

"What exactly did he say when you talked in the basement yesterday?"

She tucks her knees and her arms tightly against her body. "That he cares about me but he's not sure what he wants."

"Can you blame him? You broke his heart."

"I know." She bites her lip.

I glance up at Fitz. He quickly dips his head and pretends he's not trying to eavesdrop.

"Let me talk to him and see where his head's at. Then I'll figure out a plan."

"Thanks, Paige. You're a good friend."

I smile tightly as she brushes the snow from her pants and heads inside.

"Can I help?" I ask. Without quite meeting my eyes, he finds me a shovel and we work silently for a long time.

After last night, I'm not sure how to approach the subject of Molly, so naturally, I turn it into a joke. "Bet you wish you'd cuddled with Bernie last night, huh?"

His eyes snap up to meet mine, looking too offended to respond.

"Because of the hypothermia . . . you could have kept her warm—" Never mind. Better just spit it out. "What's the deal with you and Molly?"

He sighs. "She wants to get back together."

"Do you?"

He's quiet for the length of three shovels of snow. It feels like longer. "I don't know yet." Another shovel. "What do you think?" Eyes still down. Still won't look at me.

My stomach clenches. This is my chance to sabotage their relationship. But what's the point of doing that? If he's not going to be with me, why not Molly? Why not any of the other ones? At least when he has a girlfriend, there's a reason he's not with me. When he's single, it all comes down to the same thing: He doesn't want me. Full stop.

If it's not going to be me—no, *since* it's not going to be me, does it really matter? "I think you should do whatever you want."

"You must have an opinion." He spikes his shovel into the snow so it's standing up straight and rests his palm on top, his face a smooth mask of nonchalance.

"Not really. I don't care who you date."

"You don't care?" He blinks once, his voice flat.

I shrug. "If it's not her, it'll be someone else." And knowing Fitz, the next girl will be as great as Molly. I said Fitz doesn't have a type, but the truth is, his girlfriends are nice. I like them. He doesn't date mean girls, because that's not the kind of guy he is. So whether it's Molly or Bernie or whoever, it'll be the same knife in the gut as always, and I'll hate that I can't even hate her.

"I dunno. Maybe I should take a break from dating. I keep screwing things up." He swallows hard, his jaw straining. His eyes search mine, looking lost. My heart breaks for him. I'd do anything to keep that look out of his eyes.

"What if I can promise that Molly won't break your heart again?"

It's a terrible thing to promise; I have no way of knowing the future. Obviously. I mean, that's basically the source of all my problems. But she seems sincere. Why shouldn't they have another chance?

Besides, Fitz and I? We already tried this. First that night of the spring carnival, and then again on the train. And being close to him triggers something in me that makes my insides panicky and scared. My heart is not nearly fearless enough for Fitz Wilding.

Fitz's vulnerable, tortured expression is wiped clean in an instant. His features smooth and his shoulders square as he returns to shoveling.

"Is that a yes?"

He laughs bitterly. "Whatever you say, Collins."

My stomach twists. I step back, mumbling something about the cold. In reality: It's time to find Molly and fix what's broken. That'll make everything right. Better. Normal.

I'm in love with Fitz, and I'm going to help Molly plan the rom-com grand gesture of his dreams.

What could go wrong?

"What did Fitz say?" Molly's waiting for me in the basement, her hands wrung together.

I sit on the hearth, remove my boots, peel off my socks, and bring my feet close to the fire. Slowly, my body begins to thaw.

"Well?" She finally bursts. "I'm dying over here. What did he say?"

I've already decided to help her, but admitting it out loud is harder than I expected. "He has reservations."

"Because I dumped him? Or because he's not interested anymore?"

"He's protecting his heart."

"But I love him." Her eyes shine with an expression I recognize well: foolish hope and a good dose of heartbreak. Molly has resting love face. I have it too. The only difference between us is that she has a chance at a happy ending. Or, at the very least, a happy right now.

And yet. I still can't bring myself to push them back together, so I stall a little longer. "Tell me why you broke up with him."

She worries her lip. "I'm not supposed to say anything."

"To me? Or to people in general?"

"You. Specifically."

Well. That's a punch in the gut. I don't want Fitz to have secrets about me. I'm the only one in our relationship allowed to have secrets.

"He's my best friend, and you shattered his heart. I need to be sure you won't do it again."

And okay, maybe shattered is a *tad* dramatic. But I saw his expression out in the snow when I brought up the topic of Molly, and I feel confident that he's miserable. And maybe this makes me pathetic, but I love him too much not to help.

"I was jealous," Molly says.

I sigh. "I get that, honestly, but if you love him, then you shouldn't punish him for his past."

"It's not like that. I don't care about his exes or anything."

"What were you jealous of?"

"You."

I blink, confused. "He doesn't like me like that."

"I know that now," she says easily. "But I didn't get why he was inviting you here. And it felt like a trick, the way he invited me, waited for me to say yes, and then was all, 'Oh, yeah, Paige is coming too.'"

My ear snags on this last part. The part where she says that Fitz was inviting me *too*. It was *always* his plan to ask me to come? But then my brain catches up, and I have to ask. "You said yes? But I thought you dumped him because he didn't know you were afraid of heights?"

"Seriously?" She shakes her head. "That's a lousy reason to dump someone."

"So why did you break up with him? And why'd you change your mind?" I concentrate very hard on keeping my voice steady. Unaffected. It's fine. I'm fine.

"Promise not to say anything to Fitz?"

"Yes," I answer immediately, without even stopping to consider if I mean it. Let's face it, I'd promise to stick my feet in the fire to get this information.

"He told me that Darcy was going to be here . . ." She trails off meaningfully.

"And?" I prompt.

"And he wanted you two to meet."

"Why?"

She raises her eyebrows, as if it should be obvious. I shrug, my way of saying *obviously* I don't get whatever hints you're dropping so spit it out already.

She sighs and puts a hand on mine, not unkindly. "Fitz invited you here to meet his sister because she's a psychiatrist, and he hoped she could help you with your problems."

"Fitz talked to you about my problems?" My voice is the coldest thing in this entire frozen town.

Molly withdraws her hand slowly. "He thinks that maybe you have anxiety because of the way you get stressed out by simple things."

Simple things. Tears burn the backs of my eyes as the words echo in my brain, but I refuse to cry in front of her. Not about this.

"At first, I didn't believe him. You seem so normal—"

I suck in a breath, and Molly quickly backtracks.

"Sorry! Wrong word choice. Not that you're not normal, I just mean, you know, I never would have guessed that you have trouble making decisions and stuff. But I missed him, and when I saw you in the grocery store, you convinced me I made a mistake. So, I decided to come figure things out for myself. When I got here and saw the thing with the app, I realized he was telling the truth."

I wrap my arms around my stomach, fighting the urge to puke. Shame and embarrassment burn my cheeks. How stupid could I be, thinking that Fitz *wanted* me here, even as a replacement for Molly. All he wanted was for his sister to fix me. He probably gave her a detailed list of everything that's wrong with my brain and told her to diagnose me. No wonder she cornered me over the puzzle this morning. My head spins. I close my eyes, trying to make sense of this new information. But worse than all that, worse than Fitz lying about the reason he invited me here, worse even than him talking to Molly about me, is the one fact I can't ignore.

Fitz thinks I have problems.

I always knew my brain was broken, but I foolishly thought he didn't mind. I hate to have been so wrong about him.

"Did I say something wrong?" Molly frowns, clearly distraught. "I shouldn't have said anything."

"No, it's okay. I'm glad you did. I'm going to help you."

She squeezes my hands, gratitude radiating off her in waves. "What do I do? How do I get him back?"

"His favorite movie is *When Harry Met Sally . . .*" I wipe my eyes as Fitz's footsteps pound down the stairs. He appears, and I burn with hurt and anger and embarrassment, but also with longing. When cool girls in romantic comedies get their feelings hurt by a guy, they stand up for themselves and say, "Screw you! I don't need you!" But the fact is I've never been that cool and I'm still hopelessly in love with him. Even when he breaks my heart.

Fitz glances at us warily as he sheds his layers, unsure whether to stay or go.

"You two should go upstairs." I nudge Molly to him. My heart breaks, but I'm doing the right thing. At the end of this trip, I'll go home alone with SIM, his lists, and overwhelming regret for not going to New York when I had the chance.

But at least Fitz will be happy with Molly, and for once I'll have done something right.

The lights in the cabin flick on as the heater wheezes to life.

Time to make a plan.

But first, I'll call Jay and fix what I broke.

FATE ONE

December 26 | 2:42 p.m. | Upper West Side, Manhattan, New York

"What the hell?" Harrison looks at his dad and my mom with a mingled expression of fury and disbelief.

Because apparently philosophy quotes go down the drain when you walk in on your parents acting like teenagers.

Tyson and Mom spring apart. Mom's hands are everywhere at once: covering her mouth and smoothing her hair and straightening her blouse. Tyson is equally caught, but flails about awkwardly, stammering and gesturing wildly as he sputters. "We, um—"

"Paige—" Mom says.

"I wish you hadn't seen us like this—"

"We didn't realize the time—"

"It wasn't planned—"

"You've got to be kidding me," Harrison groans.

My heart is in my ears and my throat. Sweat prickles the back of my neck. It's too much. And it's hot in here. *Oh my gosh, why is it so hot in here?* I want to crack the window above the sink, but that would involve moving closer to our parents, an option that is very much off the table.

Harrison and his dad are fighting, and the sound is too much. Too loud. Too hot. Too awful. Too everything.

"I can't breathe."

"Harry, you have to understand—"

"Dad! You're sick! You shouldn't be—"

"Happy?" Tyson's tone matches his son's.

"Tyson—" Mom lays her hand gently on Tyson's chest, which has an instant calming effect. He deflates.

"Harry, we'll talk about this," Tyson says.

"Screw that." Harrison throws his arms up.

"I can't breathe. I have to get out of here." I turn to leave.

"Wait up. I'm coming." Harrison follows me out the door as Tyson shouts, "Harry, wait!"

"Where do you want to go?" Harrison asks darkly as he follows me down the steps of his apartment building. I pick a direction without thinking, desperate to put space between myself and them. I gulp for air, but it's icy and painful in my chest. The sun is gone, replaced by a thick layer of clouds.

"I can't breathe," I gasp. I double over, hands on my knees, and fight for air.

Rainbow. I need to find the rainbow. Everything is gray and black and muted and I can't see anything red. Never mind. "Five things. Five things I can see."

Harrison puts his hands on my shoulders. "Calm down. Stop freaking out."

I shrug away from his hands. They feel wrong. "I see the street, taxis, tree branches, buildings, clouds."

He takes a step back. "What?"

"I feel cold." I left my coat in the apartment. No going back there now. I'll abandon my suitcase and buy new clothes. I rub my hands up and down my arms. "I feel goose bumps." I still need two more, except now I can't feel anything except the freezing temperature seeping into my bones.

"Paige!" Harrison snaps his fingers in my face. "What the hell is going on? Our parents were being gross, but it's no reason to spin out."

I look in his eyes, and I can't tell him. I can't tell him that for twenty breathtaking minutes I dared to imagine a life beyond Fitz, a life where I could possibly want someone else as much as I wanted him. And it's not like I'm in love with Harrison. Not even close. But now it's another door slammed shut, because I'll never be able to kiss him again without thinking about our parents, and what if they get married, and what if I'll always be haunted by the memory of my stepbrother's tongue in my throat, and what if— tears prickle the corner of my eyes, and I feel so stupid and full of regret, and life really does come full circle.

On every parallel plain in the entire freaking multiverse I'm the same girl with a broken brain who's stuck playing what-if.

I dig through my pockets for the Post-it of options and come up short. Right. I'm in different pants than I wore last night. When I find it, I'm bookmarking that website and finding a way out of Gilbert and out of New York and as far away from my life as possible. China. Russia. Australia. Who cares? As long as I can leave.

I fumble with my phone and call Fitz.

"I was beginning to think you'd forgotten about me!"

"I can't breathe."

"Where are you? Is there a place to sit down?"

"New York. Sidewalk. There's a porch."

"Sit," Fitz says. I walk midway up the steps of a brownstone and sink down.

"Tell me five things you can see." He walks me through the five-four-three-two-one game, and by the time I get to one thing I can taste (car exhaust), my heart has slowed in my chest and SIM has stopped his furious scribbling.

Harrison is hunched on the bottom step, fiddling with his phone. I wonder vaguely if he's listening, and if he thinks I'm crazy.

I wonder if he's right.

"Thanks, Fitz."

He pauses for a long time. And when he says, "*Always*," it's quiet.

"How's your trip?" It's a weird transition, but I hate myself for demanding so much of his attention. I wish he didn't have to fuss over me so much. I wish I didn't love it when he does.

"Epic blizzard. We lost power for the night."

"I saw Molly's pictures." I force myself to say the next words, even though they taste worse than the exhaust. "I'm glad you two worked it out." If I say it enough, maybe it'll be true, and maybe that's the first step toward getting over him.

"Oh. Um."

Oh. Um? The words blaze like a signal fire. "What's going on?"

"When do you get home?"

"A few days. Why?"

He exhales a huge breath, and my world tilts on its axis. "Because when you do, we should talk."

"About what?" I ask too loudly, even though I know *about what*. There is only one possible thing that could make Fitz's easy voice sound that pained.

Another deep breath. Another tear in my paper-thin heart. "I read your letter."

Four simple words that detonate my entire life.

He knows that I love him and that I hate him, and it's all over.

"I told you not to! I told you it was a mistake. I didn't mean it, I didn't—" I sound hysterical.

"Paige—"

"I gotta go." I hang up the phone as Harrison turns.

"He read the letter," he says. The corner of his mouth twitches, and I realize he's holding back the urge to say I told you so.

"I don't wanna talk about it."

"Relax, it's not a big deal."

Not a big deal.

Another bomb, this time blowing up whatever this is between Harrison and me.

"I'm gonna lose him."

Harrison reaches out to capture my hand. "What about the multiverse? What about Kierkegaard? Or hey—" He folds his arms, closing himself off. "Maybe he'll choose you." He shrugs.

Maybe he will. Maybe there's a microscopic chance Fitz will choose me. And I'll never be able to trust that it's not because he's trying to fulfill his wildest rom-com dreams.

Something cold and wet lands on my arms. Harrison and I realize what's happening at the same moment, both of our eyes turning skyward.

It's snowing. Because of course it is. I laugh harshly. "I've never seen snow."

Harrison's eyes spark. "I'll show you."

"No thanks."

"C'mon. Let me introduce the small-town desert girl to winter in the city."

I step back, ignoring his outstretched hand. He's glad to have another new thing to show me, like science and philosophy and the High Line. That's all this is. To him, I'm a quaint, hot-chocolate-swigging girl who makes him feel smart. And the thing is, I want to experience all these new things. But that doesn't mean I want to experience them with him.

Harrison can cast me as his new girl, holding my hand and showing me the city, but that doesn't change the fact that he's trying to fill the hole Kate left in his heart. I can hold his hand and fall in love with the skyline, but that doesn't mean I don't miss Fitz.

And maybe I'll never have Fitz, but I don't have to settle for someone who makes me feel crazy, someone who uses Philosophy 101 quotes as a substitute for vulnerability. Someone who barks at me to calm down instead of helping me find a way to do it.

I jog down the steps of the brownstone, brushing past him without a word.

"Where are you going?" He reaches for my hand and I tug it free.

"I don't know. But I need time to think."

I step off the curb as he yells "Paige!" in a voice of pure annoyance.

I turn just in time to see the taxi that slams into me.

FATE TWO

December 26 | 8:14 p.m. | Williams, Arizona

Step one: Fix Clover and Jay's relationship.

My fingers shake as I dial Jay's number in the basement, and my stomach squirms when Clover answers the phone. "What do you want?" she says.

"To apologize."

"No need. Jay told me what you said, and I told him it was a lie. Sorry not sorry to disappoint you, but we're already back together."

Huh. It turns out that even my bad decisions aren't powerful enough to disrupt fate or stop true love.

After nearly an hour of groveling, it seems like Clover and I will be okay, though it'll take time for things to go back to the way they were. With that done, I set to work on fixing Fitz and Molly's relationship. I'm a veritable matchmaker now. An hour later, I call Molly to the basement to see what I've done.

"Are you sure?" Molly wrinkles her nose and looks around.

And look, I get it. A few balloons and a portable speaker don't look like much. But it'll do the trick. I know it will.

"Trust me. It's perfect." Okay, maybe perfect is a stretch. But I only had so much to work with.

"Explain it again? This is from a movie?"

I clench my teeth. It takes everything I have not to roll my eyes at this girl. She's in love with him. It shouldn't be so complicated.

"*When Harry Met Sally* . . . is Fitz's favorite rom-com. You're re-creating the final scene." It's ironic, actually, because the final scene in the movie doesn't have a grand gesture. The main character Harry *finally* realizes that he's in love with his best friend, Sally, so he finds her at a New Year's Eve party and tells her how he feels. I downloaded "Auld Lang Syne" to Molly's phone and synced it with the speaker. As soon as we're done here, I'm going to go upstairs, where Fitz, Darcy, and their parents are watching this movie. That part was a minor miracle, but the power of suggestion is real, apparently. "When I go upstairs, wait two minutes and then start the song."

"And he'll get it?"

"He'll get it," I assure her. I found a package of old birthday balloons in the kitchen junk drawer and blew them up and scattered them around the room for good measure.

"What do I say?"

"Tell him the truth."

"You think this will work?"

"I can't make any guarantees, but yeah. I do."

"Okay. Thanks, Paige." She hugs me tightly. I hug back, because why not. If I'm doing this, I may as well go all in.

I walk halfway up the stairs and listen for the closing credits of the movie. Harry and Sally are talking about serving side sauce with their wedding cake. Close enough.

"Two minutes," I remind her, and take the steps two at a time. I pause under the mistletoe, watching Fitz watch his favorite movie. He's lying on his stomach on the carpet, his chin resting on his hands, and I want nothing more than to join him. I close my eyes and take a deep breath.

"Hey, Fitz." I'm surprised how normal my voice sounds.

He turns and sees me standing under the mistletoe. His eyes widen. I hastily step forward so he won't get the wrong idea. "Molly needs your help with the fire."

He stands. "Sure." He brushes by me, the back of his hand grazing mine. And then he goes downstairs to get back together with his ex-girlfriend. I head straight for the front door and yank on boots, a coat, and a hat.

"Where are you going? It's dark and it's freezing," Darcy says.

"I won't go far. I just need some fresh air."

She stops me on the porch, closing the door behind us. "Are you okay?" Her breath puffs in the yellow glow of the porch light.

I'm fine. I'm fine I'm fine I'm fine. My heart is not breaking. I'm not in love with your brother. I don't hate him for talking about me. My brain is not broken and my life is not a trash fire. "I don't know."

"I hate the way our conversation went this morning. I wasn't trying to diagnose you. I was being nosy, and I'm sorry."

"Don't apologize. I might—" I squeeze my hands tight, trying to summon the courage I've never had. "I might, you know, talk to someone when I get home. Try to figure out if there's something I can do to manage my, you know." I gesture to my general brain region.

"Oh, Paige." Darcy looks like she wants to hug me. "I hope you find someone who can help."

"Thanks. So now you can report back to Fitz that your job is done. I know he invited me here so you could fix my messed-up brain."

"No, he didn't."

"Don't lie for him. Molly told me."

"What you're saying is impossible. When did he invite you?"

"The twenty-first. Why?"

"I wasn't planning to come, hadn't even bought a plane ticket on the twenty-first." Darcy twists her expensive scarf around her fingers, winding and unwinding it. "I was nervous about facing the family after the wedding, because I knew Meg was furious. And I wanted April and me to spend our first married Christmas together. She talked me into coming at the last second because she wants me to smooth things over with Meg. I didn't even buy my ticket until the twenty-second. It was an astronomically expensive miracle that I even got here."

"But Molly told me that Fitz said—"

"I don't know what she said or what he said and why, but I'm telling you the truth. I can show you my bank statement if you don't believe me." She crosses her arms, looking frighteningly like her brother.

"Okay, so maybe he didn't know. But he obviously told you about my problems. Why else would you have taught him grounding techniques?"

"I taught him grounding techniques because he asked me to.

He wanted to know coping mechanisms for stress. He didn't once mention your name."

"Oh." My eyes wander to the door. I squeeze them shut and try not to drown in images of Fitz and Molly.

If I had known . . .

Nothing. If I had known, nothing would be different. "Thanks for telling me. I've gotta go."

Racing down the porch steps, I venture into the dark forest. I circle around to the back of the cabin and walk straight, praying I don't get lost. I didn't bother charging my phone after my long conversation with Clover, because I was distracted by my efforts to push Fitz into the arms of another girl to the tune of "Auld Lang Syne." That song is ruined for me now. As is *When Harry Met Sally . . .*, and all Meg Ryan movies, and anything resembling a rom-com. Not that it's such a tragedy. My favorite thing about them was watching with Fitz, anyway. I walk, making a mental list of all the things I'll never enjoy again. Baseball. (Heartbreaking.) Snow. (Tragic.) Any food made with vinegar. (Good riddance.) I snap out of my daze as I come to a frozen lake.

The branches around me are heavy with magical snow, like something out of one of Fitz's movies. It's disgustingly romantic, and when I get home, I should put Jay and Clover in a car and drive them up here so he can properly propose.

I press my foot against the ice, testing it. It doesn't crack. I try not to picture what Fitz and Molly are doing now, but it's impossible. I see him wrapping his arms around her, whispering in her ear, kissing in front of the fire.

"Why'd you do it?" Fitz's voice cuts through the trees.

Surprised, I turn and slip, falling hard on my butt. Fitz jogs the rest of the way to me and reaches a hand to help me up. "Are you okay?"

I ignore him and scramble to my feet. "I'm fine. Why aren't you with Molly?"

"I asked first. Why did you set that up for her?"

"I don't know what you're talking about."

"Cut the crap, Collins." He sighs, tugging on the brim of his hat. "Don't you think it's time we stopped lying to each other?"

I want to protest, but his words catch my attention. Stop lying to *each other*. "What are you lying about?"

"Please, tell me why you're trying so hard to get Molly and me back together. I need to know."

"I want you to be happy."

He takes a deep breath, and then another, steeling himself for whatever he's about to say. I've never been so eager or so petrified.

"I like Molly a lot—"

It's worse than a snowball down my shirt. "Cool. You came out here just to tell me that?"

He rolls his eyes. "I like Molly a lot, *but* I don't want to date her. I've been trying to tell you that but you haven't been listening."

"Okay. Well. I hope you let her down easy, I guess." I don't know what to say because I don't know what he's doing here.

He starts to say something, stops himself, starts again. I have never in my life seen Fitz Wilding look so unsure of himself. "I want to talk about that letter."

My heart freezes. "Did you hide it from me? Did you know it was in your truck the whole time?"

"I—"

"You did! I was so desperate to find it that I had an actual panic attack in your basement: shortness of breath, numbness, racing heart, all of it. And you knew where it was the whole time! Did you and Whit laugh about it behind my back?"

He looks crestfallen. "I would never do that. I wanted to know what it said, okay? I wanted to know if—"

"If what?"

"If it said something important. And I knew you would be too scared to let me read it. So, can we please talk about it? It might help."

"I don't know, okay? I don't know what I want."

This is more than decision fatigue. This is paralysis. My heart beats wildly, like I'm being attacked. I fumble with my phone before I remember it's dead. This stupid brick has one job, and that job is to *stay on* so it can decide my every last decision and take responsibility for my life so I don't have to.

Is that too much to ask?

"Collins?"

"I, um . . . I don't know . . . my phone is dead." He can't expect me to make decisions under these circumstances. He understands me. He won't push it.

"Hold up. Are you kidding me?" He takes a deep breath and starts again, his voice gentler. "I'll rephrase that. Let's talk about this."

"It's not a good day for this conversation."

"What did the letter say, Paige?" His voice is so soft, like he's preparing to let me down gently. Which means he already knows. On some level, he's probably known since he saw the envelope.

I swallow. My heart feels frozen in my chest. "It said that I hate you."

Fitz blinks.

"It was a friendship breakup letter. It asked you to stop talking to me."

"Wow." He takes his hat off and runs his hand through his hair. "I'm an idiot."

"I hate that you're the first person I think about when I wake up in the morning and the last person I think about before I go to sleep at night. I hate that you're the one person who doesn't make me feel crazy. I hate that you don't touch me when you have a girlfriend. I hate that I don't hate you."

His mouth twitches. "*10 Things I Hate About You.* Now you're speaking my language, Collins." He steps toward me. "Is all that true?"

Yesterday, I might have had a different answer. But I can't stop the one that comes to my lips. "It was when I wrote it."

"And now?" He swallows, and my eyes can't help but watch the movement. The subtle clenching of his jaw, the bob of his Adam's apple. The way his chest expands and then freezes, literally hanging on bated breath. It feels like I've been doing this, tracking his movements, for a lifetime. A lifetime of loving him. It was so easy, because it wasn't ever a choice.

But now I'm being given the choice, and my phone is dead, and my heart is racing and my knees are trembling and my neck is sweating under an itchy wool scarf and I have to choose.

"Now it's not."

He nods slowly, taking this in. "But . . . are you sure? It hasn't been that long since you wrote it. And this week, I thought, under the mistletoe, and on the train . . ." He trails off, an invitation for me to fill in the gaps.

"I changed my mind. Isn't that one of my *problems*?"

His face falls. "I guess I shouldn't be surprised. Not with the way you reacted to Jay's engagement ring."

"What does that have to do with anything?"

"You think a wedding would ruin Clover's life because it's not the choice you'd make. Admit it. You're terrified of becoming attached to anything that would make you want to stay in Gilbert."

"That's not true."

"Isn't it?"

"No! Maybe. I don't know! But that doesn't mean I don't love—" I stop myself before I say the words I'll regret tomorrow.

He steps closer, his eyes the only bright spot in the dark night. "Tell me."

"No! It doesn't matter what I thought. I was wrong." I turn and step onto the frozen pond.

"Hold up! Don't walk away from this."

"Why not, Fitz? There's a gorgeous girl back at the cabin who is willing to tell you exactly what you want to hear, so why don't you go get her?"

"I'm not leaving. Not like this. This is the part of the movie where the couple fights because of a misunderstanding, and it's ridiculous and everyone knows it's ridiculous. I don't want to lose you over a misunderstanding."

Couple. My heart stutters over the word. Fitz and I have been a lot of things, but we've never been that. And honestly? I've always related to that part of the movie. The misunderstanding. The everything-would-be-fine-if-they-would-just-talk part.

Just talk.

As if revealing your feelings and secrets and weaknesses and neuroses in a way that's honest and authentic is anything other than the scariest thing in the world.

Talking to the people you care about is not *just* anything.

"Did you talk to Molly about my 'problems'?"

"Paige, listen."

"Answer the question."

"Yes, okay! I said that. But I didn't mean it. She was mad, and I panicked. I had to tell her something."

"Did you talk to your sister about me?"

He sighs heavily, looking resigned. "Indirectly."

"I trusted you." My voice breaks as tears spill over my cheeks.

"I lied to Molly, okay! I invited you here because I *want* you here. It had nothing to do with Darcy. I wasn't even sure Darcy was coming!"

"You shouldn't have talked about me. Full stop. I'm not interested in your opinion of my problems."

"You're really gonna yell at me because I want you to be happy? If you're gonna resent me for trying to help you, then maybe we shouldn't be together. If you'd rather live your life on the whim of your app—"

"You think I like being like this? I hate that this is how I am! I hate lying awake at night wondering how I screwed up my life this time, or why you're not in love with me, or what I could do to make you fall in love with me. It's torture. And I hate that you're so good at grounding me, because it makes me worried that no matter where I go or how much of the world I see, I'm always going to wish I were here with you. But my staying won't do either of us any good, because I can't watch your fearless heart try to win every girl but me with gesture after grand gesture. You wear the title *Hopeless Romantic* like a crown, falling in and out of love at a dizzying rate, but for those of us on the sidelines, you just look reckless."

"You think this is my idea of fun? You think I haven't spent the last two years chasing the high I got from creating that snowstorm for you?"

"You didn't make that for me."

"Of course I did! I just didn't understand what that meant. Seeing the look on your face when you saw it, the spark in your eyes . . . it felt so good I literally thought my heart was gonna explode in my chest. I was young and naive and thought it'd be that way every time. With Ruby and the rowboat and Molly and the fireworks, but they all fell flat. And I couldn't understand why none of the other girls made me feel the way you did that night. I haven't felt that way since, until we hid behind the Christmas village and you saw snow for the first time. The missing piece was you."

I stop breathing.

I stop breathing, because Fitz just said the thing I've always wanted him to say, and none of this is real.

And then I'm gasping for breath, because apparently, it is.

"I thought you were addicted to love," I say quietly.

"I'm addicted to you, Collins. Molly didn't want me to invite you to the cabin, but that was my deal breaker. I've been waiting to show you a real snowstorm for years. And it's because I've been in love with *you* this whole time."

I shake my head, unwilling to believe the words. "That's not true."

"I love you, and I think a part of me has always known I did, but I was scared."

"You've never been scared of anything. Especially not love," I accuse him.

"Look at the walls of your bedroom. It's not exactly a secret that your number one goal is to be anywhere other than here." His eyes soften. He passes his hand over the back of his neck, self-conscious. "I never said it out loud, but that night you bailed on our carnival date hurt like hell, Collins."

"For me too."

"Ever since then, it's been hard to imagine the concept of you and me, of a world where you even *want* me, when all you can focus on is finding a better life."

"I—" My heart slams into the walls of my chest. I have to act fast before paralyzing fear and an endless list of what-ifs take control. "I love you. It scares me how much I love you, because what if it doesn't work and what if we're not friends anymore and what if I stay in Gilbert forever and being with you means I miss my chance to leave?"

Fitz winces, his head falling.

I gulp the icy air and force out these next words, despite how foreign they feel. "But what if you're the best thing that ever happened to me?"

He looks up, and his expression mirrors mine, eyes wide with wonder and hope. "What if I kiss you right now?"

"And what if it's better than I imagined it would be?" I breathe in a shaky, unsteady voice.

He steps onto the ice and threads a trembling hand through my hair, his eyes glued to my lips. When his mouth presses against mine, we melt together, years of friendship paving an easy path to something more.

He pulls away with a grin. "Seventh-grade Dance Unit, when I was shorter than you and stepped all over your toes."

"What about it?"

"Eighth-grade Spanish class, when you said 'Estoy caliente' instead of 'Tengo calor,' and your cheeks went an adorable shade of red. Ninth grade, when you ran onto the field and hugged me after our team won that extra innings game against Desert Ridge. Sophomore year, when—"

"What are you doing?" I can't help but smile at the memories, including the horrifying time I told my Spanish class I was horny instead of saying I was hot.

"Making a list of the times I wanted to kiss you."

Oh. His eyes burn through me, smoky enough to melt the ice beneath our feet. This time I kiss first, grabbing the front of his shirt and pulling him into me. I press my lips to his and am shocked by the electricity that snakes through my body.

When he eventually pulls back, his eyes are dark and wild. "Collins—" he rasps, shaking his head. "Never in my life has it been like that."

"No kidding," I gasp. He leans in again, and the ice cracks, soaking us in icy water up to our shins. We both shriek with surprised laughter. He takes my hand in his and pulls me to the snowy shore. "Let's go warm up," he says, a wicked grin on his face.

"What about Molly?"

"She left. It's just you and me."

"Plus your mom, and your dad, and Darcy, and Jane," I point out.

"Don't you get it, Collins? This trip is just the beginning of you and me." He squeezes my hand. "So what's it gonna be. Are you in?"

"I'm in."

FATE ONE

December 28 | 5:05 a.m. | Manhattan, New York

Everything hurts and I'm dying. It's the only explanation for the screaming pain in my body. If I'm not dying, I want to be. Put me out of my misery. My eyes flutter open. I'm in a hospital bed, and the room is dark. Makes sense. That's generally where people go to die.

Slumped in the chair next to my bed, Fitz is sleeping. He's rumpled. Hair and clothes and the crease between his eyes. It doesn't make sense, because I remember now: I'm in New York, and he's in Arizona. But maybe the rules of this universe are different than I thought, and I can manifest him in front of me simply by wanting him enough. *I should have tried that ages ago.*

Or maybe I'm hallucinating.

My eyelids are heavy, but before I sink back to sleep, I can't help but think that everything hurts a little bit less.

When my eyes open again, the room is lighter, and Fitz is awake.

Huh. Not a hallucination, then.

He pushes himself upright, eyes wide. "Paige! Can you hear me?"

I nod.

"Can you talk?"

"Who are you?" I ask.

He looks stricken.

"I have amnesia. Selective amnesia. Are you—are you the guy who sells subway tokens?" I crack a smile, amused by my own reference to one of Fitz's old movies.

Fitz groans and adjusts his baseball hat. "Not funny." He sticks out his wrist so I can see evidence of his racing heart. "I cannot believe you *While You Were Sleeping*-ed me."

"Couldn't help myself." I grin. "Where's my mom?"

"In the cafeteria. Wait here. Well, I guess you don't have another choice." His shoe slips as he races across the room, and he grabs the doorframe to stay upright. He announces to the entire hall that I'm awake and then disappears. Seconds later, the room fills with nurses, one of whom bends over me and shines a light in my eyes.

"Do you remember what happened?"

"I got hit by a taxi. What day is it?"

"December twenty-eighth. You've been here two days."

"Am I dying?" I ask, even though I'm pretty sure I'm not. But it never hurts to double-check.

"No, sugar. You're not dying." She inspects the monitor next to me and strings together a bunch of medical jargon while someone else types it into a mobile computer.

"What's wrong with me?"

"A few broken ribs, some cuts and bruises. It could have been a lot worse."

"Paige!" Mom's in my face, sobbing happy tears and

apologizing on a loop. It takes me a while to piece together the fact that she holds herself responsible for my accident.

"If I had known that you had feelings for Harrison, I wouldn't have—"

"It's fine."

"I thought you were in love with Fitz, and Harry was stuck on Kate—"

"I am, and he is. I'm not mad, and it's not your fault. I want you to be happy, and if Tyson makes you happy, well, that's cool."

She smiles and takes my hand. "Tyson's still working on Harrison, but we're hopeful."

"Where is Harrison?" I ask as Fitz walks into the room holding a bag of sour gummy worms. We make eye contact and he pauses, a question in his eyes.

"Did you buy those for my funeral?" I ask, recalling the night on the water tower when his reaction to my potential death was to serve candy. Fitz shakes his head with a small smile and walks in.

"Harrison's at home with his dad," Mom says.

"He stopped by a few times, though." Fitz chooses his words carefully, but he can't hide what's written all over his face. He hates Harrison. This realization gives me a small thrill.

"Oh. Okay," I say, trying to imagine a scenario with the two of them in the same room. It's too weird. I prefer to keep them in parallel universes. I wonder if Harrison quoted Kierkegaard. I wonder if Fitz quoted Ephron.

"Do you want to text him?" Mom asks, handing me my phone. "I'm sure he'll be relieved to hear from you."

"I don't have his phone number." I can't help but laugh. It's a small thing, but it feels like we might have skipped a few steps on our way to getting to know each other. Maybe I skipped *all* the steps in my quest to be a different version of myself.

I open my phone anyway, and am bombarded with dozens of messages from Clover. She doesn't hate me after all. I blink the tears out of my eyes and lock my phone. I'll read them when I don't have an audience, and then I'll apologize at least a hundred times.

Mom fusses over me, smoothing my blanket and checking my water cup and wringing her hands. Fitz sets the candy on my bedside table and takes the chair, eyes scanning me, as if he can't quite believe I'm real. Like I'm a shadow version of myself and he doesn't know what to say to me because—

Oh. Oh yeah. He read the letter, and now he doesn't know how to exist in my orbit. Everything is terrible and life is trash. Or something like that. SIM knows the deal. "Why are you here?"

He ducks his head, his cheeks turning pink. "Uh—"

"I mean, how did you get here?"

"Darcy transferred her plane ticket to me, and I rode the train in from Boston."

"Wow. I must have been on my deathbed for you to go to all that trouble."

Fitz hesitates, his eyes flicking to my mom. He couldn't be more obvious if he tried. She kisses me on the top of the head for the fiftieth time before announcing that she's going to run to Tyson's to take a shower and change her clothes.

"Wait!" I scramble, desperate for her to stay, because as soon as she leaves, Fitz and I are going to have to deal with the letter, and I'm still not sure how to do that. "When do I get to leave?"

"You're staying another night or two for monitoring. But the doctors say it's a miracle you don't have more injuries. We won't be here long." She smooths the hair out of my eyes, blinking away more happy tears.

"Can I leave now?" I sit up, wincing in pain.

She places a hand gently on my shoulder and urges me back down. Her eyes follow mine to the beautiful boy waiting to talk to me alone. "We'll talk later. And you need to call Dad. He's worried sick."

"I will. Can you bring me clothes and stuff? From the apartment?"

She nods. "I'll be back soon." Then she leaves, and Fitz and I are alone.

Lines from the letter come rushing back to me, so vivid it feels like I wrote it this morning. My face burns with embarrassment. I play with the oxygen monitor on my finger, clipping and unclipping it, when I notice a blue sticky note fastened to the plastic rails by my bed. I reach for it, gasping at the pain in my side. "Where'd this come from?"

"Harrison," Fitz says darkly.

Huh. It must have fallen from my pocket. Or maybe he took it when his hand was in my pocket in the elevator. My face goes miserably hot. "Did you snoop?"

"Wouldn't you?" He's right. I would. "Lots of options on that website," he says.

"Yeah, well, I've still got a few months to decide where I'm going."

Fitz grimaces. He looks so uncomfortable; I have to put him out of his misery. "I kissed Harrison," I say, hoping to relieve him of the pressure he's feeling. *No need to let me down gently, Fitz Wilding. I've already moved on.*

He makes a face. "Yeah, I figured that out, somewhere between Socrates and Nietzsche."

"He didn't." I groan into my hands, which makes Fitz smile.

"'You cannot step in the same river twice.' Heraclitus. I googled it after he left."

"That's kind of beautiful," I say. "But hang on, am I the river in this scenario? Is that his way of breaking up with me?"

"Sorry to deliver the bad news."

"We weren't even together! And if we were, I broke up with him first!"

"Why?"

"'Cause I didn't want to see the snow with him."

Fitz leans forward, his face intensely serious. "Go on."

"He's not a bad guy," I start, which makes Fitz scowl. I bite back a smile and continue. "A bit pretentious and surly, but I had a good time touring the city with him." The scowl deepens. "But then I had a panic attack and his reaction wasn't anything like—" *You*, I almost say. I try again. "Anyway, it started snowing, and I realized I didn't want that experience to be with him. I wanted it—" Ugh. Did it again. Fitz opens his mouth to say something so I keep talking.

"Can you believe I was hit by a car? All that careful planning, all that painstaking deliberation and Magic 8 and the what-ifs and the endless lists and my brain whispering all the ways it could go wrong. All of it, basically, to make sure that I don't either blow my life up with a nuclear bomb and or get in a horrible accident, and I did both anyway. I'm never going to be a different version of myself."

"Why would you want to be?"

I slant him a look.

"What's Magic 8?"

"It's a thing I did to avoid dealing with my own problems. It worked until it didn't anymore."

"And the nuclear bomb?" He leans toward me, elbows on his knees. Even here, in hospital lights with rumpled clothes and sleep-mussed hair, he's the most beautiful boy I've ever seen.

"The letter."

So much for avoidance.

Fitz pulls a worn, folded-up piece of paper out of his pocket.

"No. Don't. It's too embarrassing."

"Paige—"

"Please. Just forget about it. I shouldn't have written it! I'm sorry."

"For what?"

"Saying that I hate you. Why'd you come here anyway? I told you to stop talking to me." I'm in agony. This has to be the worst moment of my whole life.

His face softens. "Come on, Collins. Don't you think I know you better than that?" His voice is so tender I want to scream.

"I'm sorry this is so awkward. I told you not to read it, I—"

"I love you," Fitz says.

Time stops, and for a perfect heartbeat, I know Kate is

wrong about the multiverse containing every possible scenario, because there is no other scenario but this one. In every universe, in the whole space-time continuum, there is only Fitz and me. He was made to say those words and I was made to hear them.

And then reality kicks down the door and I remember my aha moment on the High Line, and all the reasons I can't trust Fitz's reckless heart. As desperately as I want it to be different for us than it was for the others . . . what if it's not?

"You don't mean that," I say, creating the first layer of armor around my tissue-paper heart. He frowns in confusion. I make my armor tighter. "This is all very romantic, isn't it? You reading the letter, me almost dying, you flying across the country. How could you resist?" I mumble miserably. The words feel all wrong in my mouth, and I hate myself for saying them.

"What's that supposed to mean?"

"You're a sucker for a romantic gesture, but you can't build a relationship on gestures. You don't love me any more than you loved Ivy or Priya or any of the others."

Fitz blinks, looking shocked. This is not the reaction he was expecting. But if I tell him that I love him and let him kiss me senseless in this hospital bed, I'll never know if he's doing it because he wants *me*, or because he wants the story.

And despite the fact that I've imagined enough versions of the story to fill all the books in all the universes in the multiverse, being a short-term player in Fitz's fantasy isn't enough.

"Paige, I need to explain—"

"You need to leave, and I need time to think. Please."

His face crumples, and then he leaves.

It doesn't take long for the panic to set in. Fitz leaves, I cry, and SIM starts a new list, full of all the reasons I'll be alone for the rest of my life.

It's one line:

Fitz is my guy. Always. And if I won't let myself be happy with him, what chance do I have with anyone else?

I'm also in pain, and the small room feels claustrophobic, and it's not long before I'm playing the five-four-three-two-one game.

A nurse comes in and bustles about, tidying dishes from room service and making notes about the numbers on my screen.

"Two things I can smell. Alcohol from the hand sanitizer. Onions from my soup. One thing I can taste. Also onions." I take several deep breaths.

"I do that too, when my anxiety spikes," she muses as she checks my chart. "Are you due for a dose? I don't see any medications listed on your chart."

"Oh, no, I'm not taking anything."

"Good. I was worried the intake nurse missed something."

"Like what?"

"Prozac, Zoloft, Lexapro," she says as she changes my IV drip. "How's the pain? Do you need more medicine?"

I shake my head. "Those other medications, what do they do?"

"They're SSRIs, which increase levels of serotonin in the brain."

"Why did you think I need them?"

"The grounding technique you were doing is common for patients with severe anxiety."

Anxiety. It's not an unfamiliar term; Mom mentioned it when she tried to get me into therapy. But it's not often I hear the word on its own; it's usually one half of "depression and anxiety." *Depressionandanxiety.* And since I've never suffered from depression, I assumed I was more okay than not. Not "bad enough" to warrant help. Whatever that means.

"Is that why my brain feels broken?" I ask. She frowns in response. I press forward, because I need her to understand. "I make lists in my brain, all day, every day, of all the things that could possibly go wrong. I can't make decisions. I'm scared all the time. Is that—" I take a deep breath. "Does that sound like anxiety?"

"Have you ever spoken to anyone about this? A doctor or a therapist?"

"No."

She appraises me for a long moment. "Would you like to?"

It's the easiest question I've ever been asked. "Yes. Please."

SIM turns over a new piece of paper. *But what if—*

Shut up, SIM. I smile as I settle back into my pillows, feeling instantly lighter. I might not have to spend my life paralyzed. It's a gift I never dared to want because I didn't even know it was possible.

"Hot chocolate?"

I startle at the sound of Harrison's voice in the hospital lobby when I'm discharged two days later. With his hair pulled back and his artfully torn skinny jeans, he looks cuter than I remembered. But my stomach is blissfully free of butterflies. Mom excuses herself to meet the Uber outside while I accept the warm drink from Harrison.

"What's the occasion?" I wiggle the cup in my hand.

"I'm sorry. It's my fault you're here. If I hadn't—"

I hold up my hands. "I'm done with that game. No more blaming myself, or other people, for things beyond our control. I've been doing that for a long time, but I'm hoping to do it less now that I know my anxiety is at least partially to blame."

"You have anxiety?"

"Officially diagnosed this week." It's a relief to admit it out loud.

He fidgets with his own coffee cup. "I should have reacted better when you were upset."

"Thanks, but you didn't know." My mind flashes to Fitz. He didn't know either, but he understood me enough to react the right way. Harrison isn't *my* guy, but I meant what I said to Fitz. He's not a bad guy.

"So we're okay?"

"Like brother and sister." I smile, and Harrison looks torn between laughing and cringing.

"I can't believe you're walking out of here with no wheelchair or crutches," he says as we exit the hospital. "You're making me reexamine my stance on miracles."

"Who knew miracles could be so painful?" I joke. My ribs hurt like crazy every time I bend, or lie on my back, or laugh, or cough, or, heaven forbid, breathe. But I'll heal. Not even this is unfixable. As for my messed-up brain, I talked with a doctor from the psychiatry department. She gave me a preliminary diagnosis of generalized anxiety disorder and panic disorder and referred me to someone local. When I get home, I'll meet with the new doctor and set up a plan for treatment.

All the times I wrestled with SIM and had panic attacks and felt like one more decision would send me over the edge, I assumed that's the life I was destined to live. For the first time in years, I don't feel the heavy weight of my future anchoring me to the ground. I had no idea a label could be so empowering.

I say goodbye to Harrison and meet up with Mom. She opens the Uber door (she's boycotting taxis, naturally) and helps me into the back seat. Our return tickets are booked for this afternoon, and we're headed straight to the airport. She packed up our luggage from the Blairs' and brought it to the hospital.

Fitz went home on a red-eye last night. While staying in the city he slept on Harrison's couch. He stopped by the hospital yesterday before he left, but thankfully the letter wasn't mentioned again.

I buckle my seat belt, wincing in pain. Broken ribs take weeks to heal, and it turns out there's no way to treat them. Kind of makes me grateful for my broken brain and the modern medicine that's supposed to help.

She reaches across the back seat and squeezes my hand. "How are you feeling?"

"I'm fine." It's both true and it's not.

"How did you leave things with Fitz?"

I shrug and lean against the headrest, wishing for the

hundredth time that I'd said goodbye before he got on that plane. I'll see him in Arizona, but the way he left feels wrong, and I wish he were here with me. I bet a part of me will always feel that way, whether I'm at home in Gilbert or scaling ruins in Peru.

I close my eyes and let the tears slide down my face.

The car slows to a stop and Mom shakes me. I wasn't asleep, though. Just lost in a daydream. I unbuckle my seat belt and open the door.

"Where are we?"

It's not the airport, and it's not Central Park. *Riverside Park.* How do I know that? A picture from my wall, or a scene from a movie, maybe. A long, wide stone path unfurls at my feet. Bare tree branches line the path. Sitting on the bench closest to the car, with his head in his hands, is Fitz.

He looks up, and my heart catches in my chest.

"What's he doing here?"

"Go on." Mom hands me her credit card. "Use this to grab a ride to the airport. You have a couple of hours before you need to meet me." I step gingerly out of the car. The door shuts behind me and the car pulls away.

Fitz slowly moves toward me, his hands up in the universal signal of surrender. "This isn't a gesture!" he calls out, stopping several paces away. Leaving it up to me to close the gap.

"It's not?" I'm drawn to him by an invisible force.

"No. It's come to my attention that you hate them." He smothers a smile. "Have you always hated them?" He stuffs his hands into his pockets and moves toward me.

"Only 'cause I was jealous. And then 'cause I was scared."

"I'm scared all the time. When I got the call about you and the taxi—" He shudders. "I've never been so scared in my entire life." We stop, the fronts of our shoes bumping together. I don't know if we've ever been this close. Not since the day I realized I loved him in the homemade snowstorm. "I'm scared of you leaving Gilbert and forgetting all about me. I'm scared that you'll never be able to see me as anything other than an irresponsible screwup, the boy who couldn't make up his mind or keep a girl."

"I don't think of you that way." Not really. Harrison messed with my head, made me doubt my relationship with Fitz, but the truth is, I've always loved his fearless heart.

"I'm terrified out of my mind right now." He swallows, his face an open book of hope and dread. His fingertips brush lightly above my right eyebrow. "This is where my tooth busted open your forehead."

"I wasn't sure if you remembered that."

"I remember everything."

This seems to require a response, but my brain has stopped working. "Being this close to you is against my rules," I confess.

"You have rules?" This perks him up.

"Oh, yeah. You have no idea how many times those rules saved me."

"From what?"

"Ruining everything between you and me."

"You could never." He shakes his hair out of his eyes and my bones puddle at my feet.

"I could have."

"Show me." He bites his lip, fighting a smile. "Show me what you would have done that would have ruined everything." Clearly, he's loving this. Judging by the wild skip of my pulse, I am too.

"The rules are as follows: No touching unless it's accidental, helpful, or necessary."

I expect Fitz to unleash the full force of his grin, but instead his eyes turn smoky. I stop breathing. "We're not touching, Collins."

"True," I say in a shaky voice.

"And when I do touch you, you better believe it'll be necessary."

I swallow. My breath turns shallow.

"But first I have some things to say. I should have known I was in love with you the moment I created that snowstorm, and your reaction was all I thought about for weeks. Every gesture, with every other girl, was an idiotic attempt to chase that high I felt when I made you happy. I knew I was *probably* in love with you the moment I chose to invite you to the cabin even when it meant losing Molly. I knew I was *definitely* in love with you when you went to New York instead."

"It wasn't the letter?"

He shakes his head. "But I wanted the letter to say what it did. So badly. You have no idea."

I reach my hand into his back pocket. Fitz's eyebrows go sky-high. "Is this accidental, helpful, or necessary?" He grins wickedly.

I'm extremely relieved when my letter is still there. He tries to snatch it from me, reaching around my back. "Hey. Look at that," he says when he realizes his arms are around my waist. "Clever. Are you hitting on me, Collins?"

"I'm burning this letter."

"No! I love it! I'm gonna frame it and hang it above my bed. I'll read it every night and cry into my pillow when you're gone."

"I said horrible things."

"You? Never." His smile grows.

I take his chin in my hand and lock his eyes on mine so he'll know I'm serious. "I love you, and I've never regretted it. Not for a second."

His eyes are smoke and ash and fire, burning right through me. He tilts his lips to meet mine, and I'm lit up. I'm every firework in the whole Fourth of July parade. I didn't know it could be like this. I wrap my hands around his back and pull him closer, determined to stay here until we're forcibly kicked out.

"Wow," he breathes, his breath hot and sweet. "That was the best kiss." He rests his forehead against mine, his eyelashes fluttering as my stomach responds in kind.

"For me too. In all the universes in the multiverse."

Fitz's grin explodes.

"What?"

"Look up," he whispers, gently squeezing my waist.

Light, fluffy snowflakes dance around us. Fitz and me, in our own personal snow globe. I smile at him, dazzled by the snow and the nearness of him and his hands around my waist. "You, Fitz Wilding, are the best decision I ever made."

EPILOGUE

I kneel on the tile floor and peer into the oven. The rolls inside are rising steadily and I sink back onto my heels, smiling.

Magic. Every time.

The squeak of the garage door alerts me to Mom's presence. Thirty seconds later she's in the kitchen, dropping her purse and a stack of mail on the counter. "What smells so good?"

"Cinnamon rolls."

A pause. "How was therapy today?"

"Good." The timer dings and I pull the rolls out of the oven.

"Should I be worried that you're baking again?"

"Nope!" I still have bad days, sure, but thanks to daily medication and therapy, the panic attacks and stomachaches are gone. Combined with my grounding techniques and exercise, I can handle the small decisions of daily life, and the bigger, scarier ones too. I set the pan aside to cool and begin whisking together powdered sugar and cream cheese to make icing.

"Glad to hear it. You know, I'm thrilled that you're doing well enough to not need to bake, but I have to admit I've missed it." She reaches into the pan to swipe a hot drip of butter and cinnamon sugar. "What's the occasion?"

"I'm testing a new recipe for the bridal shower next week.

Speaking of—" I glance at the clock on the microwave as I drizzle hot icing on the rolls. "I've gotta go. I won't be home for a few hours, so feel free to have your gross Skype date with Tyson."

Her laughter rings down the hall as she goes to her room to change out of her scrubs.

My phone beeps with a text.

I'm here.

I untie my apron, throw it on the counter, and head out the front door into the warm March air, where Fitz's truck is idling by the curb. He's leaning against the passenger door, his legs crossed at the ankles. My heart flutters at the sight of him in his snug baseball tee and snugger pants.

"It should be a violation of the rules to look that good in uniform."

His responding smile is blinding. He casually wraps his arm around my waist, and my heart collapses. "You have flour on your nose," he says.

I duck my head in embarrassment, but he catches my chin gently in his hand and kisses my nose. A dusting of white covers his lips. His free hand traces a wandering line down my neck, over my shoulder, to my side. My cheeks flush and my heart quickens, despite the layer of cotton between our skin. A familiar side effect of being near Fitz. His fingers trace a gentle path across my ribs. "How're you feeling?"

"It was a *good* day," I sigh, leaning into him. "It's better now."

He kisses me again, and after several seconds I bring my hands to his chest and gently pull away.

"Do we have to leave?" he groans.

"You have a game. And I have maid of honor duties."

Fitz groans again but opens the passenger door for me to climb inside his truck. He holds my hand in his while he drives, taking care to steer with his left. "How's the research going? Find anything irresistible?"

"Intriguing? Yes. Irresistible?" I slant a glance at him, attempting to transmit my thoughts straight to his brain. His answering smile tells me he gets it. "I'm still looking." I've been looking for ways to travel on my shoestring budget. My walls are still a tribute to the world, but it's less scary than it once was. I know I'll get out of here. I'll find a way to make it happen. But I'm also enrolling in community college in the fall, because I'm no longer drowning in the claustrophobic feeling of wanting to escape my own skin. It's a mixture of the medication and Fitz and all the things in my life aligning in a way that feels too good to be a happy accident.

Fitz drops me off at the curb of a small dress shop in a strip mall, gives me one final, lingering kiss, and leaves for his baseball game. Steeling myself, I open the door. Clover spots me from across the shop. Her excited squeal settles my worried stomach. *I love Clover, and Clover loves Jay.* I can do this.

"Can you believe this is finally happening?" She wraps me in a happy hug.

Behind her, the shop is filled with every shade of white: ball gowns and mermaid silhouettes, lace and tulle, glitter and crystals and beads. Next month is our senior prom, but today we're picking out a wedding dress. After Christmas, it took a while for things to go back to normal between us, but we're in a good place now, and I'm so relieved.

I squeeze Clover's hand, and she drags me over to a rack of dresses that look like they were pulled straight from a Disney movie.

"I love this place so much," she says as we rifle through the dresses. "The plus-size collection is amazing. I was afraid I would have to order something online and have it altered." We each pick out half a dozen dresses and hand them to a nearby sales associate to bring to the dressing room.

"I guess I should get started." Her eyes flick to the couches outside the dressing room, where the rest of the group is waiting. Jay's mom and two sisters are sitting on one couch, laughing and talking and flipping through bridal magazines. On the next couch, Clover's mom sits stiffly, a grim expression on her face. She looks like she'd rather be sitting through a congressional fili-buster than watching her eighteen-year-old daughter try on bridal gowns. "Does my hair look okay? What about my shoes? I should have worn a different bra." Clover wrings her hands.

"You look gorgeous. Go on." I give her an encouraging push toward the changing rooms and take my seat next to her mom.

"Hello, Congresswoman."

"Good to see you, Paige." She smiles, but her eyes are wary, and I get it. She worries about Clover's future. I do too, and I almost ruined our friendship over it. But things are different now.

"They're going to be okay."

"How can you be sure?"

I bite my lip, thinking. "Let me rephrase. Clover is going to be okay. She's smart, and she has family and friends who can love her through anything. And besides, maybe she and Jay will be the lucky ones."

Stranger things have happened. And although Fitz and I aren't running to an altar *anytime* soon, it'd be hypocritical of me to doubt Clover and Jay's love based solely on their age. Not when I know how it feels to find the person who makes me the happiest possible version of myself.

Clover emerges from the dressing room and stands on a pillar before a sea of mirrors in a snow-white ball gown. The sales associate places a tiara on her head, which I think is going to be over the top, but instead looks perfect sitting in Clover's blonde waves.

"What do you think?" she asks the group, but it's obviously a question directed at her unmarried mother. She's soliciting her opinion on a white princess ball gown, fit for a church wedding. I bite the inside of my cheek to keep from smiling.

Ms. James swallows. "You look beautiful, darling." She turns to Jay's mom with a small but genuine smile. "Your son is a very lucky man."

"Doesn't he know it," Mrs. Bryant agrees.

Clover catches my eye in the mirror. "Thank you." She mouths the words.

I hold my hands up in the sign of a heart.

Clover is happy, and I'm happy for her.

End of sentence.

Later, when the gown has been picked out and paid for (she tried on more than a dozen, and yes, she bought that first tulle dress), Clover drives me to the old water tower in Gilbert and drops me off.

The sun is low on the horizon, the spring air warm and still. A small flutter comes to life in my chest, building with every step. I'm antsy with the need to see him again, and it takes me forever to get to the tower, despite my quick steps. I stop short in front of the ladder that ascends five stories into the air, and there's no question about what I'm going to do.

Climb.

Five. Ten. Twenty stories. Whatever it takes to get to Fitz.

"It's me!" I call up. But my announcement is unnecessary. Fitz's head is already hanging over the platform, his smile blazing and his eyes locked on mine in the low evening light.

"Hurry up, Collins."

I climb quickly and am rewarded for my speed with a kiss at the top. He smells like soap from his post-game shower, and the ends of his hair are still damp under his hat.

"I missed you," I say, not worrying whether it's too much or too clingy or whatever. I still get the urge to make lists in my head, but I'm working on it. My therapist tells me to be patient with myself. So that's what I'm doing.

"I always miss you," Fitz says as we sit on the edge of the platform, our feet dangling off the edge. "In fact, if I miss you this badly after three hours, I'm not sure I'm going to survive your trip abroad. Put me in your suitcase; take me with you." He smiles against my lips, kissing me deeply again.

"I wish."

"Then let's do it."

"You'd really want to come with me?"

He pulls back and makes unwavering eye contact. Something swoops low in my stomach as my breath catches in my throat. "From now on, consider me the Darcy to your Elizabeth. I'm just a player in your story."

"Dramatic, much?" I roll my eyes, but he captures my face between his hands.

"If you want me with you, I'm with you."

"What about baseball? Don't forget you're now a Sun Devil. You can't just take off on your team."

He drops his hands. "Stupid real life getting in the way of everything," he mumbles, and I know what he means. In two months, we're graduating. Two months after that, real life starts. For me, that means Mesa Community College and a job, as I slowly save up money for a study abroad program or a mission trip with Clover's church or some other opportunity I haven't thought of yet. For Fitz, that means Arizona State University and a spot on their baseball team. It's tempting to panic at life tearing us apart when we only just realized we belong together.

I lean forward against the railing and peer down, flashing back to that night just before Christmas. Instead of dwelling on it, I tip my head back and gaze at the stars. "Statistically, the odds are against us."

"Why do you sound so okay with that?" Fitz frowns.

I scoot closer, taking his hand in mine. He's spent so many nights comforting my anxieties, and now it's my turn to soothe his. "Because I believe in us. If it takes a miracle to keep us together, we'll create the miracle. I'll write love letters in every city in this whole damn world if it means finding my way back to you. We don't have to worry about time spent apart or how the future is going to play out."

His mouth crooks up in a smile. "You really believe that?"

I drop my head against his shoulder and close my eyes, thinking back to the moment Clover downloaded Magic 8. If I've learned anything since then, it's that I don't need to panic about the future. Life is going to be hard and wonderful, and if I have a say in any of it, I'm going to see the world. And one way or another, Fitz will be by my side when I do.

ACKNOWLEDGMENTS

One Way or Another is the most personal story I've ever written. Paige isn't me, but I put so much of myself into her. I set out to write the exact kind of book my romantic yet anxious heart has always wanted, and I'm endlessly proud of it. There are so many people who helped me in this journey, more than I can possibly list here, but I'll give it a try regardless.

To Katelyn Detweiler, you are everything I dreamed of having in a literary agent. I still feel so lucky that Paige's story landed in your hands. You understood what I wanted from the very beginning, and I knew you were the perfect agent for me when you encouraged me to add *another* kiss scene at the end of the book. Thanks for that advice, and for all the emails, phone calls, guidance, and support. This past year has been filled with wonderful milestones and I can't wait for what comes next. To Sam Farkas: Paige's dream of traveling the world is coming true, thanks to you. Every time your name pops up in my email, I scream with delight, and I can't wait to hold my first foreign edition in my hands. Thank you thank you thank you. And a massive thank you to Mary Pender and Olivia Fanaro at United Talent Agency for all your enthusiasm for this project!

To my brilliant and kind editor, Mallory Kass, who understood

Paige's story in a way no one else did. You not only believed in my ending, but you also wanted #TeamFitz *and* #TeamHarrison shirts. (I do too!) Thank you for all your insights, for refusing to let me settle for jokes that aren't funny, and for reminding me that you're here to bring out the best in my story. And thank you to the whole team at Scholastic, especially Rachel Feld, Shannon Pender, Lauren Donovan, Taylan Salvati, Lizette Serrano, Emily Heddleson, Maya Marlette, Josh Berlowitz, Yaffa Jaskoll, David Levithan, and Nikki Mutch. And thanks to Dr. Peter Kass for his expert read and his insight into Paige's anxiety.

To RuthAnne Snow, Kelly Coon, Sam Taylor, and especially Kimberly Gabriel, thank you for being the first to read Paige's story and fall in love with Fitz and Harrison, and for helping me shape this book into what it is today. Kimberly, I'm not sure I would have survived debut year without sliding into your DMs every other day; thanks for being there to celebrate and commiserate. Thank you also to Leah Crichton for the support and encouragement on the days writing felt impossibly hard. Sara Faring, when I wasn't sure if this story was worth writing, you sent me a copy of *Light the Dark* and changed everything. And thank you to Lillian Clark, Tiana Smith, and the rest of the Class of 2k19 for helping me launch my first book baby into the world!

To the AZ YA/MG writer's group, especially Abigail Johnson, Kate Watson, and Joanne Ruth Meyer, thanks for taking me in. Three years later, and I still feel lucky to be among your ranks. Thanks for inviting me to participate in my first-ever panels and events, and for always being willing to chat about books and publishing and how insane it is to try to write novels while also raising busy toddlers.

To everyone that I call family, the Durkins and the McDowells, thank you for all the support and love. To Owen, Graham, and Emmett: It's not always easy or convenient to have a mom who rushes away from dinner to write down the "one" sentence that won't get out of her head. *I know, I know!* But my life is better because of you. *I'm* better because of you, and so are my books. Thanks for being the best little motivators and for thoroughly distracting me when publishing gets rough. And to Scott, your support for my career is unwavering, just like you. I love you, and I can't wait for a lifetime of adventures with you by my side.

ABOUT THE AUTHOR

Born in the mountains and raised in the desert, **Kara McDowell** spent her childhood swimming, boating, and making up stories in her head. Now she lives in Mesa, Arizona, where she divides her time between writing, baking, and playing board games with her husband and three young sons. Find her online at karajmcdowell.com, on Twitter at @karajmcdowell, and on Instagram at @karajmcdowellbooks.